The Beautiful One

M. Lee Musgrave

Black Rose Writing | Texas

©2023 by M. Lee Musgrave
All rights reserved. No part of this book may be reproduced, stored in a retrieval system or transmitted in any form or by any means without the prior written permission of the publishers, except by a reviewer who may quote brief passages in a review to be printed in a newspaper, magazine or journal.

The author grants the final approval for this literary material.

First printing

This is a work of fiction. Names, characters, businesses, places, events, and incidents are either the products of the author's imagination or used in a fictitious manner. Any resemblance to actual persons, living or dead, or actual events is purely coincidental.

ISBN: 978-1-68513-320-7
PUBLISHED BY BLACK ROSE WRITING
www.blackrosewriting.com

Printed in the United States of America
Suggested Retail Price (SRP) $20.95

The Beautiful One is printed in Calluna

*As a planet-friendly publisher, Black Rose Writing does its best to eliminate unnecessary waste to reduce paper usage and energy costs, while never compromising the reading experience. As a result, the final word count vs. page count may not meet common expectations.

As an artist and author, during my many decades within the international art community I have met and worked with a vast array of engaging individuals. I am especially thankful to those who have enthusiastically encouraged and championed my creative efforts. Among those helping with this project are long-time ally and mate Doug Walsh; new colleague, author Alison Hubbard; and Heidrun Anita Orbitz-Musgrave, of whom, despite their extremely full schedules, took time to suggest ideas and changes thereby helping to make the story unique and a joy to write. I honor and value their love and friendship.

FOREWORD

This story is a work of fiction. Names, characters, businesses, places, events, and incidents are either the products of the author's imagination or used in a fictitious manner. Any resemblance to actual persons, living or dead, or to actual events has been altered for art's sake; for the self-expression of the author; as a process of introspection and contemplation for the purpose of creative thinking.

The Nefertiti bust, discovered in 1912, is one of the most loved and copied works of art from ancient Egypt. It has become an icon of international feminine beauty and allure; a celebrated artistic image of a mature woman whose cultural potency is enhanced by her mystique and captivating enigmatic smile. One can only imagine the joy royal sculptor Thutmose felt when she posed for him in his studio in the new city of Akhetaten in 1345 BCE. His insights, discernment, and sensitivity in capturing the very essence of her beautiful soul are a gift to all humanity.

The Beautiful One

CHAPTER 1

With visions of golden tombs half-way to the stars of Orion filling my thoughts, the cold and rainy night made it a struggle to steer clear of the treacherous pot-holes proliferating the south road out of Cairo. It was late in the season for a downpour, even a light one and I was surprised the normally firm dirt road was not welcoming to the motorcycle I'd barrowed, though I eyed its ponton sidecar as a possible kayak should the next boggy area turn out to be a significant sink-hole instead of the firm throughfare I'd traversed so often.

I laughed to myself in the rainy, cold darkness for I have never been much of a nocturnal traveler though I enjoy the solitude and simplicity of night. Its state of balance invites reflection and its lunar dreaminess coerces the sheen of ambitions yet formed. Plus, I enjoy the feeling it stirs within me, but its limited optical-ness can be inhibiting, impeding, and deterring.

The Tell El-Amarna excavation was my worksite destination again. I was to be there by dawn and traveling at night had the advantage of cool air as well as less encounters with any local unsavory elements. Or so I was thinking when the rain abruptly intensified and I attempted to swerve passed a large puddle, but instead my careless grip on the motorcycle caused it to slip side-ways right into the middle of the mire.

The Peugeot 500M was a new 1912 test model with a parallel twin-cylinder engine and dual overhead cams designed by Swiss engineer Ernest Henry, a friend of my father. No doubt the mud I had been traversing overwhelmed it.

Soaking wet, tired and disgusted 'what can you do now?' I said out loud in hopes of hearing an answer emerge from the blackness enveloping me. "With only 50 known motorcycles in Egypt, at well past midnight, you get yourself stuck miles from the only repair shop." The bike did not answer my snivel nor did the deepening surrounding shadows.

Drenched and exasperated, I pushed the soggy mud-coated bike to the side of the road and placed it beneath a lonely, limp looking palm. Finding a couple of fallen fronds nearby, I placed them over the sidecar and saddle bags along with my coat in hopes of keeping my new photography supplies from getting completely sodden. I sat beneath the tree trying not to doze-off should a car or carriage happen along. Which given the late hour and dismal conditions was not likely.

To keep myself alert, I pondered the exciting artifacts the dig had uncovered earlier in the week, but my frustration at probably having to miss the next day's finds was overpowering my joyful reminiscences with a deeply felt dose of disappointment. As my head lowered my self-inflicted aggravation quickly turned to wild expectation for the glow from lights of an approaching car on the road from Alexandria emerged from behind a small sandy knoll.

The vehicle was heading south, exactly the direction I needed to go. My mind was reeling. Will the driver stop, do they have room for me, for my supplies and what of the 500M? Probably not I quickly surmised. Maybe they are only going to Beni Suef, less than half the 200 miles to my destination of Amarna. I cannot abandon the 500M, my father would never forgive me, but perhaps I could ride with them to Beni and find help to quickly return and retrieve the bike.

As the vehicle's lights crew brighter, I could see it was a truck, not a car. I cautiously stepped out into the middle of the muddy road waving my arms frantically. The truck weaved a bit, slowed, and slid to a stop less than an arms-length from my boots. "I recognize this machine," said a dark, hat covered head as it leaned out the side tarp. "Is that you Asim?"

"Yes, yes, Herr Borchardt, it is I Asim. Are you returning to camp?"

"What has happened to your motor bike?"

"Maybe it is just the mud that has fouled it," I replied. "May I ride with you? Do you have room for my miserable self?"

"Why of course my good fellow. The men will help you. Load your motor bike quickly, we need to schnell for we must arrive before the digging resumes at the dawn." He looked at the bike with a trace of suspicion in his eyes. "That is a very impressive motor bike even covered by mud."

"My father is testing it for Peugeot to see how it holds up in the desert. He will be surprised when I inform him it does not do well in rain." I said this so Borchardt would not worry as to whether I had stolen the machine. He chuckled a bit and gestured for his workers to get the bike.

The men loaded it as I struggled to put my coat back on over soaking wet clothes. My befuddled-ness was of little concern for I was deeply gratified I was on my way again and would arrive on time for the reconvening of the excavation.

The relentlessly bouncing open bed truck had a leaky canvas tarp roof, was crowded with men and supply crates requiring me to cradle my saddle bags containing expensive, new photography glass plates, in my arms like a newborn. The light-sensitive emulsion of silver salts coating the plates made them thinner than common window glass which demanded they be handled with a high level of care. If I were to damage them, Herr Borchardt would surely insist I repay him and maybe even dismiss me.

"How is your work progressing Asim?" asked Herr Borchardt as he flicked rain from his hair with the back of his left hand. "You must make sure we will be able to see the details of each artifact. Has the new tent made it possible for you to better control the light?"

"Yes, very much. I pray it has remained waterproof against this unforeseen weather."

"Right you are, I hope the excavation is not flooded either." His eyes and voice were drowsy with trepidation. His receding hair, nose, chin, and mustache were all dripping wet plus his usually strong impersonable voice was sounding overwrought and he looked uncomfortable as he gazed at each of the three Egyptian men, including myself, seated opposite him. He seemed to be scrutinizing more than our appearance, almost as though he was expecting to see our souls revealed within our eyes. The moment reminded me of one of my father's favorite maxims 'rain in the desert is considered a blessing, but to Europeans it is looked upon as a curse' or at least an annoyance it seemed to me.

"The dig is a success is it not?" I said hoping to elicit at least a grin. "You have discovered many wonderful artifacts. You will be praised when you return to Berlin Herr Borchardt."

"Perhaps. It will depend on whether inspector Gustave Lefebvre is generous with his partage of the artifacts and if our crates are not pilfered during shipment." He listened to the sound of his voice as though he had used that sentence before and looked at each of us again with his analytical stare. "Youssef assures me everything discovered to date is accounted for, but I believe I should hire more armed guards for the excavation and the Cairo warehouse. There are thieves everywhere."

I noticed at the mention of Youssef's name, the excavation diggers with us paid heed.

"Is there one individual you suspect?"

"I'd rather not reveal whom or what I suspect." He glanced around as though he were ill at ease again, then reluctantly returned to writing in his journal and frowned over the scrawling he was doing there.

I could not help but wonder if it ever occurred to him, we Egyptians view the English, French and Germans as criminals who are constantly appropriating our ancient cultural heritage. However, I dared not speak of it for I would be discharged, thrown off the truck and never awarded such a privileged position on an excavation team ever again.

The drizzle resumed as a dark moon peeked from behind foreboding clouds and the truck slid about a bit as we rounded another challenging curve to traverse more potholes. As the hour grew late and the lunar light darkened, we all became lethargic and impervious to the relentless thumping of the rutted road. However, somehow the pummeling sound caused me to contemplate if the people of China were content and joyful they had proclaimed themselves as a republic. I pondered if Egypt were ever so fortunate, would it celebrate such a momentous change? Could it even handle it?

CHAPTER 2

Finding all the tents dark and no guards in sight, the driver unobtrusively slowed the truck as we approached camp. My fellow Egyptian companions gestured to me, I reached across and lightly tugged Herr Borchardt's sleeve. "Good morning, Sir." He shook his head, glared at me, stood up quickly and strained to look about into the obscurity of the murky pre-dawn.

"Where are the guards?" he shouted as he reached over and hit the truck's horn repeatedly. "Youssef," he yelled.

A light came on in one tent, then another and Youssef emerged fumbling with his clothes. "Yes, yes I am here Herr Borchardt."

"Where are the guards?" Borchardt shouted even louder. To my surprise, Youssef looked toward the women's area.

She was leaning forward from a new tent, watching us intently. Our eyes met for an instant and Borchardt looked at me too. She looked back at Youssef and walked calmly past him toward the truck. "I instructed them to remain inside Asim's tent to protect the artifacts and his equipment Herr Borchardt."

His face twisted sourly. "Who are you Fräulein?"

"This is my ward Chione Khnum-Rekhi, Herr Borchardt," replied Youssef with his head bowed.

"Ah, the language interpreter for our customs and shipping documents."

"Yes, yes, she will make sure all translations are accurate," said Youssef repeatedly bowing in a reverential and overly servile manner I found incensing.

"And how do those responsibilities allow her to station guards inside the photography tent rather than at the excavation site as I instructed you to do?"

"Before the rain began, we covered Room 19 of the quadrant with canvases and heavy wood planks plus left one guard stationed there. The other guards are inside the photography tent to keep it from collapsing due to the weight of the rain," she said as a sweet smile brushed her delicate face. Her tone was both assertive, but lacking in self-confidence.

There was just enough sunlight emerging to reveal Borchardt's unshaven mug working with a terrible effort of discontented thought. The moment slowly lingered to a level of rising anxiety amongst us all.

"Vielen Dank, ah, thank you Fräulein. That was very good thinking. Did much water enter the room?"

There was a communal sigh of relief as Chione bowed slightly and stepped back. Youssef moved forward.

"We were able to cover it before the cloud burst started Herr Borchardt," said Youssef no longer bowing. "We will check now to see if our efforts kept it dry."

I felt as though I was in the middle of a life size chess game and it was my turn to make a move. "I will check the photography tent and report my findings to you immediately Herr Borchardt."

"Right you are Asim and take Fräulein Chione with you to make sure the inventory ledger is dry. The rest of you join me at the dig schnell."

"Natürlich," I uttered under my breath. Borchardt looked at me not sure of what I had said, but none-the-less gave me a stiff, but affirmative nod.

Chione caught my gaze and held it, as if she were trying to read my thoughts. Her eyes were dark, intense, and resistant to decipher.

Everyone scattered about quickly and the emerging sun appeared to push the clouds further away. Chione inclined her head toward me as her glistening dark hair swung forward, framing her fine features. Captivating and demanding my attention.

She began nervously nibbling the inside of her upper lip. I let the silence stretch out. I just wanted to look at her in the morning glow. She did not mind. Her skin was a smooth natural brown and I wondered if she was tawny all over. She looked close into my face and then beyond into the vast awaking desert before speaking. I smiled and she decided to respond.

"Youssef told me you are a professional photographer. That must be very exciting. What do you photograph besides old artifacts?"

The rhythm of her voice was hypnotic and the golden rays of sunlight streaking over the horizon and reflecting in her auburn eyes left me transfixed. "Why are you a ward of Youssef?"

"Ugh ... both of my parents were killed in the Mahdist War."

"I am sorry. So, Youssef is a relative, perhaps an uncle or something?"

"In a way possibly."

I wanted to ask what that meant and on which side did her parents fight in the war, but her unexpected contriteness suggested a hint of malice. I left the question for another time.

"I did not mean to pry. It is just that you and he do not seem as though you are of the same background. You are refined and, as nice a fellow as Youssef is, he is not. In fact, if you do not mind me saying, he is a bit-coarse at times."

She turned toward my tent. "Herr Borchardt is not paying us to gossip aimlessly. Shall we check everything inside?"

"Right, but you could live anywhere, and yet, you choose to wither away in this dreadful sun in the middle of the desert looking at bits and pieces of an old, dead culture. Why?"

Her eyes focused on me with a fierce sharpness, but her voice was soft. "Because I have no other choice. I must do as Youssef commands. That dead culture as you call it, is very much alive especially, with regard, to women. Are you not an Egyptian man?"

I did not answer or ask any further questions. We went about our business checking the equipment and supplies without speaking, all the while keeping my eyes on her. Every move she made was sensual and alluring. My mind felt scattered and aflame with carnal thoughts.

"That's it, we are finished," I said as I looked at my watch.

"Would you mind, if I report our findings to Herr Borchardt?" she said with her demeanor and eyes sharp focused again. "I'd like to make sure he is not angry with Youssef about how we protected Room 19."

"Not at all. Go, I need to take care of my new photography glass plates and check to see what can been done to repair the motorcycle."

She graciously smiled and walked away with purpose in her heart and stride. I was already missing her and looking forward to our next encounter.

The Peugeot 500M was not looking as exciting as it did just a few hours earlier. It was just a mud coated machine whose fire had been easily harnessed. However, Chione's inner inferno seemed infinite to me and I wanted to get closer to it, to be warmed by it, maybe even singed. Plus, my manhood felt challenged by her femininity.

CHAPTER 3

Considering how humid and damp the day before had been plus how suffocating the night air was, the morning was surprisingly pleasant and crisp. I looked about in hopes of finding Chione in the camp, but she was not there. Everyone was a buzz because today the main effort in the Quadrant is untouched Room 19, which could be the personal workshop of the royal sculptor. A bust of Pharaoh Amenhotep IV had already been found along with other busts, glazed amulets, amphoras and interesting stone fragments with carved images of the Pharoah's family. Today, everyone's hopes were high more significant artifacts would be uncovered.

At mid-day messengers arrived and informed Herr Borchardt the steamship bringing the Prince and Princess of Saxony would be docking soon. Borchardt dusted off his clothes and hat, "Keep working as you are. I will return with our Royal guests soon." He dashed-away looking nervous and a bit ashen. It occurred to me perhaps the night truck ride did not provide him with sufficient respite for he usually did not appear so stressed when notables where present.

The team work of the excavation crew was impressive as always. They carefully filled and lifted each sieved bag of sand out of the room with studied care. As the last bag was taken away to be emptied some shifting rubble from the stone brick walls near the northeast corner revealed what appeared to be a flesh-colored neck. Everyone abruptly stopped, set their tools aside and began digging cautiously with their hands only. First a neck with painted red ribbons was laid bare, above the neck the lower portion of the bust appeared, below it the back of a queen's wig-like form. It took some time, however, before the piece was completely freed from the rubble and sand, because first another portrait head of the Pharoah, found directly north of it, had to be carefully retrieved. Only after that was the colorful bust lifted out by Youssef and we had the most lifelike Egyptian work of art any of us had ever seen before, staring one-eyed back at us.

As Chione and I watched in awe, a car arrived and to our astonishment Prince Johann Georg, his wife and sister-in-law plus Princess Mathilde stepped out. They looked about for Herr Borchardt or for someone to officially welcome them. Excavation supervisors Herrmann Ranke and Paul Hollander cautiously welcomed them and invited them to approach. As they watched Youssef carefully wiped some of the dirt from the back of the bust and turned it over judiciously revealing an almost completely intact life-sized portrait sculpture of a woman. He took special note that the colors were still bright.

"It looks freshly painted after maybe 3000 years buried right here in the womb of mother Egypt's sand. We must see if the missing parts of the ears and eye are here. All, of those last bags must be resieved."

"It will be done," said Chione. "Is it Queen Nefertiti?"

"I believe so, she is wearing the crown. The beautiful one has come," said Youssef with pride.

Everyone slowly stepped back as he gently carried the sculpture out into the sunlight allowing his eyes to survey and savor every inch of it. "Even unfinished her charm and repose are absolutely enchanting," I said.

Youssef bowed slightly, smiled and handed the sculpture to Prince Georg. It seemed noteworthy and completely unexpected the first person in this new century to be introduced to the Queen, as it were, was a Prince, a Royal if you will, who immediately turned and held the sculpture out for each of his family to view.

Senussi, one of the more experienced excavation diggers reported he had felt 3 more plaster heads and one granite foot under the sand nearby. Youssef immediately ordered four guards to stay at the site.

"Perhaps Room 19 was a storage space or personal workshop of the royal sculptor," I said. We all looked at the area again and Prince Georg handed the Queen back to Youssef as Herr Borchardt arrived obviously frustrated having missed the discovery of the Queen and the arrival of the Prince, but extremely excited at seeing Nefertiti safely cradled in Youssef's arms.

Herr Borchardt bowed to the Prince and his family, "Please come and allow me to show you all of the other artifacts we have discovered and then we can have tea where you can relax in the shade."

"Yes and then you and your staff will join us on the steamboat for dinner," said the Prince while shaking Herr Borchardt's hand.

"Oh, I'm sorry we do not have any evening attire here," replied Borchardt.

"There is no need, we will all dine in khaki."

The Prince then went to the car and retrieved a camera and began taking photographs of everyone. Seeing them staring at him, he said "Oh, I'm an amateur and these photographs will be for my daily diary."

The photographer who arrived with the Prince's entourage had taken several glass plate negatives and I was amazed at how quickly he snapped each one. I was certain the candid compositions would not be acceptable to the Prince, but he appeared to be pleased each time the man said 'hold it'.

"Maybe it was never finished," said a throaty whisper that made the short hairs at the back of my neck arise. It was Chione standing behind my left shoulder and leaning her subtle body against me. "Maybe they all had to leave in a hurry and simply left everything behind."

Herr Borchardt stood staring at the bust as if transfixed by wonder or astonishment.

"We should clean it off before I photograph it," I eagerly suggested. "It will appear as new."

"No, do not touch it. I want it photographed as it is. As it is. Do you hear Asim?"

"Yes, Herr Borchardt, I will do as you say."

Everyone looked perplexed and completely baffled. Every artifact was always lightly brushed off or wiped clean before photographing it or even before listing it in the excavation's master ledger.

Chione looked at me steadily for several seconds. Finally, a smile touched her luscious mouth and parted it with hushed tones. "Herr Borchardt has been consumed. Look at how intense he is."

"He will keep this sculpture for himself," I said as I turned and looked into her eyes. "No one else will hold her."

Chione and I returned to my photography tent. I took out my personal journal and wrote a note after the date '6 December 1912: Our first embrace'. Chione smiled and we enthusiastically put our arms around each other for what felt like stilled time until she turned, took the pen and wrote 'and kissed'.

"Meet me tonight for a walk after everyone is asleep," she said looking deep into my eyes and giving me another delicate kiss.

I smiled and shook my head in aching anticipation. She was so much more than I had ever hoped for in a woman.

The excitement of the day had been spent as Herr Borchardt and his staff returned from the Prince's river boat dinner party at 9:30pm, but it was not quiet in the camp until after midnight when Chione and I met and walked away in the moonlight. I immediately put my arm around her and moved in for a kiss. She pushed against me and said "No, we must not. Youssef will send me away if he were to discover me alone with you."

"But surely his daily ration of beer has put him to sleep," I replied.

"Probably, but I do not want anyone to see us together. It would give them something to hold over Youssef," she whispered as she took my hand and led me away from the tents.

"Tell me about Herr Borchardt," she said as we sat on a large fallen column from the demolished temple to look at the moon and each other. "Do you know why he was given this excavation?"

Her question disappointed me, but I did not want to give her reason to dislike me.

"He studied at a university in Berlin and became assistant to the Egyptian art department at the museum there. He is now a well-known Egyptologist and archaeologist who specializes in architecture. However, in the first year of digging here he did not find any spectacular objects. But during the past few weeks he has more than made up for it by discovering numerous portrait busts of Pharaoh Akhenaten and his family, a spectacular find."

"So why does he need me?"

"I asked him the same."

"And?"

"He believes he will get more cooperation with the Egyptian & French authorities if he has a local person assisting him."

"I see, but I am a woman. Does he understand how limited my standing is with anyone in authority. What can I really do for him?"

"Perhaps it is your womanly charm and beauty he is attracted to. You saw how enthralled he was with the bust of Nefertiti. I mean you do look very much like her."

"Do not be ridiculous. I am not a Queen," she said shyly as she turned away from me holding back a smile.

We walked on beyond the adobe wall of the quadrant site. "Why are you so interested in Borchardt?"

"If I am allowed to travel with the artifacts to Berlin, he may be willing to help me find a position there."

"You want to live in Europe? Why?"

"Besides Egyptian, I speak German, French and English plus I have been told, women have a better chance to improve their situation there. If I stay here, Youssef will marry me off to one of his relatives or cronies and I will be kept in a house just to bear children."

"You don't want to marry and have children?"

She turned and faced me. "I hate the idea as much as I love it." She shook her head quite sharply, as if to punish herself. "Perhaps someone will..." she made a small coughing noise of distress, but did not complete her thought.

"That sounds so unconclusive," I uttered. "And preposterous."

"Maybe," she said as she studied the night sky. "Have you ever wondered why those three bright stars are in a straight row? They are so close together their gravity must hold them in place. You can always clearly see them this time of year."

I was impressed and thankful to know she is well educated.

"Orion's Belt is always visible in the night sky from November to February from just about anywhere in the world. The stars are named after Greek gods Alnilam, Mintaka and Alnitak, but they are not actually next to one another they only appear so from earth," I said as I stared at their reflection in her eyes.

"Have you ever walked beyond those cliffs to the high desert," she asked pointing.

"Yes, there is an old quarry and wadi there," I replied while studying how the lunar light revealed the gentle curves of her neck. "It is where most of the stone for Pharoah Akhenaten's city came from. He had it cut into talatat-blocks so each one could be easily carried by a man or donkey."

"Is it true, what the old ones say, that he made life easier for his people."

"I suppose you could think so, but more likely he simply wanted to make it possible to build his new city quickly."

"Did you hear about the man that jumped out of a flying airplane wearing something called a parachute and he floated to the ground?" she asked.

"Yes, it's remarkable and wonderful," I replied.

"But it is not good the way the Italians are using air ships to spy behind the Turkish lines in the war," she said starring deeply into my eyes.

"Not all new inventions are used for good purposes, I said embracing her.

"The collision of the big ship and iceberg where all the people drowned was terrifying. Have you ever seen an iceberg? I cannot imagine one so big floating in the sea."

"Can you imagine a woman flying an airplane over the sea?" I asked.

"No, did that really happen? They let a woman learn how to fly an airplane?"

"Yes, in Europe women are allowed to do many things."

Her pretty mouth twisted in thought as she walked away into the shadowy stillness of the desert. I watched her from a distance as she safely made her way back to the women's tent. I suspected she would fall to sleep dreaming about flying an airplane.

My tent was dark, but I could see the night sky through the open flap as I lay back on my dusty cot gazing at the stars of Orion's Belt again. Visions of the real Nefertiti with her husband, the Pharaoh Akhenaton, at their royal court, playing with their daughters and at the workshop of the royal sculptor flickered through my tired mind super-imposed with images of Chione roaming carefree about Berlin. I did not sleep well.

• • •

A few days later, Borchardt went to Cairo to send some special communications to the Berlin Museum so I took the opportunity to go to Assiut, a nearby small hamlet. I was looking for a local historian named Karim whom Youssef claimed had a vast knowledge of Nefertiti and Akhenaton.

I found him at the end of a narrow passage in the old quarter of the wadi. He spoke respectively of Youssef and invited me to sit and share a beaker of honey-ginger beer.

"You are an Egyptian photographer who works for a German. That is most unusual."

"My father is Egyptian, my mother Turkish so I was allowed to apprentice in Istanbul with a Turkish photographer whose wife is German."

One of Karim's eyes was a little unlevel giving his face an amorphous appearance as he pondered my answer. He turned away and did not speak as he looked out toward a well-formed, but relatively short-lived dust devil swirling out of the open desert.

"How can I be of help to you?"

"I would like to know why there are no Egyptians who can read hieroglyphics."

The dust devil dissolved and again Karim studied me as he picked up his spoon and stirred his beer. "Is your father or mother a Christian?"

"I see, so it was forbidden to read hieroglyphics because of the possible religious content?"

He swallowed a sip of beer and smiled.

"And this was of concern to the Christians?"

Another dust devil sprung up and dissolved just as quickly as the first.

"Only to the greedy ones," he replied.

A mature woman emerged from a dusky room behind us and refilled the beaker as he recounted how European and British archaeologists had gone to great lengths to keep Egyptians from understanding their own history and possibly finding the location of unspoiled tombs.

"Do you know what happened each time a new pharaoh took over as ruler?" he asked.

"No, that was not part of my schooling," I said.

"Pharoah Akhenaten and his wife Nefertiti made many changes. They replaced the animal gods with the sun god Aten and started a new religion which caused social upheaval. Then they moved the royal palace and temple to Akhetaten, which you call Amarna, but there was no city there. They ordered one to be built quickly."

"Is that why every building there was made with small adobe and stone blocks instead of the traditional large ones?"

"Yes, Akhetaten reflected a vision of the ultimate society, dedicated to the idea of the sun as the only life-giving god. The newly founded city housed temples for him, palaces for the royal family, residential areas, work-shops, and burial grounds for the people. It was all beautiful until the death of Akhenaten."

"What happened then?"

"Akhetaten was destroyed and abandoned. All of Egypt turned its back on the sun religion," he uttered through a dry cough.

"So Amarna's, ah Akhetaten's sudden-destruction was forgotten and the desert returned?" I asked.

"It was barely 20 years old when it became a city for the dead. Those that took power sought to erase all traces of Akhenaten, his followers, and his capitol Akhetaten. No new buildings were ever constructed on top of the ruins."

"So that is why the buried artifacts are so well preserved and that brief life of the city is what has made Amarna a treasure trove for Herr Borchardt and his team of archaeologists. Their excavations have discovered countless fragments of the city's history and treasures," I said.

"That is Egypt's history, our history. You must share it with our people.

He spoke with dislike for the French archaeologists and Louvre emissary who controls the Conservator of Egyptian Monuments office and opposes training Egyptians as professional archaeologists. "They are afraid Egyptian professionals will replace them. We are not even allowed to copy hieroglyphic inscriptions. Their fear is why so many of us have learned. You must help."

"How can I. I have not the time to study hieroglyphs."

He glanced around as though he were ill at ease then grinned with tobacco-stained teeth as his hairy nostrils sniffed the air. Perhaps he suspected I was not who I said I was.

"You are the official photographer of the Tel El Amarna excavation, give us copies of every photograph you make. Photographs of what rightfully belongs to Egypt."

"That would be difficult. I have what sounds like an important title, but I must account for all the supplies I use. Making copies of all the photographs would use up more paper and chemicals than I have access to. Herr Borchardt would have me arrested as a thief."

"Leave it with me. I will talk with Cairo to see what can be done. Perhaps you will be given the glass plates at the end of the dig? I understand more treasures were found."

I smiled, but did not answer as I left feeling as though I had made a mistake. If word spread, I was working with dissents or worse with smugglers I would be shot.

My tent was dark when I arrived back at the compound, but there was a pleasing hint of roses lingering around my cot and a small bag of fresh dates had been placed on my pillow. I laid down and fell asleep gazing at the night sky while my slumbering mind again ushered in wonderful visions of Nefertiti and Chione.

In the coming days a variety of artifacts were found including a ivory horse blind engraved with hieroglyphs stating the royal sculptors name was Thutmose which meant this house and workshop were most likely his. I was instructed to photograph everything and knowing the name of the artist made the process so much more personal for me.

Besides the bust of the beautiful Nefertiti also discovered were small maquette models of sculptures and full-size unfinished ones, rare flint and bronze carving tools, fragments of steatite, granite and calcite plus a delicate ivory plate painted in a rare red pigment.

Above all, a series of plaster casts were found that represent the different stages of the rendering of a future sculpture. All of these, precious artifacts were discovered in the personal complex of royal sculptor Thutmose and many revealed the varied processes he used such as making clay and plaster molds directly from the living patron.

I was impressed with how these discoveries showed making life size portrait bust has changed very little over the centuries.

• • •

Several days later, after everything had been inspected, listed in the ledger, and photographed, Herr Borchardt carefully placed the Nefertiti bust inside a shipping crate along with several ordinary unimpressive items. He insisted I take photos of the open crate to show how the items had been packed. He had not made such a request of any of the other crates.

The crate was then sealed and labeled. I was instructed to develop my photography plates and make prints immediately.

I reminded Borchardt the photos were only black and white while the Nefertiti bust was in glorious color. "Would you like me to hand color at least one photograph of it so inspector Monsieur Lefebvre will have a better understanding of its beauty?"

"If he wants to inspect the bust, he has only to have the crate opened. Besides, as you are well aware, there are several other plaster busts and some very fine stone ones of Nefertiti that he has designated to remain in Egypt."

"The bust photograph Borchardt placed in the envelope for inspector Lefebvre was the one showing the most dirt and sand still on the sculpture," I whispered to Chione.

"It is obvious he doesn't want to draw attention to it," she replied has she gestured for us to back away.

"Chione," said Borchardt as he watched the lid of the crate being secured. "Did you make copies of all the shipping documents as I instructed?"

"It has been completed and is placed on your desk, Herr Borchardt." Her face drew pale as she clasped her hands together behind her.

I must have dozed for a moment for a dream rushed into my consciousness causing me to shake my head in a negative motion. I could see Chione in Berlin with Herr Borchardt as plain as the address on the side of the crate.

Turning toward Chione he spoke again. "We will leave for Cairo in the morning. Be sure you are packed and ready to go at dawn," he snapped as he tried to smile without showing his teeth. The smile was a failure and only served-to-show more of his age. He did not look at me. "Oh, and make sure Asim gets his letter of introduction." He swallowed whatever taste he had in his mouth and assumed a guarded manner nodding in my general direction. "Asim, I assume you packed all the glass plate negatives? If there are any photographic supplies remaining you may have them. Just make sure everything is out of the tent by nightfall."

"It will be done Herr Borchardt and thank you, most generous."

He walked away and waved without looking back.

"He seems annoyed, is he angry about something? I asked.

"He met with a member of the German Oriental Company and a senior Egyptian official this morning. They discussed the final partage of the artifacts from the excavation, reviewed the inventory list and looked at the photographs you took of each artifact," whispered Chione. "Including the Nefertiti bust."

"The one with all the dirt still on it?"

"Yes, but the bust was left wrapped up in the crate when Monsieur Lefebrvre came in for his official inspection and I watched him read the description on the inventory list, but I did not see him look at the photograph.

· · ·

There was nothing left in the tent after the crates were packed except a few half-empty jars of chemicals and a small box of print paper so there it was, my worst nightmare and my dearest dream all at once. Chione will leave and I will have a few photographic supplies to make prints for private clients.

Borchardt walked out to the shipping truck while Chione and I stood in silence looking at each other from opposite sides of the crate containing the Nefertiti bust. It was also leaving for Berlin.

"So this is it, you will get your chance to experience living in Europe," I said with a forced smile.

She stood there in a rigid pose and begun walking back and forth quickly. The vigor of her youthful figure was stunningly beautiful and I hated the thought of European men looking at her as I so enjoyed doing.

"You will like Herr Borchardt's letter of introduction," she stated firmly.

That was not what I had expected. "Why, because it says he was happy with my photography work? No Egyptian clients will care about that."

Her eyes flashed and her breast rose and fell with the appearance of genuine feeling as she darted out of the tent. I felt a rash of stupidity clouding my mind. I bowed and leaned my head against the crate hoping for some ancient Egyptian wisdom to emit from Nefertiti and penetrate my cranium.

I had very little money, no house and only a dream of opening my own photography studio. Chione would be traveling surrounded by rich men, to a rich country, to mingle amongst the most modern of life styles at the start of this new century. I doubted I would ever see her again. I would end up living in my father's house and working in his automobile garage for the rest of my life. I reminded myself, I should be grateful for there are thousands of others who have far less than I.

. . .

The warm breeze off the desert shifted as a lone cloud passed in front of the sun and the unnatural smell of motor oil-soaked sand made the garage feel more crowded than usual. It had been several weeks since Chione had gone to Berlin and I was once again cleaning the Peugeot 500M in hopes it would run strong again by just getting all the dried mud out of the carburetor.

"Probably dirt in the vaporizer," said Youssef. "Camels are better adapted to the desert than internal combustion engines. Ah, but then if you are going to Berlin, a camel will not work as well as a motor carriage there."

"I did not hear you come in Youssef. It is good to see you. Are you working on another excavation and what makes you think I am going to Berlin?"

"Oh, Chione made me promise to give you this before I leave. The new dig I am working at is called Babylon."

He handed me an unsealed envelope with 'Anneliese Brantt, Istanbul' written on the outside. Starring at it, I stood reminiscing about my many weeks in Istanbul as a photography intern.

"Well take out the letter, she obviously wants you to read it."

The name rang a bell in my head and I remembered reading about Ms. Brantt in a magazine at the Grand Bazaar in Istanbul and in another one at the studio of the photographer I apprenticed with. "It's a letter of recommendation to a photographer in Istanbul."

"Istanbul, but Chione is in Berlin. What is in Istanbul?" Youssef asked with a scowl.

"I guess Herr Borchardt believes I'm not suited for Berlin." The sun disappeared and everything turned grey or so it seemed to me at that moment.

"He wants to keep you away from Chione," he replied looking at me incredulously.

"What are you talking about?"

"Everyone knows you and my Chione have feelings for one another. Do not deny it. Herr Borchardt must feel, as do I, you need to improve your station in life before pursuing her in marriage." His eyes held a curious mixture of plea and threat.

"It does not make sense this photographer is a woman of about my age. How could she possibly help me to advance?"

"Would Herr Borchardt take time to write such a letter only to embarrass himself. I do not believe so. He knows something about this photographer woman you do not." He gave me an impervious stare.

I must have drifted for a few moments again for a dream rushed past the threshold of my consciousness causing me to shiver. There was enough truth in his statement to tie my tongue and cause the obscure pain of memory to return. It was of the image centered in my mind; the face of my loving Chione.

"Youssef, you are a cunning and astute fellow. Chione is smart to follow your council. Which reminds me. Did Herr Borchardt get everything he was hoping for from Lefebvre's final examination of the excavation artifacts?"

"Lefebvre's cursory exam of the photographs you provided were all he looked at."

"He did not open even one crate?"

CHAPTER 4

Ms. Brantt's face had a little starch in it, but not enough to spoil her natural beauty. Her hair was pulled back from her forehead and left to curl at the back of her head or at least that was the impression I got from looking at her self-portrait photographs posted outside the door to her studio in Istanbul. I knocked and a voice said "Die Tür ist offen" I entered.

She was standing at a desk with the phone to her left ear and listening while using her right hand to fuss with the curls of her hair. Indecision was twisting her lips, but her eyes were firmly focused on me. She let go of her curls and cupped her hand over the phone mouth piece "I dislike contacting the Police, but I guess I must."

I leaned forward and whispered. "What is the problem?"

"Nichts," she said and hung up the phone. She looked radiant and slightly disorganized.

"The problem is I must have everything packed and to the station before noon or I will miss the next train to Berlin. Ah, no, what I mean is, the men hired to help me have not arrived and I am running out of time."

"I see. Perhaps I could be of assistance?"

"Oh, I would not want to impose on you. After all you came here to have your portrait photograph made, not to do manual labor."

I was obviously over-dressed, though it did not seem so to me. "I am Asim Khalifa Lateef and…"

Her eyes seemed to focus inward, on an image in her memory. She blinked and said: "Oh, oh, yes, the letter from Herr Borchardt. Well, needless-to-say I cannot offer you a position now. I have received a very important photography assignment in Berlin and must leave today."

I was amazed. Berlin, the very place I had been hoping to go to.

"Will you need an assistant? I would welcome an opportunity to work with you in Berlin," I gushed out.

She paused and sat down in the only chair. The taut curve of her back made her overall posture impressive. "You are willing to move to Berlin just to be my assistant?"

"Herr Borchardt believes I could benefit from working with you."

"Does he now? He wrote the same thing about you."

"I do not understand."

"He thinks I could benefit by working with you. He wrote it in the letter he sent me."

"I see, well we are wasting time. Are we not?"

She stood up quickly, put her hands on her hips and smiled. "I will empty out this desk, you see if you can finish loading the crate in the studio. Oh, do you have money for a train ticket?"

"May I use your phone? I will reserve one now." She still seemed dubious and tense. "I will have them send a truck to pick up the crate."

That made her smile. "I must remember to thank Herr Borchardt properly." Her voice was low and resonant.

We shook hands and quickly packed everything. I had just enough money to pay for my ticket, the transporting of Anneliese's crates to the station, and for a few small meals on the journey.

. . .

The Istanbul railroad office told me the Balkan Zug train trip to Berlin could easily take five days because of the winter weather. I reserved a sleeper in the men's 2nd class car which left me with very little money for meals. The first night we got as far as Sofia and made a brief 30-minute stop and continued-on while the tracks were still clear of snow, but the following night in Belgrade we were informed the tracks ahead were impassable. We stayed there until almost noon the following day before being able to travel on.

Fräulein Brantt was in a railcar much further forward than I, so we met in the bar car for drinks. She was not overly talkative about herself, but I gathered she was more interested in art and industrial design than general photography. She was an accomplished painter, sculptor and metalsmith as well as having designed several household objects such as teapots and lamps. I wondered if Herr Borchardt was trying to tell me I was not good enough to be just a photographer and I should expand into other fields too.

We agreed to meet at the bar again the next day. I arrived a little early and it was interesting to hear such a vast array of languages being spoken by an even more diverse looking ensemble of individuals than yesterday's group. It caused my thoughts to drift to visions of Chione probably surrounded by a similar throng in Berlin.

"Do you understand many of these people?" Anneliese asked as she stood opposite me at a small table. "I can tell what a few may be talking about for they look as though their conversation is mostly gossip," I said as we both leaned against the table.

"Yes, their tell-tale whispers and raised eyebrows do make it seem so."

I glanced about and everyone was in a group of two or three except one lone man standing at the far end of the bar. He was slim and appeared as though he may be tall if he were not leaning his elbows on the bar. He wore a dark suit with his hat pulled down to shade his face and was smoking a short, thin cigar.

"As the only person we both know is Herr Borchardt, there isn't much we can tittle-tattle about unless you want to start a rumor about him," Anneliese said with a mischievous smile.

"No, that would not be appropriate, especially since he may be friends or a colleague of any one of these people. Besides, I know only two mysteries about him," I replied as the waiter came to our table.

Anneliese ordered a gin and tonic while I asked for ginger beer.

"Well you are ahead of me. I know practically nothing about him other than he is considered an authority on ancient Egyptian architecture. What are the two mysteries you are referring to?"

A faint, attractive wave softened her eyes as she stared into mine while tasting her drink. I was thinking about the Beautiful One and Ms. Brantt herself, but I really should not talk about the first one. "Well, you are one," I said with a sly grin.

"Me, what do mean?"

"While I did not get to know Herr Borchardt well during the excavation, I do know he does not do anything off-hand or in a casual manner. So, I wonder, why he feels you and I should work together."

Her generous smile turned to laughter. "Yes, that mystery could easily be turned into a juicy rumor. However, it is one I ponder too."

The sudden silence in the room got her attention and she shifted her relaxed pose to one of apprehension then lit a cigarette with a lighter in the shape of a lipstick holder. Something I had never seen before. Her hands shook slightly, but I could see the sharp edges of fear behind the careful expression on her face. "I have only met him once. He came to the opening reception of one of my art exhibitions."

"That's all? You must have made an impression on him."

She took a slow view around at the crowd, forcing every one to resume their own conversation and in an incredible reserve attitude of presumed innocence she found the energy to blush. "It was probably my artwork which moved him. I talked more with his wife than with him."

A gentle ripple of laughter lifted above the chatter which told us everyone was still listening to everything we said. "Shall we get some air?" I suggested as I finished the ginger beer and offered Anneliese my arm. Her face was contorted and I thought she was trying not to cry, but she shivered, hunched her shoulders up and looped her arm around mine.

We exited the bar and entered the next car when she turned to face me. "Do you think it was our conversation or just Herr Borchardt's name which captured everyone's attention?"

"Well it certainly was not me or my name. No one knows me."

"And I doubt any of those people know me either," she said as she narrowed her eyes and watched me with a faded kind of guile. "If you know something important now is the time to tell me before we arrive at the Museum."

I shrugged. She began walking away. "Good evening," she said quietly as she put out her cigarette and did not look back. "Be careful about what you dream for."

I turned to return to the sleeper car and discovered the slim stranger from the bar was now standing only a few feet away with his back turned to me. As I approached to pass him, he turned to face the window, keeping his back to me. I passed and saw only a quick glimpse of his face reflected in the window. He wore a black mustache over thin lips and had an offensive rancid odor about him. I did not like his shaded aura at all.

• • •

The train managed to arrive in Berlin before noon and it was a fine, crisp day with only a mild cold breeze coming out of the northeast. Anneliese had arranged to share a small apartment, near the Hotel Excelsior, with a girlfriend from her hometown of Chemnitz. She suggested I could probably find a room in the Wedding District. I recalled Chione had mentioned Tiergarten Park, but I was quickly informed it was in the opposite direction.

"Well, Herr Borchardt assured me we would be given space in the Museum to store the camera equipment plus a darkroom to develop and make prints," said Anneliese. "So, there is no need to find a studio immediately. I will have our crates delivered to the Museum."

Hearing some of the train luggage porters speaking Turkish I asked them where I might find a room for the night and was given several suggestions, all of which were some distance from the Museum, Tiergarten Park or the Potsdamer Platz which Chione had also mentioned in one of her short letters. I decided to go to the Museum and begin walking toward the first address the Turks suggested in hopes of finding a room they knew nothing about. To my great surprise within a few blocks, I found a basement room with a side entrance off Erna-Berger Strasse. The house mistress, or lady of the house, was very impressed when I told her I would be working at the Museum even though she gave me a very skeptical look as she studied my black hair, eyebrows and eyes while correcting my very inadequate attempts at speaking German.

The room was small with a low ceiling, one table, one chair, a bed more suited to a woman or child, a single window, an aged wash basin and a half-melted candle, but the rent was also modest and the room felt surprisingly warm considering how cold it was outside. It was also getting dark and I was ravenous, but felt exhausted. I ate the last of my small bag of dates and fell into a deep sleep dreaming about Chione.

The rent fee included a complimentary breakfast of bread, Lingonberry marmalade and coffee. All of which was very fresh and tasted wonderful which made me wonder what Chione was eating, what her day would consist of and where in this massive city she could be for all of her letters bore only the address of her business employer, but not of where she was lodging.

The walk back to the Museum was long and challenging. Every street was filled with cars, motorcycles, horse drawn carriages, bicycles, and an endless parade of people. I felt out of place. My suit was of thin cloth and light colored while everyone else wore heavy clothes in dark colors. As I scurried along the sound of the city seemed horrendous and I noticed many people wearing earmuffs and wondered if they were for protection from the racket or the cold.

As I crossed a major intersection a blast of icy air reminded me it was still winter. By the time I arrived at the Museum I was shivering from the chill and trembling with the anxiety of not knowing what to expect. I fully believed as soon as whoever was in charge saw me, I would be thrown out. Perhaps I could get a position as a railroad baggage porter I thought, but if another Balkan war starts all trains will be halted again.

"You must be Asim," a young woman said as I reluctantly stood on the sidewalk in front of the Museum. "Staff enter around the side. Follow me," she said. "Anneliese, ah Ms. Brantt asked all of us to keep an eye out for you."

All I could do was to smile and nod. I knew if I spoke, I would sound like an imbecile. I followed my guide down a hall to a small room filled with men and women close to my age. They were all drinking coffee. Someone handed me a cup. I nodded my gratitude and smiled. "Sugar and milk are over there," she said with a polite gesture. "The Museum opens at 9 so you best finish quickly."

I nodded again and smiled, but had no idea as to where to go next. As I stood sipping my coffee and nodding to those who smiled at me the instant, I lowered my cup I was over taken by an array of aromas and fragrances that filled the small room. I hoped whatever scent I was contributing was not offensive.

"Herr Lateef, I am Hans Herbster. Ms. Brantt requested I bring you to the Photography Studio." His voice had a slight whine and it seemed to cost him some effort to speak. "If you have finished here, we should go." He was wearing a conservative dark gray suit and matching tie with highly polished black ankle boots. Which immediately reminded me I needed to get a new suit and shoes. He smelled vaguely of pine.

I set my cup near the sink. "Yes, of course, please." I gestured toward the door. Herr Herbster was short, but his hair stood erect on his scalp, like magnetized iron filings, making him appear taller than he was. He had a long stride which was challenging to keep up with as we went down a few stairs and through a labyrinth of hallways.

"The Photography Studio is the second door links. Welcome to the Museum Herr Lateef," he said as he shook my hand limply and walked away at a brisk pace.

The hallway was poorly lit and smelled musty. The second door on my left had a hand written note pinned to it that read simply: Photography Studio. Anneliese Liebe Brantt, Asim Khalifa Lateef. I was stunned to see my name posted next to Ms. Brantt's especially in a world-famous museum in an even more famous city.

I was not sure if I should knock or just enter. I chose to enter. "Hello Ms. Brantt, it is I, Asim."

"Guten Morgen, ah, good morning," she said in an excited manner. "Pick up those lights and put them on the cart next to the tripod."

I was amazed to find both of the crates we had packed in Istanbul delivered and emptied. "Did you unpack these?"

"No, I think Herr Herbster had some of the cleaning staff do it early this morning or late last night."

I smiled and nodded. "Where are we going?" I said as I noted she was wearing a gray smock over her own clothes.

"To the library. We will be taking portrait photographs of several of the Museum's general staff," she said as she moved to open the door. "Oh, there is a lab coat for you over there. We are required to wear them whenever we are working inside the Museum."

As we made our way through the halls to the Library, Anneliese told me in the coming days we would also be taking portraits of the Museum Volunteers, Exhibition Installers, Curators, and Secretaries as well as all the Administrators and Trustees. The list seemed endless and I wondered where all these people were in the building.

"I had assumed we would be photographing items from the Museum's permanent collections," I said when she finally stopped to catch her breath. "I have very little experience making portraits."

"Now I understand," she replied with her hands on her hips. "I have experience as a portrait photographer while you have specialized in photographing artifacts. Herr Borchardt is quite right, we can learn from each other." She looked very pleased with herself.

"How did you find out about all of this? I mean I arrived at 8:50, what time did you arrive?'

"I apologize, I neglected to tell you we are required to be here at 8:00 and stay until 6:00 every day except Sunday naturally. Are you familiar with Hans Holbein?"

"Ah, no, does he hold a position here at the Museum?'

She laughed. "Oh Asim, we have so much to learn from each other. Holbein is a very famous portrait painter and printmaker who lived during the Northern Renaissance. We are going to use some of his ideas when we stage the sitters we photograph," she continued to giggle to herself. "There is sure to be a book about him in the library."

"Are we allowed to take books from the library?" I asked still unsure of how much authority I had, if any at all.

"I do not know. We will have to ask. By-the-way, are you familiar with the Lumiere brothers autochrome technique?"

"No, is it something Holbein used?"

The look on Anneliese's face was unlike any I had ever seen on anyone and especially not on a woman. All I could tell for certain was she appeared completely frustrated and charmed at the same time.

"It is good we may only be photographing two sitters today because you have a lot to learn. Autochrome will enable us to make color photographs. Which means we will have to be very careful with the lighting."

I had heard about color photography made with a special kind of film and a mix of chemicals, but could not image how I would be able to learn the process in time to help with this photo shoot. "How much time do we have to set up before the first sitter arrives?"

"Less than an hour."

"How many lights does the library have?"

"I do not remember. I did not have time this morning to check and it has been a long time since I was last in there, but I seem to recall sechs, ah, six ceiling mounted lights."

"Who set up this schedule?" I said as we struggled to move our loaded carts through the halls without dropping anything.

"I do not know. Hans Herbster told me about it when he showed me to the Photography Studio. He appears to work for the Museum Director."

"That makes it two fellows my inner voice has told me to be watchful of," I said under my breath.

"What? Who are you talking about," she said as she abruptly stopped and inhaled deeply. "And what is your inner voice?"

"Don't you have a voice inside your head or a feeling right here in your gut that tells you when something does not seem right? I thought all women had one," I said as I pushed against my growling stomach.

"Oh, you mean intuition. Yes, I have it. So, who or what are you referring to?"

"Herbster and the slim, wiry looking fellow on the train."

"The one in the bar?" she said with a pause. "You are right, both of them have the same suspicious disposition and the slim one seemed creepy too."

Just as I was beginning to feel we were lost in the bowels of the Museum, Anneliese said, "The library is that door over there. You take everything in and set it up. I will be back in a few minutes, there are some things I need to check."

She dashed away before I could respond. I pushed the two carts in front of the door, but felt hesitant to knock. "Here, allow me," said Hans as he stepped passed me, opened, and held the door while gesturing like a waiter showing me to a table. "If the space we've prepared isn't appropriate, let me know before you move anything." His quick back glance vanished as he darted down the corridor.

The library, smelled much like the ones in Alexandria and Istanbul, the only libraries I had ever been in. The door I was shown through was not the main entrance so I was not sure what part of the library this was. I wanted to look around, but as the nearby staff were all focused on me, I nodded to each of them and went about setting up the camera and the two portable lights. The camera was not one I was familiar with. It appeared to use film instead of glass plates. I aimed it toward the empty chair someone had placed in front of a wall of shelves filled with books.

As I stood there staring aimlessly, Anneliese swiftly entered with a young woman following her whose tortured teeth showed in a small smile which drew the corners of her lips up unnaturally. She appeared worried about her hair and kept fluffing up her dress too.

"This won't do, we need much more color," said Anneliese as she began rearranging the books on the shelves, taking out black and brown ones and replacing them with those in brighter colors. "There, now sit," she said to the young woman.

The woman looked completely overwhelmed by the large chair. Her feet did not even reach the floor and her diminutive girth spanned less than half the sitting area.

"No, definitely not. Asim, please remove the chair."

I did as she asked, placing the chair completely out of view of the camera lens. She guided the young woman to the center of the books with colorful spines and handed her a soft yellow folder. "Turn your body left about 20% and your head right 10% keeping the folder left at waist height."

The young woman did it perfectly. "Bezaubernd," said Anneliese. "Now do not move. Azim lower the light and move it back zwei meter bitte."

I did as asked, watched Anneliese load the film into the camera, adjust its height and focus the lens all in a one choreographed movement. It was flawless. "Look Azim."

I quickly moved to her side and looked through the lens. I was amazed.

"Do you see it?"

"Yes, I will take it away," I replied as I picked up a large book and held it up to block a small shaft of light reflecting off a hair clip on the young woman's head.

"Perfect," said Anneliese as she snapped the lens shutter. "Now shift the folder to your other hand and look to your left."

This time Anneliese moved the camera half a meter closer, raised it higher and told the young woman to tilt her head down just slightly and look upward, but only with her eyes.

Everything was progressing very well until I realized someone was behind us. I turned and found Hans standing against the door leading to the hall. His dark suit blended in with the wood wall paneling to where only his face was noticeable. I nodded to him and reached over pretending to adjust the camera in a manner Anneliese would be concerned about. She glared at me and I darted my eyes in way that made her understand someone was behind her. She walked backward until she was against a table then turned completely around and saw him.

"Ah, is that you Herr Herbster? Is there something we can do for you?"

"No fräulein. I thought you might be ready to stop for lunch and the director would like to have a word with you before you leave."

"Thank you Herr Herbster. We will take the last photograph now. Inform the Director I will be there presently."

He looked at her mutely and his unmoving frown fitted the lines of his face like a worn glove. "As you say fräulein." He vanished quickly.

Anneliese took one more photograph of the young woman, thanked her for her patience and composure; directed me to take our equipment back to the studio and said she would meet me at the Hollerbach Restaurant in 15 minutes. I assured her I would be there, even though I had no idea where it might be located or why our other portrait subject was not coming.

"Does the young lady work here at the Museum?" I asked.

"No, she is Herr Director's granddaughter. I told him we would need to take a test photograph to make sure the camera and lights are in good order after the long trip. He asked if it could be of her."

"That was very nice of you and a very wise decision too."

Anneliese smiled and nodded. "See you at Hollerbach."

When I reached the studio, I realized I did not have a key, but it did not matter for the door was unlocked. After unloading both carts, I hesitated to leave everything unattended. It seemed prudent to simply take the exposed film from the camera and put it in my coat pocket. If any of our equipment was stolen or damaged, it could be replaced, but todays work would be saved.

The Hollerbach was easy to find, the first person I asked with my limited German vocabulary recognized the name and by using hand gestures was able to set me off in the right direction. The only other thing I was worried about was my lack of money after having paid a week's rent in advance, plus needing to save to buy a winter coat and suit, I had very little left for meals. It felt odd having to decide to spend my money on a warm coat or lunch.

The noon day traffic noise was even more overwhelming than it had been in the morning, plus it was cold standing on the side walk waiting for Anneliese. Everyone who passed by looked at me as if I did not belong there and while I did not understand most of what they were saying it was obvious they disliked seeing me in their presence. I wondered if Chione was experiencing the same unpleasantness where ever she was having lunch.

A car stopped at the curb. Not wanting to draw any attention to myself, I turned and walked away from it. "Surprise," said a woman leaning out the car's window. Her voice was low and throaty to match her manly appearance. "It is my fault we are late. Please forgive me."

Anneliese stepped out of the car followed by the woman. "Asim, allow me to introduce Ms. Romy Stern. Romy this is my colleague, Asim Lateef." She stepped down and moved toward me with a queer awkwardness; wore what appeared to be a man's suit but with a multi-colored sheer scarf instead of a tie; and dark red women's shoes. I was not sure if shaking her hand was appropriate or not, but she offered hers so I did. Her grip, armed with multiple rings, was as hard as a man's. Releasing her hand, she placed it behind my elbow, ushering me forward like a warden.

"Romy is administrative aid to Herr James Simon," said Anneliese as the two of them stepped to my sides and interlocked my arms to enter the restaurant. "Anneliese has been telling me many engaging things about the Museum and all of the wonderful artifacts you photographed at the Amarna excavation site Herr Simon funded."

Her last comment captured my attention, but rather than respond I deposited it in my memory vault for future reference.

The maître d' was somewhat taken aback by Ms. Stern, but did not hesitate to show us to a table. "It is nice to see you again Fräulein Stern. Will there be a fourth joining you?"

"No, this is the party for today. Herr Simon is engaged elsewhere this afternoon."

I felt as though the maître d' was not impressed by my suit or general appearance. He seemed especially displeased with my shoes.

"Today's lunch is my welcome to Berlin gift to you both so please order whatever you desire," said Ms. Stern as she focused her attention on the maître d' first and then on her two guests. I was greatly relieved by her gift for the prices listed on the menu where beyond the meager funds I had in my pocket.

As the lunch proceeded Ms. Stern carried most of the conversation, I was feeling more and more out of place, maybe even of another generation. When she finally got around to enquiring from her guests as to what we would like to see in Berlin, Anneliese immediately said she wanted to visit the studios of several of the new Expressionist artists she admired all of whom Ms. Stern knew personally. I had no idea what Expressionism was.

"What about you Azim? Is there something special you want to see here?"

"Well, obviously I need a winter suit and coat so as soon as we receive our wages, I will find a tailor," I said with a flush of embarrassment. "Then I want to find my Chione."

"Do you mean Chione Habib Khnum-Rekhi, the volunteer interpreter at the German Oriental Society? I think she also works for antique importer Har-shaf Uga. That Chione?"

I let out with a sound that must have been too loud and too improper in manner for the waiter and maître d' both came running. "Sir, please control yourself. I must insist Fräulein Stern your guests restrain themselves."

Stern rose from her seat, took the maître d's arm and calmly walked him away from our table. The waiter straightened up the table and left with a look of disbelieve I had not been thrown out.

"So Chione is a friend from Cairo?"

"She is, yes. I'm just surprised that of all the people I could meet in Berlin, Ms. Stern knows her," I said still reeling from astonishment.

"Mmm, Romy does seem to be well informed about everything going on in this city, but she was born here, graduated from Friedrich Wilhelm University and is very active in the women's rights movement."

"The what?"

"She is a suffragist."

"Oh, you mean one of those who think all women should have the same rights as men including to vote. I should have realized the moment I saw her clothes," I said shaking my head. "Plus, she is administrative aid to Herr Simon. Which is perhaps even more surprising."

"Why do you say that?

"Herr Simon funded the entire Amarna excavation and owns all of the artifacts selected for him by the French partage inspector," I stammered still striving to catch my breath.

"That is good to know and another reason why it is extremely important we both become Romy's friends. If the Museum director knows we are her associates he may be more willing to extend our contract to beyond just shooting portraits of his staff."

As I fidgeted with my coat and tie, I recalled I had not told Anneliese I had to leave the studio unlocked. "Here is the film from today's shooting session. Since I was not able to lock the studio, I felt it would be safer with you."

She looked at me with a sweet smile and placed her hand on my arm. "You are a treasure. Herr Borchardt was right to recommend you to me. When Ms. Stern returns lets finish lunch and go directly back to the Museum. I will show you how to develop color film and I will see about getting you your own studio key."

"Thank you. You are most kind. I am anxious to learn how to make color prints," I said with a shiver. "I assume we will make proofs for the Director to review before making the finished prints."

Ms. Stern returned looking very pleased with herself. "I apologize for being delayed, the maître d' needed reminding of how many friends and colleagues I bring here. I told him you are an Expressionist." We all smiled and finished our drinks, made our selections for lunch, and had an unforgettable meal filled with aromas and flavors I had never experienced before. I especially enjoyed the Sauerbraten. I was not sure as a newly anointed Expressionist, if I should do something odd or not. I decided I had drawn enough attention to myself for the day.

• • •

"Now let's go directly to a seamstress, ah, sorry I meant to say tailor and see about getting you a new suit and coat Asim."

"Oh, we cannot today. We must develop the film we shot this morning of Herr Director's granddaughter."

"It will be fine," said Anneliese. "I will take care of the film. You need warmer clothes before you become ill."

I was beginning to feel wan or at least depressed. "I have to wait until we are paid," I said. "Perhaps this will be at end of the week. Saturday, maybe?"

"Nonsense," said Anneliese. "It is far too cold for you to wait until then. I will advance you funds. You can repay me next week."

Miss Stern was shaking her head back and forth and said: "You go to the Museum Anneliese and take care of your film Asim and I will go to a wonderful tailor I know. I will bring him back to the Museum in a new suit before 6 pm."

"Lovely," responded Anneliese. "Most generous of you."

"Wonderful, besides, I want to hear all about your relationship with Ms. Chione Habib Khnum-Rekhi," replied Ms. Stern with her raised eyebrows aimed directly at me. "You know she has become very popular with several of the young men in town. Another good reason for you to have a new suit. Have you known her long?"

Ms. Stern had a look of radiant self-satisfaction about her. Anneliese had a neutral look slowly melting into one of relief, while my anxiety was racing in all directions of my brain. We all laughed, but I was feeling miserable. How was I ever going to be able to compete with the rich young men in this city? I could easily see how I could become a nervous workaholic with a permanent shake derived from too much drink, too little rest, and an undefined neuroses. After all I am basically a quiet and introverted fellow, I thought to myself.

The ride to the tailor's was quicker than I had imagined it would be. Ms. Stern asked an endless array of questions about Chione which almost convinced me I am not resilient enough to live in this city. When we stopped in front of the tailor-shop I wondered if the thousand little twinges of my imminent depression were noticeable on my forehead.

Ms. Stern had no hesitation as she walked through the door straight to a fit looking young man with crew cut brown hair above the grimace of sleeplessness in his eyes and the anxious lines surrounding them. "Good afternoon, Ms. Stern, how may I assist you today?"

"This is Herr Lateef from the Museum. He has been on assignment in Egypt and, is in need, of a new suit. Perhaps something in a deep brown?"

I simply smiled and nodded to the young man.

Ms. Stern moved toward the door with a flair that caused her coat to open. "I have a task to complete. I will return within the hour."

The young man quickly stepped passed her and opened the door for her exit. "I will have a suit for Herr Lateef ready by your return," he said as he bowed slightly.

When she turned to face him, we both noticed the delicate pink nipples of her generous breasts pointing up at us through her sheer lavender colored blouse. Their beauty took our breaths away. She smiled slily and swayed her hips as she left. The young man appeared to lose his self-confidence and took on a wilted look while I stood with my mouth agape. I could not help but wonder what she was wearing under her slacks if anything at all.

"Ah, ah, may I ask Herr Lateef, what position you hold at the Museum? Ah, so I can select an appropriate color and fabric for your new suit."

The words suddenly sounded strange coming from his stupefied mouth.

"Assistant photographer," I said. "I photographed all of the discovered artifacts at the El Amarna excavation for Herr Borchardt and I'm now assisting with photographing the entire Museum staff for the Director."

He stiffened, nodded, and gestured for me to enter the next room. "Shall I open an account for you Sir? A man in your position will certainly need more than one suit."

My stupid name-dropping ego had led me into a fool's corner again as my mind raced with a vague intention of appearing completely attentive to everything around me so I would not seem fragile or incapable of taking care of myself in whatever the circumstance.

"Not, at this time, perhaps after my travel trunk has arrived. I will then know of what further needs I may have."

"As you say Sir and that being the case, perhaps you would consider selecting one of our fine special seasonal suits. This one has two sets of pants and a winter coat as well. It is of a very good fabric in dark gray and I believe it is your size. Shall we see." Having recovered fully from Ms. Stern's unintended display of her feminine charms he was fast, smooth and obviously able to understand my situation without offending me.

"Yes, let's see if it does."

Wearing a European style suit is very different from the traditional jihab robes I wore in Cairo. They were made of flax plant linen and I usually wore pants underneath. All of which were loose fitting compared to this suit. The weave has stark lines and the structure is tight and restrictive.

As I looked about, I noticed there were also plaid suits in muted greens, mild ochre and burnt umber. I liked those colors, but not the plaid design. The tweed also came in appealing colors and I liked the texture and look of it, but it would probably make me stand out too much especially considering there is a general gloominess to all the suits in this shop.

The tie that came with my suit was one shade darker and the socks slightly lighter. I wondered why. Perhaps it is a requirement? Plus, now completely transformed from a common looking Egyptian I appeared to be a fairly-well-off European, except for my hair. It looked mussed compared to every man around. "Please excuse me sir, I do not mean to be blunt, but your hair is looking a bit stodgy, ah, old-fashioned sir. I can recommend a barber for you."

"Yes, please do, preferably one near the Museum."

"Do you prefer X, Y or H suspenders sir?"

I was beginning to feel I had clothing anxiety for I had no idea what he was referring to.

"What do you recommend for this suit," I said sheepishly.

"Well, all of them will crease and wrinkle your shirt sir, I would select a fine leather belt. Suspenders are for older men and can slow one down when dressing or un-dressing," he said with one raised eye-brow.

"A belt it is then."

As I stood looking at myself in the full-length mirror I felt as though I was wearing a thin veneer of western civilization. "No hijab, turbans, ghutras, or gallabiyahs. What have you done to yourself Asim," I whispered under my breath. The mirror also caused me to wonder how Chione might look in her new western attire. I hoped she was not dressing like Fräulein Stern, except maybe for the blouse.

. . .

Her gloved hand lighted on my arm and lingered. She had an electric touch, even though the cloth in the suit consisted of several layers. "The color and fit are just what you need," said Fräulein Stern as she walked around me. "And there is no need to adjust the fit. Wunderbar. Shall we go, Anneliese will surely be waiting for your return."

I was at a loss as to how to inform the young man that Fräulein Stern would settle the bill. I looked at her with a noticeable level of apprehension and her natural ease revealed a lifetime of experience with such situations. "This is to be put on Herr Simon's account for now," she said with the grace of a member of the aristocracy.

The young man nodded and helped me on with my new overcoat. "What shall I do with your ah…"

"You will not need that Khaki suit any further will you Asim? Why not donate it to the needy," she suggested with a wave of her hand.

"Yes, please donate it," I said as I took the few things from the pockets.

Fräulein Stern had a charming habit of rolling her eyes without moving her head which I took as a sign all was well.

I put my hand forward to shake the young man's. He however, stepped back with a blush of embarrassment and bowed slightly. Fräulein Stern took my arm and we walked out to her waiting car. As we approached, she said, "you must always remember your station, Asim. As a member of the Museum's staff, you are above those in service." I did not like the feeling, but understood the implied implication of her concern.

When we arrived at the Museum, I thanked Fräulein Stern profusely and waited for her car to meld into the flow of traffic before walking around to the side entrance. As I looked back, a carriage arrived from which Hans exited, but what caught my eye was the slim man, from the train, seated inside it who reached out and shook Han's hand. Seeing these two men together worried me, but I was not sure why.

They did not seem to hide their relationship and obviously were not concerned about being seen together, but there was something about the way they acted that veiled an overly tense liaison. To my surprise Hans entered the Museum via the main entrance, I continued to the side door. The slim man's carriage vanished into the harried traffic and once again I became aware of the overwhelming noise of the city.

A new hand written note, attached to the Photography Studio door, instructed all to knock before entering. I did so and Anneliese replied "Herein" as I entered. I was amazed to see the entire room had a heavy black curtain installed separating the front half from the back.

"Ah, the darkroom is now functionable," I said to the curtain.

A pleat in the curtain opened and Anneliese stuck her head out with a big smile. "Almost, for now we will have to carry water from the restroom to fill the rinse tray and we do not have a red light, but I believe we will be able to function."

We spent the rest of the day setting up the darkroom and our small front office area. By 6pm we both were exhausted. As we started to leave, there was a knock on the door. I stepped forward and opened it.

He was old, his hair was mostly gray with patches of black here and there and his pale, rounded nose had visible red veins sprouting above his moustache. Plus, his blue eyes were murky at the edges with lids drooped wearily over them.

Dressed in a black suit and vest over a crisp white shirt with flying collar he sported a gold-tinted tie. His heavy dark overcoat and highly polished dress boots were covered with a light mist of rain. As was the hat in his hand.

"Oh, Herr Director, Willkommen, bitte treten Sie ein," said Anneliese as she bowed and stepped back. "May I introduce Herr Lateef … oh, darf ich meinen Assistenten vorstellen Herr Asim Lateef."

"Herr Lateef, welcome to Berlin and our museum. We are very happy to have you as a member of our staff."

I was greatly relieved he spoke English and I had on a new suit. Anneliese looked stunned. "Is there something we can do for you Herr Director," she said still bowing.

"No, no, I was out the door when I remembered I wanted to officially welcome Herr Lateef, as I did you yesterday Ms. Brantt." His voice was thin and somewhat dry sounding, but sincere and assertive.

We all smiled, but I could tell Anneliese was not able to control her nervous need to fold her lower lip under her upper one. I decided to speak first.

"May we show you how we have arranged the darkroom Herr Director," I said hesitantly.

"Why yes please do."

I gestured with my eyes at Anneliese and she quickly stepped forward. "Ms. Brantt is the expert. She knows all about how to make the new color photographs."

Anneliese inhaled, smiled, and lead the way as I pulled the curtain back and turned on the light. We all entered and she began by talking about the camera and then moved on to the color film, the enlarger and all the chemicals and paper we would be using.

"Very impressive and intriguing," he said. "I hope to live long enough to see more of the new inventions I keep hearing about. When may I expect to see the portrait photograph you took of my granddaughter?"

"Soon Herr Director," replied Anneliese as her nervousness returned. "Since all of this equipment and darkroom are new, it will take a few days to test everything, but soon, it will be soon."

He looked disappointed, but smiled as he turned to walk toward the door. "I understand Herr Lateef you photographed all the artifacts discovered at the Tell El Amarna excavation. That must have been challenging and exciting."

"It was Herr Director. I was very honored to have been given the responsibility by Herr Borchardt."

"Good, perhaps when you both have completed making the portrait photographs, we can talk about photographing some of the special artifacts in the Museum's collection," he said as he reached for the door handle. "Well, thank you for making my visit so enjoyable and informative. If you need anything do not hesitate to let me know. Good evening." He opened the door, stepped out and closed it behind himself. Anneliese and I looked at each other and embraced with elation at our good fortune.

"Isn't it curious how the three of us speak different languages, but the only one we all speak well enough to make ourselves understood to each other is English," I offered as we stepped back from one another.

"I'm impressed you noticed the difference between the Deutsche Herr Director speaks and my humble home dialect."

"In Egypt there are at least a dozen or more dialects and those that are educated also speak either French or English."

"Do you read Egyptian hieroglyphs?"

"Egyptians are not allowed to learn to do so."

"Why not, for heavens sakes, it's your history."

"We might gain a little power back over our own land and lives."

We stood in silence looking at one another until Anneliese pulled the curtain closed. "You of course know of the Rosetta Stone right?"

"Yes, the Rosetta Stone was a spoil of war. The French found it and then it was transferred to the British after the defeat of Napoleon," I said as I turned off the darkroom light. "The British and French have paid little attention to any kind of international rights for the objects they've spirited out of the Ottoman territories including those from Egypt."

We took off our lab coats. "I recall reading the French implicit rhetorical justification in doing Bonaparte's expedition was to gather study materials as part of a broader civilizing mission to regenerate Egypt by restoring the land to its ancient greatness under the Pharaohs," she said staring at me again.

"And that's why the stone stele has been in the British Museum for over a century," I said as I held the door open for us to leave. "It will be interesting to see what artifacts Herr Director selects for us to photograph from the Museum's collection. Do you think they will be Egyptian?"

"I have no idea, however, it reminds me, I saw a notice posted on the bulletin board in the entrance foyer the Deutsche Orient-Gesellschaft (the German Oriental Society) is meeting here tomorrow morning. Perhaps your Chione will be here with them."

"Is that so, perhaps we should invite them to view the new Photography Studio?" I suggested in an impulsive stammer.

Anneliese smiled and looked about with her hands on her hips. "No, this space is too small for all of them. We should shoot a group portrait of them all. Surely Herr Director would like to have one for his office. We can stage them in the library. I will go now and ask the librarian if they have enough chairs."

"Make a special place for him to sit in the middle," I suggested as she hurried out.

As I reached to turn off the lights, I discovered a door key hanging near it with a little tag that read Asim. I used it to lock the door and then placed it in the watch pocket of my new suit. Pressing my fingers over the outside of the pocket and feeling the key inside gave me a warm, welcoming feeling. "You are a long way from your father's garage," I whispered.

CHAPTER 5

There was a slight dusting of snow falling as I arrived at the Museum, I took some of it and cleaned off my old scuffed shoes. Then I thought, perhaps I should leave them as they are and just tell anyone who stares at them they are Expressionistic.

The new note on the door simply said, 'come to Library. Wear lab coat.' I took the note and entered the Studio. As I took off my suit coat and put my lab smock on, I noticed in the small mirror Anneliese had mounted above the sink, the studio door slowly opening. It was Hans.

"Good morning. How may I help you Herr Herbster?"

"I am to assist Ms. Brantt. Is she behind this ... this curtain?" He looked bewildered and a little angered.

"No, she is in the library. Come I will accompany you."

We stepped into the hall and I locked the studio door. Hans raised his eyes slowly has if they had weight and required and effort to lift. When they met mine, he grinned and walked past me, I assumed to take the lead position or perhaps he was annoyed I had my own key to the studio.

"That is a different suit you are wearing today. Did your travel trunk arrive?"

"Why no, this is new. I purchased it yesterday after lunch, but you knew that already, didn't you Herr Herbster?"

He stopped. I walked on past him. He seemed reluctant to follow.

• • •

As I entered the library, I saw her amongst a group of people coming into the room with the Director. A small worry crawled across her face when she noticed me. I smiled, but did not run and embrace her as my heart so wanted to do. As the group reached the single chair in front of the camera, a young man moved to Chione's left side.

His face was lean and intelligent looking with curly hair, a well-defined brow and chin, but his nose was chiseled causing his nostrils to flare making his upper lip appear small while his blue eyes radiated a haze of dreamy idealism. My paused mind was thinking he seemed an odd man to have caught Chione's attention for he had an air of snooty elitism about him.

The Director sat in the chair and everyone else gathered around him. Anneliese began moving the tall ones to the back. I was immobile, stock-still starring at Chione.

"Asim, sorry to inconvenience you, please move the lights further back so no one is in shadow," said Anneliese when she stepped directly in front of me blocking my view and looking annoyed.

"Yes, yes, I will make sure," I mumbled as I darted toward the tall standing lights.

Chione appeared fascinated while watching me. Her eyes were large and wonderfully alive, but lost in blossoming concern.

"Everyone is to look directly at the camera, Bitte," said Anneliese. "Those on this side of Herr Director turn your left shoulder 10 degrees toward the camera, those on the other side turn your right shoulder."

Chione looked beautiful, but still apprehensive about what I was doing. As I adjusted the second light her curly haired admirer noticed her attention was focused on me. He turned his head and shoulders toward me.

"Sir please face this way and look directly at the camera," said Anneliese.

Curly hair's scowl revealed he was not pleased by her direct confrontation. His face stiffened and his eyes narrowed.

The Director stood up and turned to see who was not following directions. Curly hair immediately turned back and stared at the camera. "Thank you," said Anneliese as she nodded to the Director. "Asim, please check through the lens for any light reflections or shadows." The Director slowly sat down with a grimace. I nodded to him, smiled at Chione and looked through the lens.

The grouping was perfect except for a couple of people on the outer edges. Using hand gestures, I was able to move them into better positions and Anneliese quickly stepped in and looked through the lens.

"Perfect" was all she said and took the picture. "Do not move please. Asim, reposition both lights back 1 meter, Bitte."

Everyone fussed a bit. Anneliese raised her left hand while still looking through the lens. Everyone stopped. She took the photograph. "Vielen Dank an alle, wir haben was wir brauchen. Thank you everyone, I believe we have what we need for today."

Anneliese signaled for me to turn off the two large portable lights. I did and began rolling up the electrical cords while watching curly hair escort Chione out with everyone else. Chione looked back and winked at me with the smile I had dreamt about for weeks.

"Asim, may I have a word?" said Herr Director.

Anneliese and I looked at each other. I did not move or respond. "Is there something I can assist you with Herr Director," she said.

He moved with a slowness suggesting his thought was far out in front of his actions. "Perhaps you both can."

"Yes, certainly," she replied as she smiled at me and walked toward us.

"Would you see if you can locate Hans for me Vielen Dank Fräulein," he said in a friendly, but firm manner.

Anneliese stopped, nodded, and walked away looking worried at what she was going to miss.

When she was out of hearing range, he said: "Asim, is it true you know Fräulein Chione?"

"Yes, she is the ward of Youssef Sadek, the overseer of the Tell El Amarna excavation diggers and she assisted Herr Borchardt with translation of all of his shipping documents," I said as I felt my throat constrict from a sudden aridness.

"I see. She is an attractive young woman, can I assume you became friends?"

"We did and we still are," I said as the parchedness increased.

"Do you also know Har-shaf Uga, the man she works for?"

"No sir, I have not met him," I was barely able to speak and coughed twice before regaining my composure. "May I ask what your concern is? Should Chione be watchful of this man? Will he try to make improper demands of her?"

"Obviously you think much more of her than just as a friend. We will leave this for now." He turned and walked away.

As he walked further into the Library, Anneliese and Hans entered from the hall. "Where is he?" she asked. I pointed toward the front of the room. Hans dashed in that direction looking bereft.

"I do not mean to be impolite, but can you tell me what he wanted?" she said with great care and hurt eyes that moved her lashes up and down slowly.

"He asked only about my relationship to Chione, but he didn't explain why."

"Well, she is lovely and after all, he is a man."

I winced under her broken eloquence.

"You know Asim, we must always support each other. Please keep this in mind when anyone on the staff speaks with you including the Director."

I agreed with her whole heartedly, but was unable to think of an appropriate response other than to smile and nod. However, I did wonder if his concern was related to Chione or to Herr Uga.

CHAPTER 6

Herr Borchardt was approaching from the far end of the hall, dressed in a suit and tie, so unlike the desert attire I had seen him wear every day at the Amarna dig. But, his stride, physical deportment and disposition were unmistakable. After a few paces he noticed me standing in front of the Photography Studio door and nodded. I took it as a signal of recognition and greeting.

Standing soldier straight I said, "Good morning, Herr Borchardt."

"It is a little chilly today, but your greeting is filled with warmth Asim. I am very happy to see you here in Berlin and to know you and Fräulein Brantt are working together. Have you mastered the new color photography yet?" He said as he gestured to our now professional door sign.

"Sicher, though I am only a beginner, Anneliese ... ah, Fräulein Brantt can certainly provide a more qualified opinion," I said as I opened the door for him.

"Yes, of course," he replied. "Guten Morgen Fräulein Brantt."

Anneliese was looking at our wall display of the most recent staff portraits we had completed. "Morgen, morgen Herr Borchardt it's an honor to have you visit our humble office and darkroom."

He put forth both his hands and gasp both of hers. She exhibited surprise and even blushed a little.

"Herr Director has told me of how professional you two are, but gegen meine Erwartung, die photographs sind künstlerisch entworfen ."

We all smiled and looked at the display in silence and I was sure Anneliese enjoyed his compliment about the quality of our work.

"Are you here to have your portrait taken?" Anneliese asked quietly.

"Not at this time, aber I'm here to inform you the portrait taking for myself and the rest of the staff will be delayed for a while."

"Delayed, is there a problem with the work we have completed?" I said cautiously.

"No, no Herr Director and I need for you to photograph in color all of the Tell El-Amarna excavation artifacts now in the Museum's Egyptian collection storage area."

"Oh, how wonderful," I said while holding out my open arms to Anneliese. She smiled sweetly, gave me an intense stare, and shook my right hand instead of an embrace.

"You will have to start today?" said Herr Borchardt.

Anneliese stepped back and sucked in her lower lip to chew on its right side while continuing to stare at me. "Asim and I have given this much thought ever since Herr Director mentioned it and we have some concerns."

"I see, tell me an example."

"Well, this small space is not very practical for staging and lighting valuable artifacts. Plus, we will need a variety of lights as well as special security and…"

She stopped talking, breathed deeply while resuming her attention to her lower lip and appeared deeply anxious.

"Well, Asim functioned very well for me with only a small tent and now has stepped up to this darkroom obviously with little difficulty, but you Fräulein Brantt are suggesting a complete Photography Department is required in order to full-fill your duties."

"Whatever do you mean Herr Borchardt?" said Anneliese looking vexed.

"Just that, Herr Director anticipated your needs and has agreed to allot a portion of the new museum wing as a complete modern staging studio, dark room and office just for official museum photography business. In fact, every artwork in the entire museum will need to be photographed in color."

Anneliese appeared petrified like an immobile statue until Herr Borchardt held out his open arms and embraced her. "This is an opportunity for you both to prove you are professionals, do not disappoint me. I am depending on you to especially show the Egyptian artifacts at their very best."

We all were smiling when we noticed the door slowly opening. Herr Borchardt took hold of the handle and flung the door open. "Fräulein Chione what a wonderful surprise."

Her eyes were large and very alive tarting about starring at each of us. "Oh, excuse me Herr Borchardt I was not aware you were here. Forgive me for interrupting your meeting. I will come back another time."

We all paused as Herr Borchardt took Anneliese's hand and guided her out the door. "Nonsense, Fräulein Brantt and I must meet with the Director. You and Asim must have much to talk about. Oh, and thank you for all your excellent assistance with the shipping of the artifacts. Everything arrived in perfect condition."

Her smile kept changing back and forth from girlish to triumphant woman. "It was an honor and I am deeply grateful to you for recommending me to the Deutsche Orient-Gesellschaft.

"I'm confident you will do wonderfully for them."

"Sicherlich," she replied as he turned toward me and smiled.

"Herr Borchardt may I ask, how much time do we have to prepare the new darkroom and studio?"

"The builder is discussing the budget with Herr Director now. Fräulein Brantt and I will accompany him to the new wing to determine where to locate the office, studio and darkroom. In the afternoon we may all meet in the Egyptian storage rooms to discuss which artifacts are to be photographed first."

"Perhaps there will be some we can photograph here or in the storage room," I suggested.

"Mmm, security is certainly superior there," he said as he and Anneliese walked away.

I closed the door and Chione stepped into my arms. Her eyes revealed she was nurturing a dozen thoughts. I kissed her lips and I walked her backwards into the darkroom as my own thoughts raced.

Barely moving her lips and without shifting her eyes from mine she said, "I have dreamed of this for a very long time." Her voice came from deep within her. "It is so wonderful to have you here in Berlin. Where are you living?" She pinched my cheek and looked at me sideways in a seductive manner I had never seen from her before.

"More importantly, where are you living and with whom?" I said pulling her closer to me.

"We should not do this here. Let's meet tonight. Somewhere warm and cozy."

She stepped out of my arms and opened the darkroom curtain as she moved toward the door. "You are right, anyone could come in a find us together."

She appeared stressed and worried as we discussed our living arrangements and concluded the weather was too blustery and cold for us to go out in the evening. We determined instead to meet on Sunday in Tiergarten Park if there is inviting weather.

"I'm very happy you are here Asim," she said through a pouty sulk as she opened the door and walked away. I lingered in the aroma of her rose scented perfume as my mind drifted in a reverie of my favorite dreams, but could not shake off the force of her melancholy.

CHAPTER 7

It was a cold Sunday morning, but my new shoes were dry and much warmer than the old ones. The sky was bright blue between the clouds and the sun was warm enough to melt the remaining snowy slush from the walking paths. I had arrived early for sitting around my empty room was wearing on me. Even opening the small window did not relieve my weariness.

No woman has ever made me feel more anxious about succeeding in life than Chione I was thinking when I spotted him moving along a short stone wall. He was so near I could see the uneasiness in his squinted eyes as his head swayed sideways to sneak a peek in my direction. I decided to bluntly confront him.

Even in full daylight, the park seemed a lonely place as I approached the wall and placed a hand on the top intending to vault over it and chase after him, but before I could, a voice I recognized shouted, "Are you planning to run away from me?" I turned to find Chione and Romy Stern approaching from a carriage. The look of suspicion streaking across their faces filled me with despair for having thought I could act so rash and foolish in a public place.

"Ah, no, I thought maybe I would get a little exercise."

Their eyes filled with mistrust and caution. I looked about for Slim-man, but he was not in sight. I turned to Romy for some kind of clue as to why Chione was not smiling at my lame comment. "It's nice to see you again Fräulein Stern."

"It would not be proper for Chione or myself to meet you unescorted in a park," said Romy. "Being single ladies, we must abide by an acceptable level of decorum."

"Of course, you being a man, are free to do as you please," said Chione as she faced into the sun and welcomed its warmth. However, she appeared aged since our brief meeting in the Photography Studio. Her mouth appeared distraught and eyes red-rimmed. I wanted desperately to embrace her and to know why.

"Oh, Chione, what is causing this pain I see in your eyes?"

"Pain? It is not pain," she whimpered as a tear slipped along her cheek.

I cupped her hands in mine and brought her to me. "Please do not push me from you. I will do anything you ask of me to see you smile."

With difficulty, she threw her head back and stared into my eyes. "Promise me you will always remember our time under the stars of Orion and will not be tempted by the beauty of the north star."

I looked at her and Romy. "Whatever do you mean? Of course, I will never forget, you fill my dreams every night."

"She was somewhat surprised to see you working so closely with Ms. Brantt. I have explained it is a professional relationship only," responded Romy.

A wave of reprieve flooded my mind and heart. "Fräulein Brantt is my supervisor. She has graciously agreed to teach me how to make the new color photography. There is no personal relationship between us and please recall it was Herr Borchardt who made it possible for me to work with her and to be here in Berlin with you."

"Are you certain he has no plan for you and her to become a couple?" she stated while touching my arm significantly and bracing herself.

"Here I've been trying to find a way to convince you to not become coupled with the obviously rich man from the Deutsche

Orient-Gesellschaft Council and all the while you've been thinking I was already joined with Anneliese."

We all laughed, but Chione drew her eye brows down and said, "Mmm, you refer to her by her first name. That does not seem very professional."

She managed to give me a rueful smile and walked along the wall with her back to me looking out at the expanse of the park. "Truth is, most everything has been easy for me here in Berlin causing me to almost forget you pay for one thing with another."

I came up behind her and whispered "The memory of December 6 will forever be in my heart, let it be the promise that holds us together."

She turned and we kissed.

"Perhaps we should find a Café for a hot chocolate to cool off with," suggested Romy giggling under her breath. "Besides, you never know who could be watching."

Slim-man slithered back into my mind. "Yes, there is a fellow here in the park who I am certain has been following me. I was about to confront him when you arrived."

Romy pulled at the corners of her mouth and made a grimace. "Where else have you seen him?"

"First, it was on the train from Istanbul to here. Even Anneliese, ah, Fräulein Brantt noticed him. Then he was in a carriage with Herr Herbster in front of the Museum."

"What does he look like," asked Chione. "Is he European?"

"That I'm not sure of, but he is tall and lean."

A look of recognition passed between my two ladies. "What? Do you know him?" I asked.

"No, but he sounds like a man we have seen a couple of times. I will need to see your fellow to be certain he is the same man," replied Romy.

"I did not like the looks of him," said Chione. "He acts sneaky."

"Why would anyone follow the three of us?" I asked Romy. "Is this something normal here?"

"Yes and no, but more importantly he certainly is not the one we should be concerned about. We need to know who is directing him. Who does he report to?"

"Herr Borchardt," I said. "He is the only one who all of us know and he is the only one who knew Ms. Brantt and I would be on a particular train."

"Well maybe," said Romy. "If Anneliese or you told anyone by letter or phone prior to leaving Istanbul or Cairo there was an opportunity for the controller to set this guy in action."

"You mentioned he was talking with Herr Herbster," said Chione. "That might be the best place to start."

Without noticing, we had strolled to the edge of the park during our conversation and could see a charming Café across the main Strasse. I gestured toward it. "Shall we?"

For over two hours we talked about everything and anything about each other, our ambitions, likes and dislikes about living in Berlin. It was heart-warming and reassuring to feel I was with friends.

"What shall we do about slim-man?" asked Romy. "I can make quiet inquiries amongst Herr Simon's staff but I'll be surprised if any of them know him."

"I will start with Herr Herbster and maybe Fräulein Brantt will be willing to mention him to Herr Borchardt."

"Here it is the start of spring and Bulgaria may be starting another war with Turkey about some city in Thrace. With the Sultan deposed, I do not understand how Istanbul can defend the Ottoman Empire," said Chione looking dismayed. "Even the trains there have stopped running."

Romy rolled her eyes. "Very correct, no one should start a war just as the flowers are starting to bloom." All of that felt distant from our lives in Berlin. We all nodded and Chione kissed my cheek, but her eyes were fixed on some distant regions of her mind. Romy rolled her eyes again and said: "Only in Berlin."

I watched as my two lovelies entered a carriage, waved, and left me standing alone again to slowly venture about on my way back toward my room. Each opportunity to step behind a tree or into some shadowed place I took in order to see if slim-man was following me, but he was never there. When I arrived at the walkway to my room, a little fellow with sallow sandy eyes set close together above a long limp nose and wide mouth reaching toward bat-wing ears, swaggered toward me. "You the Egyptian?" he slurred through alcohol-soaked breath.

"I am. Who are you?"

"I thought so," he dribbled and walked on toward the dark end of the street. I stood thinking I should follow him, but the emerging rain convinced me to go inside and besides, following him is what slim-man or his master, fully expect me to do. So, I did not.

When I finally laid down on my small bed, I could not stop wondering why Chione was lost in thoughts of another military skirmish between Bulgaria and the Turks instead of our future together. I was a teenager in the last war and hated how it destroyed everything. I had no interest in another one.

CHAPTER 8

"That was a very good suggestion you made about photographing some artifacts now," said Anneliese. "It is going to take some time for the constructor to complete our building requirements and we absolutely need Herr Director to know we are still functioning. Let's determine how many of the staff still need to be photographed and which ones to do first then we'll have time to study the artifacts."

"A staff list would be helpful and I'd like to put Herbster at the top," I said while noting her reaction.

"Why him?" she said as she resumed chewing her lip and posting her hands on her hips.

"I want to show it to some of the luggage porters at the train station."

"I see, you don't trust him do you?"

"I do not and it's always better to be informed about ones potential enemies."

"Just remember if he finds out what you are doing and it turns out you are wrong about him, it will cost you your position here and will certainly affect your hopes for a future with Chione."

Again I was reminded of how wise Herr Borchardt was to acquaint me with Anneliese. "You are right, I'll find another way to uncover what he is up to."

"The Director seems to feel you have a special understanding of the Amarna artifacts," she said looking up through the top of her eyes. "Which ones do you think we should start with?"

The question surprised me, but felt appropriate and professional which I appreciated. "The Beautiful One. It is remarkable," I said with a measure of national pride.

Ah, aren't they all beautiful? I mean which one specifically are you referring to?

"Oh, yes, yes, they are all wonderful, but the life-sized Queen Nefertiti bust is spectacular. It is Herr Borchardt's favorite as well."

"Hello," a voice said followed by a knock on the door. Anneliese shrugged her shoulders. I opened the door to find Fräulein Romy Stern smiling and seemingly overflowing with delight.

"Are you excited?" she said giving me a wink. "A Photography Department, this is going to be innovative and revolutionary."

"How did you find out? We were only just informed ourselves," said Anneliese looking flabbergasted.

"Well it might be because I have friends in all the best places."

"Of course you do. Let's go to Hollerbach Haus for lunch and celebrate," said Anneliese. "I could use a drink and I'd like to know more about those friends of yours."

"Oh, sorry I cannot today. I am modeling for Otto and he gets upset if I do not arrive on time. I just came by to congratulate you both."

She kissed each of us on the cheek and darted down the hall.

"She models for artists. When does she ever have time to work for Herr James Simon," I asked. "Does she do it nude?"

"Ah, ah, yes, she does. Assuming you mean for Otto, not Herr Simon. Remember she is a new century woman. She even poses for some photographers too, but do not mention it to anyone."

It seemed odd Romy would spend the morning doing secretarial work for Herr Simon, then in the afternoon pose completely nude for an artist. I wondered what she did in the evening.

"Perhaps Chione should not be developing a friendship with her. I would not want any of those modern ideas to become something she might want to experience for herself."

"This from a man whose culture is famous for celebrating near nude belly dancing. Besides do you really think Chione has the personality required for those kinds of escapades?"

"If she does, I hope she only expresses it in front of me."

"How typically chauvinistic."

"I do not know this word. What does it mean?"

"It means you are very much a man who believes everything a woman wants should be only to please her man. What about her own needs and desires?"

"You and I should not discuss such things, but are you suggesting Romy has a need to pose nude beyond earning money?"

"Maybe she simply wants to contribute to Berlin's cultural advancement. After all, modeling helps the artist to create new art masterpieces. You know, you should take a figure drawing class just to experience how academic it is. The open session class meets on Thursday nights and has both male and female students."

"Obviously you have taken many art classes, but I have not. I would feel completely out of place in such a situation."

"Well it takes a great deal of self-discipline and helps you to separate delusional thoughts from the merely irrational," she said with a far-away look in her eyes as a faint blush began spreading from within her cheeks. "Shall I accompany you?"

"No, no, thank you but I should learn these things on my own and please do not mention this to Chione."

"Of course not. It will be our secret," she said as she took out her note pad and pencil. "So, tell me about The Beautiful One. Why should we photograph it first?"

"No sculpture has ever captured my soul so completely before. To gaze upon it makes me proud of my Egyptian heritage and masculinity."

"Mmm, by-all-means we shall photograph The Beautiful One first. Unless of course, Herr Borchardt or the Director have another plan."

We heard fast footsteps in the hall. They stopped at our door and were followed by heavy breathing as though the individual had been running. Anneliese gestured for me to be quiet and not move. A knock broke the nerve-racking silence. I opened the door to face Herr Herbster.

"Good afternoon, Herr Lateef. Fräulein Brantt your presence is requested in Herr Directors office," he stated with a phony grin and counterfeited politeness.

"All right, I will close up the darkroom and be there shortly," she replied with a programmed smile.

"Please to hurry, Herr Director does not like to be kept waiting."

"I will take care of everything in the darkroom," I said. "And lock up."

"Don't forget about what we discussed," she said with a wink as she took off her smock and put on her coat. "Have a fun evening. I will see you in the morning to continue this discussion about the artifacts."

Herbster lifted his eyes quickly and focused on Anneliese with a sugary mask. "Is there something I can assist you with? I am familiar with all the Museum's collections."

"That is very thoughtful of you, but no, perhaps another time. Thank you. Shall we go? We do not want to keep Herr Director waiting."

Herbster was obviously perturbed by Anneliese's easy dismissal of his offer of assistance. They left and I was wondering where I might be able to purchase a drawing pad and some pencils. As I put on my coat and turned off the last light, a gentle knock on the door surprised me. I opened it cautiously.

She wore a midnight blue velvet dress under an opulent yet somehow timid fur coat and hood which was covered by a lite dusting of snow. She lowered the hood taking care to keep her hair in place and turned to face me. Her blue-green eyes, rose blushed cheeks and blond hair focused my attention on her youthful lips. "Good evening, Herr Lateef."

"Ah, good evening Fräulein Simon is it? This is an unexpected pleasure. I saw you in the group photo shoot, but did not feel it was appropriate for me to introduce myself. How may I assist you?"

She hesitated and began gently wiping the snow from the sleeves of her coat. "I thought perhaps you might be willing to assist me with walking to my carriage. It is rather slippery outside and in return I could provide you with transport to your lodgings."

Her tenderness and soothing demeanor radiated an aristocratic upper-class charm unlike any I had ever encountered first hand before. She was thin and appeared fragile against the striated studio light, arousing my manly protective instinct.

"Are you sure it would be appropriate. After all we have not been formally introduced."

"As a former employee of my uncle, it's more than appropriate," she said graciously.

"To what are you referring?"

"My uncle funded the entire Tell El Amarna excavation." Her exasperation was beginning to show. "And he approved Herr Borchardt's hiring of you as the official photographer."

"Yes, of course, I understand," I said as I quickly locked the door and offered her my arm. "Please forgive my reluctance it was only out of concern for you. I would not want you to be put in a position of having to explain my presence at your side."

"Few people in Berlin ever question my uncle or I. Now where do you live?" She took my arm and we walked out the Museum's main door directly to her waiting carriage. The Museum reception personal and main entrance guard raised their eyebrows and the carriage driver tipped his hat. Indicating they all were surprised at what they were witness to.

"If you do not mind, I was not planning to go directly home this evening, so I will leave you here. It was an honor and pleasure to meet you."

"Surely, there is somewhere we can take you," she replied sharply. "Please get in here immediately."

I assisted her into the carriage and waited until she was comfortable before sitting opposite her. "I am in need, of finding a shop for art supplies. Do you know of one nearby?"

"Yes, of course, I believe there is an art supply section in the Nathan Israel Department Store," she said with a curious look in her eyes while instructing the driver.

"Which entrance Fräulein Simon?" asked the driver.

"The main one of course," she snapped looking slightly peeved. "I sometime use the private entrance for the Fashion Salon," she said still looking irked, but strangely refined.

She was not using her charm on me exactly, it was just there naturally. "I understand from Fräulein Stern you have a special relationship with Fräulein Chione Khnum-Rekhi and she is also Egyptian." Her down-cast gaze and soft-spoken manner was suddenly lightened by a faint ghost of happiness. I wondered why.

"Yes, as you know, she also was a member of the Amarna excavation as was her uncle Youssef. He has asked me to keep an eye on her while she is here in Berlin."

She shivered and twisted her body sideways. I reached for the carriage blanket next to her, unfolded it and held it out for her to take. She placed it over her lap and legs. "Do you know her uncle well?"

"I met him for the first time when I joined the excavation as photographer."

She lowered her eyes and slanted a decidedly blue glance at me. "So, you know very little about him?"

"I know he means a great deal to Fräulein Chione Khnum-Rekhi and her well-being is of great interest to me. Is there something you feel I need to know about her uncle?"

"I only seek to advise you to learn as much as you can about him and should you discover anything questionable to inform me immediately."

"Inform you, not your uncle?"

She sensed my anxiety and answered with great care. "In the short time Fräulein Khnum-Rekhi has been here she has acquired many friends. Any scandal, legal or moral that may befall her could cause public outrage and be very damaging to them all."

"I see and because she has no family here, no local history you feel she may be needlessly reckless or unethical?"

"I see now why Fräulein Stern feels you are trust worthy. I am sure everything will be fine with Fräulein Khnum-Rekhi, but it is always sensible to be cautious and discreet."

"While we are on this topic, what can you tell me about Herr Herbster's background?"

She screwed up her eyes in concentration and again her mouth took a disappointed turn.

I was thinking I liked her. Her eyes wore an intelligence and warmth, her mouth a touch of sadness. In fact, it was a face that told me it has known suffering and seemed to be renewing the acquaintance. I hoped Chione or I were not the reason why, but wondered what her concern about Chione's moral conduct was actually concerned about.

CHAPTER 9

Finding the open session life drawing class turned out to be less difficult than I had anticipated for the young lady sales assistant, Frederique, at Nathan Israel Department Store sensed I was a beginner and assumed I would be attending the class. Her street directions to it were perfect which gave me time to eat something beforehand. She suggested I try the automated restaurant nearby.

As I entered the spacious dining area, I noted there were several other individuals carrying drawing portfolio cases. A group of them, all young men like myself, went to an empty table and placed their cases on the chairs then proceeded to the automates to make their food selections.

Seeing me standing with my case in hand, one of them asked "Are you going to tonight's drawing session?"

"Yes, I am."

"You are welcome to join our table," he said.

"Thank you. That is most kind."

I watched as they went to the cashier, exchanged their paper notes for coins, walked around selecting items from the automatic slot machine dispensers and return to our table. I did the same.

"This is a German idea. There are dozens of these restaurants on the Continent now, what do you think of it?" asked the young man sitting next to me.

"Reminds me of the holy water dispensers in Cairo, they are over 1,000 years old," I said smiling. "Of course, they only take pennies."

"Well, the first electric food dispensers were the ones at the zoo here, they were installed over 15 years ago. I was one of the first to use them," said a stately fellow with long unruly blond locks. "They have been a howling success."

Everyone laughed.

"On its first day of operation das Automatische Restaurant sold over 5000 sandwiches and 20,000 cups of coffee. My uncle, Max Sielaff designed them and presented them to the public at the Berlin Industrial Exposition in 1896. They won a gold medal at the Brussels world's fair."

All of the young men at the table raised their glass in a united salute and glanced to see if I followed. I did. They all appeared to be wearing a purged expression which failed to tell me of what.

"Are you familiar with Austrian painters Hans Makart, Alois Riegl or Gustav Klimt?" Asked a scholarly looking young man.

"Ah, no, I've yet to see their paintings. Why do you ask?" I said as I noticed everyone appeared disappointed in my response.

"Well Klimt has created a series of paintings depicting important periods of ancient art, including from Egypt. In one of them, he included a Pharaonic woman holding an ankh with the stretched wings of the vulture goddess behind her," he pronounced with obvious pride.

"All art is erotic," announced another fellow at the table near us to everybody's amazement and visual scorn.

"My father told me he saw three large wall panels, in the dining room of a palace he visited in Brussels, depicting the Egyptian Tree of Life in the background, adorned with unmistakable Egyptian symbols including the Eye of Horus, the Pharaonic falcon and the pyramid motif all by Klimt," said an extremely well-dressed man.

"There is also the published work of Alois Riegl about Egyptian ornament and other ancient civilizations," commented another fellow quite seriously.

"And don't forget about Theodor Graf, the art dealer famous for collecting several Fayyum Portraits and exhibiting them in Vienna," said the oldest looking man at our table.

"Well I think, the spandrels of the stairwell of the Kunsthistorisches Museum in Vienna are the best Egyptian inspired works Klimt has created," said a soft voiced young woman to my left who fluttered her eyelashes. "Being a museum dedicated to the history of art, Klimt took Ancient Egypt as the starting point. The whole theme of the Stoclet Frieze is based on the Ancient Egyptian myth of Isis and Osiris," she said smiling at me sweetly.

"Is Klimt celebrated in Egypt?" asked someone.

"Regrettably no artists are famous in Egypt, most people there are not knowledgeable or have ever been exposed to art from other nations," I said with a pang of shame.

"So the Vienna Secession movement has not reached there yet," replied the soft-spoken woman.

I had no idea what she or any of the others were referring to.

"So, you are a pioneer on a mission and will bring our modern art movement to Egypt," said the leader as everyone stood. "We should go, we must not be late, the Künstmeister's would not be pleased."

I stood and gathered my portfolio feeling confused about the conversation, but eager to learn more about why European artists were inspired by ancient Egyptian art. All, of the Europeans I worked with at the Amarna excavation were only interested in what the artifacts told them about history. I rarely heard any of them discuss them as works of art except for The Beautiful One. They all felt it was an artistic masterpiece.

• • •

The drawing studio was crowded with a mix of individuals young and old, but I was most surprised to see so many women in attendance, most of whom were setting up near the model platform. I chose to be near the door, I did not expect to stay long.

"Are you going to stay in this location?" asked Frederique. "It can get very chilly this close to the door. I usually set-up by the instructor's desk. It is always warmer there."

She smiled and walked toward the desk. I picked up my supplies and followed her.

As we finished our preparations several people said good evening to Frederique, I nodded to each and smiled. "Attendance is good this week," she said.

"Are there always this many women?" I asked. "Are they students or just curiosity seekers like me? Do these ladies, work in the city as you do?" I said just to make conversation.

"Are you interested in how women spend their time or trying to find out why we are not taking a cooking class?" said Frederique.

"Oh, I was wondering if they traveled into the city specifically to attend this class."

"Most of us live in town and many of us take other classes including those dealing with social and political issues as well as health and sex."

I was regretting having asked the question and instantly recalled Chione telling me she did not want to be forced to stay home and raise children. At the same time, the general atmosphere of the restaurant and the department store had felt modern and perhaps more liberal than I thought Germany would be.

"Are you concerned about modernization," asked a tall woman near the wall glaring intently at me.

"No, I would not say concerned. I was at the department store and the Automatische Restaurant earlier and noted both were popular with women which is not how I thought German culture would be."

"Do you think it is wrong for those businesses to cater to female consumers?" said a robust woman seated in the front.

"As a visitor it is not for me to determine what is right or wrong. However, I found the displays and art in the fashion section of the department store very intriguing.

"You should probably see the department store's annual illustrated catalog it has very modern fashion drawings," said a young attractive woman sitting directly in front of me.

"Were they drawn by a woman artist?" I asked innocently.

Frederique eyes grew wide and jaw set rigid. "There are many women artists working in Deutschland. They offer a fresh perspective on the most current subjects – nightlife, the self, and the human figure."

She was pretty, but her sudden stern attitude made me notice she appeared older than she did at the Department Store. She had added more lipstick, powder, and eye-shadow to her charming face. No doubt to attract attention or appear more provocative to the many men present. As I looked about, another woman was grasping herself anxiously, one even cocked her head in an attitude of retort. A third raised her eyebrows and said, "Who is your new friend Frederique? He does not appear to be an artist."

"This is Asim Lateef, Assistant Photographer at the Museum."

"Oh, of course, you are Romy's friend."

"I am acquainted with Fräulein Stern," I replied quietly.

• • •

Silence descended, the overhead lights were dimmed and a spotlight lit the model platform as a young woman walked up the steps and stood at its center. She wore slippers and a bathrobe which she slowly removed. Her figure and demeanor radiated an air of remarkable tranquility, with just a hint of sensuality in her smile. I tried to imagine her as Romy and I as artist Otto Dräger. The thought made me chuckle. Several of the ladies leered at me.

The Künstmeister's eyebrows were his most conspicuous feature, black in contrast to his hair, they merged in a single row across his forehead. Under it his eyes were unexpectedly large and crystal clear. "To warm up, we will begin with a series of ten, one-minute poses. Three standing, three sitting, three reclining and one model's choice. Remember you are striving to capture just the gesture, no unnecessary details," he said with authority filling his voice. "And remember at least two hands high, no small scribbles."

Everyone quickly started sketching. I stood staring at the model. She had one hand on her hip and her other arm extended straight out from her side. At my angle of sight, I saw her from a three-quarter view and she looked wonderful.

I had no idea of how to start a drawing so I picked-up my charcoal stick and made a series of simple thick line-like swashes to represent a stick-like figure and by the time I had completed it, she had changed the pose to both hands on her hips with her upper body turned toward me. I took a quick glance at how everyone around me was drawing. They all were far more advanced than I.

"What are you thinking about?" asked Frederique.

"The stance, the attitude of the pose."

Everyone around me stopped drawing and appeared to be staring at me or at my drawing. I sensed someone behind me and turned to see the Künstmeister moving toward me like an animal stalking prey and planting himself to my side with his wry grin changing almost imperceptibly to a look of elation.

"We have a new student with us this evening and he is a natural Expressionist. Such artists often employ exaggerated strokes in the depiction of the human figure as you see here. Their techniques are meant to convey the turgid emotional state of the artist reacting to the anxieties of the modern world," he said as he turned to me. "What is your name young man?"

"Asim Lateef sir."

"Willkommen im Zeichenatelier des Lebens Asim. I look forward to seeing more of your intuitive mark making," he said as he gestured for the model to coil herself.

The pose triggered an odd mixture of confusion and delight on my face.

"When the torso is twisted, it's called contrapposto," whispered the lady seated in front of me. "Is it causing you anxiety?"

"Oh, I just wondered if women artists see the model in the same way as men do."

She smiled as did all the ladies around me.

"I can't wait to hear what you say when the male model comes out," said the woman to my right or that is what I thought she said, her English was not good.

As I drew the next series of poses, I kept thinking about the Künstmeister's comment that my way of drawing was 'meant to convey the turgid emotional state of the artist's reacting to the anxieties of the modern world.' Which seem to imply those reactions came forth from within me, rather than from an analytical attempt to depict the external visual appearance of the nude woman before me. As I pondered the thought further, I realized the standard for assessing the quality of my drawings would be the appeal of my personal feelings rather than an analysis of their artistic merits. I was not sure I liked such an approach. It almost felt like an affront to everything I understood about art, but I was determined to take advantage of every opportunity presented to me to learn something new about art or life.

Throughout the evening everyone was very polite and respectful. There were no rude comments or gesticulations. However, when the male model took the platform, the women appeared to be more-twitchy and tense. He was tall and lanky, broad shouldered and well endowed, but most of the ladies only drew a couple of vague, imprecise squiggles to represent his manhood which made it look very Expressionistic to me. I laughed to myself as I unobtrusively and discreetly viewed how each woman approached the subject.

By the last pose several people had left. I was feeling drowsy and started packing my portfolio case. My mind began reviewing the day as I attempted to clean my charcoal coated hands and for some strange reason, I immediately wondered how Romy's modeling for artist Otto Dräger went. But given, she was modeling for only one person not a room full like tonight I was sure it would feel much different to her than it did to these models.

I then reminded myself to learn more about what it means to be called chauvinistic and expressionistic I would not want any of Chione's friends to think I was that way with her. This thought felt somehow connected to Herr Herbster's offer to help us with selecting artifacts from the Amarna collection to photograph and his insistence that he escort Anneliese to the Director's office. I wondered if those were signs of chauvinism. Plus, somehow, Fräulein Simon's surprise visit to the Photography Studio was not only unexpected especially considering her concern about Chione's family background and uncle Youssef, but her very firm insistence on providing me with transport to the Nathan Israel Department Store also felt chauvinistic. All of which made me feel there were many more reasons for her startling visit and mixed demeanor.

All of that considered, I was very happy to have visited the store, met Frederique plus all the young gentlemen at the Automatische Restaurant and to experience drawing a live nude person. I resolved to give considerable thought to whether I should share tonight's experiences with Chione or not. All though she would probably like to know about the European artists who include ancient Egyptian images in their paintings.

As I stood there ruminating, I realized several individuals had gathered around me. "We hope you enjoyed this evening's class," said one of the young men. "Will you attend next week?" asked Frederique.

"Oh, thank you. Yes, yes, it was very enlightening and I will make every effort to return," I muttered still feeling stunned and strangely happy.

"Some of us are going for a drink, you are welcome to join us," said a dapper looking fellow.

"Thank you, but no. Perhaps another time. Good evening," I said as I walked away pretending to know which direction my rooming house was in. I had gone less than a block and had to admit I had no idea where I was. I walked to the nearest corner and hailed a carriage, gave the driver my address and sat back to relax, but as I did Slim-man got into the carriage from the opposite side and sat in front of me. The driver stopped the horses and waited for instructions. I told him to precede on.

Slim-man's constricted, shadow-stained eyes looked at me down a long, notched nose as his disapproving mouth said "Your father and Fräulein Chione's uncle Youssef would not approve of your activities tonight. You should give serious consideration to any further actions you take that may bring harm to them." I was surprised he spoke Egyptian.

He reached over with a switchblade knife in his hand, held it against my carotid artery then swiftly cut the top button off my coat, stepped out of the moving carriage, and vanished into the night all in one stealth move. The oblivious carriage driver did not look back or even slow down.

Clearly, this was a warning, but about what? He referenced my activities for the evening which on recall suggested my conversations with Fräulein Simon and Fräulein Frederique and or my attending of a life drawing class ogling a nude woman in mixed company were all morally offensive or at least of questionable character.

He could not have overheard any of the conversations or perhaps it is who I talked with or the related circumstances he was referencing. Both the ladies I spoke with, I believe are Jewish; I spoke to them in public without ever having been formally introduced to them; the first was dignified and according to proper etiquette while the second was casual and in a questionable environment. Therefore, he could be a religious or cultural zealot, but I doubted it for he seemed hostile to me personally. He also mentioned my father and Youssef, both of whom knew I was taking the train to Berlin in order to work at the Museum, but he did not seem to be a man my father would know. However, Youssef was another matter. He always struck me as a man who held many secrets.

Further, the attitude of this would be assassin implied physical harm could be brought to bear on those I love if I did not stop doing what exactly? "One of these nights 'Dunner Junge', I'm going to get you," I said to myself as I felt anger welling up within me. I dislike being threatened by anyone and especially not from a fellow Egyptian, if that is what he is. I was not certain.

CHAPTER 10

As usual, when I arrived at the Photography Studio, Anneliese was already there. She was looking at our display board where we had mounted small prints of each staff member we had photographed to date. I took off my coats, put on my lab smock and stood beside her.

"Herr Director has suggested we photograph the entire cleaning staff in one group photo. Which means we have only three regular staff to photograph individually. "I informed our nemesis Hans Herbster he would be first."

"So he will be here when?"

"In a few minutes. By-the-way, how did the life drawing class go? Did you enjoy it?"

"It was a learning experience, perhaps one that everyone should have."

"Mmm, that sounds rather philosophical."

"I can see how helping others can be an evasion of oneself and it can take one's emotions a long time to catch up to the realities of the experience."

"My goodness, with all that going on, were you able to do any drawing?"

"I am not sure my scribbles could be rightfully called drawings, but the Künstmeister said I am a natural Expressionist. He seemed to like my mark making as he called it."

We stood staring at each other. The door opened and Hans stepped in. "I'm here as requested."

His hair was disheveled and it appeared he had not shaved. He looked decidedly scruffy.

"Welcome," replied Anneliese obviously perturbed he had not knocked before entering. "You have a choice. You can sit in this chair or stand beside it."

"I will stand," he answered in a low disgruntled tone. "Without the chair."

I have known his type of young man most of my life. A cloaked ego walling itself behind a bluff of vanity. Although today, he seemed to have set his vanity aside.

"Fine, stand here and turn your upper body to the right," instructed Anneliese.

"Contrapposto," I said under my breath.

"I prefer to face directly at the camera," he said with a sneer.

I quickly turned the main light stand so it would make his face appear some-what veiled. Anneliese looked through the lens, stared at me and took the photo.

"Thank you Herr Herbster," she said. "Would you like a small wallet size copy for yourself?"

"Nein, Ich weiß wie ich aussehe." He nodded to me and walked out leaving the door open. I shut it loudly.

"What is it with him?"

"He is definitely insecure and guarded," I said. "Perhaps the onset of Expressionism has dawned new standards in the formation of one's manners, conduct and public behavior," I said with a grin.

"You mentioned you saw him and the 'Dunne Junge' together in front of the Museum, did you ever find out what their relationship is?"

"No, but I've encountered your 'Dunne Junge' a couple of other times, including last night."

• • •

I proceeded to tell Anneliese about my other run-ins and she agreed we should talk to Romy about them all to see if she found anything about him.

"What is the right word for this situation, the le mot juste?" she asked. "The exact, precise word?"

"If there is one, it is probably a German word," I said without much thought.

"Verdächtig," she uttered as she closed-up the camera in a pensive mood. "If we develop and print this photograph now and the remaining two staff will not arrive for another hour what shall we do until then? However, first I want to hear about your new encounter with slim-man."

"It was after class ended. I did not feel like walking so I got into a carriage and he jumped in too. I was not sure what he was going to do, especially since he had a knife in his hand."

Her hands moved to her bosom and her face took on an uneasy guise of foreboding.

"Oh no, I've been hoping he was some kind of undercover detective. Damn."

"Why would you think that?"

"Romy said there were rumors some have been hired to investigate how copies of Egyptian artifacts in the Museum's collection are showing up on the black market." I watched fear grow within her like a sudden malaise or fever.

"From the Amarna dig?"

"No, from earlier digs," she said laughing in a hollow faint way. "That guy looked sordid to me from the first I laid eyes on him. What did he say to you?"

"Well it was obvious he had been following me all night, but more importantly he implied Chione could be physically harmed if I did not adjust my public behavior."

"What does that mean?"

"I took it to mean he is a religious fanatic. You know talking to women I have not been formally introduced to and looking at a nude woman in mixed company."

"Oh, one of those, but he was on the train from Istanbul. Do you hold some kind of religious position there or in Cairo? I mean, why would he be so interested in you personally?"

"That is the right question to ask. I believe he spoke as he did because the carriage driver could over hear him. In truth, he just wants me to know I am being watched and he can attack me anytime he chooses plus he knows about Chione, probably even where she lives."

"He should be in an asylum, but he is targeting you. Why?"

"Probably because I work here at the Museum and I'm familiar with the Amarna Collection."

"Speaking of which, let's go to the Egyptian storage room and see if we can look at the collection."

"Wait, if he is a religious fanatic, why would he know Hans Herbster? Because if he has any religious fervor, it is more likely a cover for something related to the Museum's Egyptian collection."

"You are absolutely positive neither you or Chione have no connection to any right-wing group."

Her voice and questions were taking on undertones of ugliness and despair causing me to pause and reflect-back on everything I know about Chione and her family. "Come to think of it, Chione's father fought in the religious Mahdist War, but that was over 15 years ago."

"Which side was he on?"

"I don't recall Chione mentioning and since he died in the last battle of the war, I didn't question her any further about him," I replied as I studied the photographs on our display wall. "Again, I doubt that would have any connection to the Museum. Let's go look at the artifacts."

"While we walk, tell me more about Chione."

"What do you want to know?"

"Is she religious?"

"Not overly, but being a woman, she has many daily obligations and constraints she must follow."

"Of course. Does she adhere to them here in Berlin?'

"I am not certain. However, I am sure she observes all the German social imperatives."

. . .

When we entered the foyer of Egyptian Collection storage a familiar odor wafted over us. "Strange, the air in here smells like the warehouse in Cairo where we stored the Amarna artifacts," I said as I held the door open for Anneliese. "It's reassuring," I noted as we both surveyed the foyer and first room.

There were no windows and the space had a closed musty atmosphere. Several sheeted sculptures were along the far wall that led to a dark hallway and from which a man emerged. As he approached, he pulled a draw cord to close a drape across the hall.

"Good afternoon Fräulein Brantt and Herr Lateef. Welcome to Egyptian Collection storage, how may I assist you?"

"Thank you Herr Meierdiebrück. I assume you were notified by Herr Borchardt of our desire to look at some of the artifacts for possible color photographing."

"Yes, I've set these out for you to consider," he replied as he removed a sheet from the end of a table. "These are some of the amulets from the excavation," he said stepping back so Anneliese could get a closer look.

With her hands behind her, she studied each item intensely. "This winged bug looks intriguing."

"It is a scarab, a beetle. One of the most popular amulets in ancient Egypt. Many of them have been found at each excavation. They are believed to have special powers."

"Why is that?"

"The scarab was their symbol for the sun god Ra."

Anneliese smiled and stepped back from the table. "What is under this sheet?

Meierdiebrück removed the sheet from the far end of the table revealing a small carved stone wall relief of two young women. "We believe these figures are Pharoah Akhenaten's daughters."

"You have an unusually comprehensive understanding of the Museum's collection. Do you have a university degree in Egyptology?" asked Anneliese.

"Thank you for the compliment. No, I do not have a degree, but I have completed three years toward one and have the honor of assisting Herr Borchardt with his research for the planning and organization of the *Catalogue Général des Antiquités Egyptiennes du Musée du Caire* which he began in 1897," he replied as he bowed slightly while looking up at us both.

"I see, well it is wonderful to know we have someone with such a vast understanding of the collection on staff. Herr Lateef also assisted Herr Borchardt at the Tell El-Amarna excavation so we are doubly fortunate," she replied smiling broadly.

Yes, I believe Herr Lateef and I have a mutual friend in Assiut, a local historian named Karim," said Meierdiebrück.

I felt the surprise of hearing that statement spread across my face rapidly. "When were you in Assiut?" I asked casually.

"Two years ago at the start of season 1 of the excavation. Karim helped us find skilled diggers from several of the smaller communities in the region. He is a man of many resources."

He again bowed slightly, but I did not reply.

Anneliese looked at us both and smiled. "Shall we look at what else you have to show us today?"

Meierdiebrück removed another sheet revealing the life size face of a man.

"My goodness this is remarkably realistic to be Egyptian. Are you certain it was found at Tell El-Amarna?" she said with a profound blush. "Oh, forgive me. I did not mean to question your selection."

"You are correct to question it," I said. "Most of the head bust sculptures from the dig are in a decided realism style. Apparently, Pharoah Akhenaten insisted on breaking from the traditional style of representing royals."

"So we will be the first photographers to shoot these revolutionary artworks in color?" she beamed with delight.

"Das ist richtig," said Meierdiebrück.

"Fantastisch, but each of these items you have selected for us to look at appears to be damaged. Why is that? Were they damaged in their recovery or found in this condition?" asked Anneliese

"According to Herr Borchardt and most other Egyptologists I have had the honor to meet, since many of the priest did not agree with Pharoah Akhenaten about believing in only one God, they did not think it was a crime to violate the monuments or graves of the Aten heretics," I responded.

"Yes and there was no fear of being accused of sacrilege. They probably felt they were satisfying their own religious scruples by defacing anything associated with Aten," said Meierdiebrück. "It is remarkable any artifacts have survived. Look at this ring bezel, it is engraved with the cartouche of an unknown Pharoah named Tut-ankh-atun. If he was a believer in Aten, everything related to him must have been destroyed because this is the first time his name has ever been found."

"Deshalb, ah ... therefore, we are not required to hide the damage when photographing each artifact? Correct?" said Anneliese.

"That is not for me to answer Fräulein," he said as he stepped back from the table. "I suspect whatever reforms Pharoah Akhenaten introduced in religion, art or social customs was overpowered by traditional conservatism as liberal ideas are today."

"Perhaps we should not impose on Herr Meierdiebrück any further today," I said to Anneliese as she strained to see the cartouche on the ring.

"Oh, yes, we must return to the studio. All these artifacts could easily be photographed there. Could you bring them to us tomorrow morning?"

The change in his face was sudden. His mouth took on a snarl of pain and the flesh around it crumpled as his eyes narrowed to glimmering slits. His now hoarse voice said: "I was not informed you were allowed to move them to your studio. I must receive written permission from Herr Director before moving anything from storage."

The tension stayed in his face as Anneliese and I nodded slightly. I opened the door and Anneliese said "Thank you Herr Meierdiebrück. It was most informative. I will obtain the necessary permissions for you. Guten Tag."

"Make sure I receive notification at least 24 hours in advance. We do not like to be rushed when moving artifacts."

We exited and I gently shut the door. As I looked at Anneliese, I sensed she was about to speak, so I put my finger to my lips to shush her. We walked on in silence all the way to the stairwell where I stopped and leaned toward her. "Did you smell it?"

"If you are referring to the moldy musk, yes, I did. What of it?"

"No, I mean the damp clay and the wet plaster residue."

"Well, there is obviously very little ventilation in there.

"Of course, but there shouldn't be any reason to have wet clay or plaster there at all," I said. "Unless you are making a mold."

Anneliese appeared completely mystified. "What are you talking about?"

"The odor was coming from the stone sculpture of the broken face. Didn't you notice?"

"Why would he need a mold of it?"

"Exactly, why would he?"

"Are you going to ask Herr Borchardt for his written permission to bring the artifacts to our studio?"

"Yes, I will go to his office now. Do you think I should mention the clay and plaster odor?"

"No, not at this time. We can double check it tomorrow to make sure before we make any accusation against Herr Meierdiebrück."

"Right. However, I will ask Romy about him tonight."

"She does seem to know something about everyone," I said as I paused and turned toward her. "Are you going out to dinner with her?"

"Maybe, the artist she is modeling for tonight has requested some photographs of her so he has an image to reference when she fatigues."

"Will you make them in color?"

"Yes."

"Do you need any help with the lights?" I said grinning.

She smiled in return, but did not answer as she walked away. I walked toward the studio and a distant echo of Meierdiebrück's comments concerning conservative thinking crept aimlessly through my mind as if I should pay attention to it.

CHAPTER 11

There were clouds in the distance with only a lite breeze coming from the northeast again as I walked toward the Museum through the early morning crowd crush. My mind was filled with thoughts about what Chione might be doing today; how Anneliese's photography session with Romy went and whether Herr Meierdiebrück would deliver some of the Amarna artifacts to the Photography Studio.

As I approached the Museum my eyes caught a glimpse of Hans and Meierdiebrück huddled together near the side entrance. Meierdiebrück appeared as heavy and mysterious as the nearby bronze sculpture of some old German leader with half-closed eyes and folded arms.

Hans was animated with quick hand movements accentuating his hushed voice. As they opened the door and entered their conversation was amplified and sounded heated, but when I reached the door and entered neither man was in sight and the still silence of the dark hall reminded me of being inside the great pyramid at Giza. A distant sensation of being home-sick skidded briefly across the far corners of my mind as I headed toward the Photography Studio. It may have been the first such feeling I have had since arriving in Berlin.

At the hall to the Studio, I was surprised to see a uniformed guard standing with Herr Borchardt and Anneliese. I nodded to everyone.

"This is Herr Lateef," stated Herr Borchardt to the guard who looked me up and down with a stern, sour silence that set heavily on his thick featured face. He saluted quickly. "Let's go inside and discuss how you will begin photographing the artifacts," said Borchardt.

The guard unlocked the door and held it open while the three of us entered. He then closed the door and locked it again.

Borchardt smiled. "It is unfortunate this is how you will have to function while photographing the artifacts. There are too many potential opportunities for them to be mishandled or gestohlen, ah stolen. Herr Meierdiebrück will bring a few to you each morning and pick them up at 4pm each day. When you leave for lunch or for any reason the guard will lock the door and remain on duty until either of you or Meierdiebrück returns. Is that understood?" He gestured toward our work table where five wrapped objects had been placed.

Managing to hide our surprise and joy at seeing the artifacts in the Studio, Anneliese and I only nodded and smiled.

"Utmost care must be given to ensure no damage occurs to any of the artifacts," he said as he handed me a ledger book he had been holding. "This is a copy of the original excavation ledger. It contains a written description of the condition of each item. Use it to verify each is in good order before you photograph it. Should you discover something amiss notify me at once. At once, do you hear?"

Again Anneliese and I nodded in agreement. "We certainly will Herr Borchardt," said Anneliese gently while placing her hand on his arm. "No harm will come to them while they are in our care."

"I trust you both understand by following this procedure you are relieved of the responsibility for transporting the artifacts to and from the Egyptian Collections Department. Plus, the studio will not need to be guarded at night."

"Yes, it is a very good and appropriate way for us to fulfill our assignment. Asim and I will follow it faithfully," said Anneliese.

We stood at the door and watched as Borchardt unlocked it and hurried down the hall without looking back. The guard promptly closed and locked the door.

We stood starring at each other for a moment of reflection before turning toward the wrapped artifacts. "Let's unwrap each one, lay them all out and check to make sure each matches its ledger description," said Anneliese with a question in her voice.

"We should unwrap each one together and take a deep breath, examine it, then rewrap it before moving to the next."

Anneliese smiled with a look of calm indifference. "Yes, if only to get this suspicion out of your mind and I suppose it will enable us to better determine which one to photograph first."

I looked at the five wrapped artifacts and immediately recognized two were no longer covered by Egyptian cotton. I suspected the new material was British cotton. I moved the two to the far end of the table, took a piece of paper from my note pad and tore it into 5 small pieces, numbered each and placed a number in front of each artifact.

"Is this the standard steps you took at Amarna?"

"More or less, although all the artifacts were wrapped in Egyptian cotton," I replied as I picked up artifact #1, unwrapped it, recorded it in my photography ledger as #1-E-Amphora pottery shard then placed it on the table and stepped back. Anneliese put her hands together behind her back, leaned over and took a deep breath.

"Smells dusty to me," she said as she stepped away from the table.

I moved up bent over and inhaled deeply. "I concur."

We both smiled and she picked up the cotton cloth. "Watch while I wrap it to make sure I do it correctly."

She was quick, but exact and error free.

"Perfect," I said as I moved the artifact back and picked up #4. It was wrapped in British cotton. Just holding it told me immediately it was a portrait of a man's face. I carefully removed the cotton, put it aside and cradled the artifact gently with both hands, raised it up in front of my face and inhaled deeply.

"The odor of moist clay and plaster is still strong."

Anneliese quickly came to my side so I held the artifact in front of her so she could inhale directly from it without having to worry about holding it.

"I concur. Damn, what do we do now?"

"No false pattern can be created to cover a crime without bearing upon it some trace of its creator. We must look for other patterns the culprit has left," I said with a feeling of remorse.

"You mean the use of British cotton ... implying that #5 should also smell of clay and plaster because its cotton wrap appears to be a slightly lighter shade of white?" asked Anneliese.

"It's lighter looking because the thread pitch is less than in Egyptian cotton," I said. "Plus, it hasn't been handled very often."

"We must be very careful with this information. Let's not inform Herr Borchardt until we are certain as to what it means," she said with a cunning look in her eyes. "Especially since we don't know if it is not due to something he himself has been doing."

I made the following entry to my Photography Ledger:

#5-B-Tell El-Amarna

Portrait of a Man

Gypsum, Height 18cm

Note: smells of clay and plaster

. . .

"How did the ancient Egyptians create this sculpture?" asked Anneliese.

"They took a clay mold from the real man's face; ground Gypsum into powder and mixed it with water then poured it into the clay mold."

She asked, "and you are certain the odors we smell are not from that original process?"

"I doubt they would still be there after almost 3000 years of being buried in the sand. Plus, I was present when this piece was discovered and it only smelt of dust."

"Ok, let's assume a mold was recently made of it. Why would the culprit cast plaster or Gypsum copies or would he just sell the clay mold?" I said, "Or, he may replace the original sculpture with a new Gypsum copy and sell this one.'

"How do we know this is the original and why has the Egyptian cotton been replaced by British?'

We stood and stared at the wrapped artifacts as though they were mummified living entities until finally a knock on the door caused us both to wobble our heads as we listened to the sound of the key disengaging the lock. The door opened and the guard handed Anneliese an envelope then stood waiting as if he expected her to give him an order.

"Danke schön."

The guard exited and locked the door.

The sealed envelope was addressed to her, she opened it, took out a single piece of folded paper and silently read the message.

Looking at me with a childlike smile emerging on her face she said. "Yesterday you offered to help me with lighting at Romy's photo shoot."

"Yes, how did the shoot go?"

"This note is from her and she wants to know too, so let's find out."

Her proclamation generated a smile to my mug.

"These prints will need to be larger than we have done thus far. The artist needs to be able to see the details," she said with an exotic sounding giggle.

"By-the-way, how is everything going with Choine? Oh, ah, we will need to make these prints quickly. We do not need to have any visitors see them."

"And I would not want to have to explain them to anyone. Where will we dry them? We cannot leave them hanging in here. Meierdiebrück will be here at 4:00 to take the artifacts," I said.

"You are correct, we will have to make small prints. Romy can show them to the artist and let him pick the ones he wants to have larger prints made of."

"Sure, he can take the negatives to one of the private studio's and have the prints made how-ever large he wants them to be," I said.

"Are you sure we have time to photograph the artifacts and make prints for Romy?" I asked.

Anneliese's face twisted in search of a quick answer then her eyes flickered. "You photograph the artifacts, I'll make the prints."

"Right, we'll each do what we do best."

. . .

As we worked through the day it was obvious the prints were not going to dry before Meierdiebrück arrived. We would have to make certain he did not enter the dark room.

"What shall we do," I asked.

"Let's put them in my central desk drawer and lock it. I will sit there and complete the Studio Ledger entries about each of the artifacts you photographed today. Oh, did you have any difficulty photographing any of them?"

"I actually photographed each twice and varied the lighting accordingly," I said while studying her eyes.

"That sounds very prudent. We should develop the negatives today to make sure that process works before photographing tomorrow's delivery."

"Let's make small prints first," I suggested. "We can keep them with our official Ledger."

"Let's check the prints of Fräulein Stern to see if they are dry enough to package," she said while unlocking her desk drawer.

As she slid the drawer open, I felt a rush of joy at having good eyesight, but still found myself leaning forward for Romy was an exceptionally physically attractive young woman.

"I can see you like the images, but are they worthy of being considered kunst?"

I felt speechless, as I was when I watched The Beautiful One emerge from the ancient sand of Amarna. "The poses are staged with natural ease. There are no prissy or prudish gestures and your lighting is remarkably sensitive. The artist will have a challenging time of matching your superb sense of discreet, unobtrusive subtlety."

Anneliese smiled, collected the photographs, put them inside an envelope, sealed it, closed and locked the drawer, then stood up and strolled back and forth across the office in silence. I watched for a minute or two until I realized it was almost 4pm.

"Herr Meierdiebrück will be here any moment," I whispered.

She stopped, looked at me and said, "We will wait and let the Guard officially record his admittance and unlock the door. You stand near the curtain and do not allow him to enter the darkroom." Her voice had become cool and contained with very little expression in it except sounding tired.

"I understand."

The clock struck 4 bells and we instantly heard Meierdiebrück talking and the guard responding. The door was unlocked and opened, Meierdiebrück entered pushing a cart.

"Good afternoon. It is time for the artifacts to return to Egyptian Storage."

I did not like his voice any better than his sly grin. There was not quite a sneer in both, but close enough. My jaw clinched.

He loaded the artifacts onto the cart and Anneliese moved over to stand next to me. As he pushed the cart passed us we both nodded and she said dryly "Danke schön."

He went out the door, did not speak or look back as he proceeded down the hall. The guard closed the door, but did not lock it.

"I'm surprised he did not ask if we found any irregularities in the artifacts nor checked our rewrapping," I said, but Anneliese seemed perplexed in more of a mystified manner.

"I've always thought of myself as an artist. Do you think of yourself as such?"

"My training in Istanbul was more technical than artistic, besides no two people move in the same way, just as no two sets of fingerprints match exactly," I responded. "What are you thinking about?"

I felt an aura of righteous indignation in her mood.

"Do you think the photographs of Romy are works of art or do you view them as erotica?" she said.

"This may be unfamiliar to you, but that is like asking if the artifacts are sacred pious objects or commodities of art history."

"At the very least, the photographs are worthy of appreciation as creative expressions of humanity. Would you agree?"

"Yes, and may I add, since you know Romy and by extension, Romy knows the individual who will receive the photographs, it could be seen as a benevolent act of assistance," I responded.

"That is a wonderful way to think about it, but would you feel the same if the photographs were of Choine?"

Once again I felt trapped. Yes, I would like to have photographs of Choine nude, but I would definitely not want other men to view them. I wondered if that meant in my heart, I am chauvinistic? As I stood considering that thought, I also wondered if Choine were to pose for me as a drawing model, would I represent her looking natural or Expressionistic? Would I be concerned with evoking powerful reactions to my drawing by using bright colors and jagged strokes, completely abandoning all expectations of aesthetically pleasing and easy-to-process art?

CHAPTER 12

It was late in the afternoon and we had completed photographing all the artifacts except the Nefertiti bust. Anneliese and I heard Meierdiebrück's squeaky cart approaching. We took our usual positions blocking the entrance to the darkroom as the click of the door lock simultaneously sounded with the chime of our desk clock bell. The door opened and we were again subjected to Meierdiebrück's sour expression. But this time his leathery skin, tightened lips and winkled eyes appeared strained more than usual plus he was stooped some causing his disheveled thin hair to part revealing a glistened scalp and a sprig of bluish veins. I wondered if he was ill.

As he finished loading his cart, I noted he stared at my drawing portfolio case. "As you are aware, you have only to photograph the Nefertiti bust," he said.

Anneliese looked up sharply. "That is correct. Is there a problem?"

"I have been instructed to deliver it to the new Photography Studio on Monday morning," he said. "Will you have completed moving your equipment by then or should I wait to hear from you?"

His half-hearted friendliness did not meld well with his customary foulness.

"Two days will be time enough for us to get the new space ready," replied Anneliese as she rose from her chair.

"Wie du sagst Fräulein," he said with a slight nod. "Herr Lateef, perhaps you would like to join me for a drink this evening."

Anneliese and I stood staring at one another and the guard opened the door. "Ah, I will return shortly and we will begin packing," she said stepping quickly passed the guard and scurrying down the hall.

I looked back at Meierdiebrück, "Thank you, I will. Where shall we meet?"

"At Ratskeller Haus," he said in a hoarse, choking way.

I nodded and he pushed his cart passed me, glanced at the guard and proceeded through the hall. The guard paused for a moment as though he wanted to say something, but closed the door instead.

• • •

I had completely filled the first cart with photography chemical containers and trays when I moved it aside thinking about what to put into the second one and the desk clock chimed 5 bells. "Leave this," said Anneliese. "We will have plenty of time tomorrow Herr Director has assigned two of the cleaning staff to assist us."

"What do you think Meierdiebrück wants to talk about," I said as I sat down to relax for a moment. "I mean surely he hasn't decided to be sociable."

"Maybe there is something wrong with the Nefertiti bust?" she said pulling her chair over close.

There was a quick knock on the door and it opened instantly as the guard leaned in and gave his door key to Anneliese. "I was instructed to give this to you Fräulein."

She took the key, he saluted us both, closed the door and we heard his footsteps quickly fade away.

"Here, these are for the new Studio and Dark Room," said Anneliese as she handed me two new keys. "I insisted we be able to lock the dark room."

I smiled and put both keys into my pocket. "If there was something wrong with the Nefertiti bust, I'm sure we would have been told. No, I think he may want to talk about our ledger."

"What? Why?"

"I noticed this morning there is an odor of fresh clay on the cover and on a couple pages inside. Someone looked through it."

"How would they have gotten access?"

"Perhaps that's why the guard rushed away," I said with raised eyebrows. "It does not really matter. We are not the ones who need to explain the change in wraps or the odors on nearly half of the artifacts. We need only to decide on whom to mention them to first, Meierdiebrück, Herr Borchardt or the Director. If Meierdiebrück has read our ledger, as I suspect he has, he will have noted each of the questionable artifacts are listed differently than the others."

"Our first loyalty is with Herr Borchardt," said Anneliese.

"I agree. Shall we tell him together?"

"No, you go meet with Meierdiebrück and I will speak to Herr Borchardt," she said. "But don't mention anything about what we found to Meierdiebrück."

"What if he comments on it or questions me?"

"Tell him you are not at liberty to discuss anything related to the Amarna Collection."

"That will imply that there are others beyond us involved and will certainly make the evening a short one."

We had turned off the lights and locked the Studio door and were walking through the hall when I remembered about Romy. "Oh, did Romy like the photos you took of her?"

"Yes, so much so she is going to give only one of them to Otto. She said seeing photographs of herself nude feels entirely different than looking at a drawing or painting. It is a lot more personal and she is reluctant to share that intimacy, especially with the variety of people who visit Otto's studio.

"That's easy to understand," I said. "Which photo did she give to him?"

"The same one you spent so much time admiring and she is going to tell him that it is only for his eyes. If he shows it to anyone, she will not model for him again."

I smiled, but thought it would be more appropriate to not say anything further on the subject. "Was she able to find out anything about 'Dünner Junge', ah slim-man?"

"Nothing, no one in her circle of friends or contacts has any idea who he is."

"That's unfortunate."

We went our separate ways; Anneliese to Herr Borchardt's office and I to the side exit to find a carriage to the Ratskeller Haus.

• • •

The evening was becoming cool, but it was still light outside. I found a carriage and was surprised when the driver asked which Ratskeller I wanted to go to. I quickly determined going to the nearest one would be best choice. It took only 15 minutes to reach the dark building and the driver gestured the bar was in the basement. As I approached the obscure stairwell, there was a strong stench of beer and pong of urine. I considered turning back and yelling for the carriage to stop, but my vacillation was slow, the carriage had already reached the corner and turned.

Upon opening the heavy wood entrance door, I was overwhelmed by a heavy veil of tobacco smoke and the deep murmur of grouching and bellyaching gripes or so I imaged since most of it I could not understand. Judging by their clothes, the patrons were tradesmen and low-level civil servants and while Meierdiebrück held a higher position in life, he seemed to fit right in when I spotted him alone in a far booth.

He was twisting a piece of paper with one hand and drinking from a glass of beer with the other. As I approached, I noted for the first time, how thin and sullen his attitude was and when he sneered, he looked as though he had too many teeth for the size of his mouth.

"Guten Abend," he said as I sat opposite him and he signaled to the waitress to bring me a beer. "Agh, we will need to speak English, since your Deutsch is limited."

I grinned and nodded. "Do you come here often?"

"No, I have a wife and family who expect me home."

I had never given any thought to his private life and knowing he has one made him look entirely different to me. "How many children?"

"Zwei kinder and Schwiegermutter ... ah, two plus mother-in-law."

I took a couple of swallows of the beer, which tasted very good. "Do you live far from here?"

"We have a small apartment in Wedding, not far from the Strassenbahn. I see you are carrying an artist's portfolio. Have you been making drawings of the artifacts?"

"No, I am a beginner. Was there something specific you wanted to talk about?"

"Did you find anything amiss or improper with any of the artifacts?"

We starred at each other and I took a long draft of beer. "Do you enjoy your position at the Museum?"

He paused and then finished his beer. "The work is interesting, but as a family man, I'd like to earn more wages."

"Well, I hope someday to be a family man too," I said and then finished my beer. "So, I am sure you will understand, I am not permitted to say anything about the artifacts. Now I do not want to be late for my drawing class." I placed some money on the table, picked up my portfolio and started to leave. "Oh, how is everything between you and your friend Hans?"

He looked startled and crumpled the paper in his hand, but did not speak. I walked outside and went only a short distance, stepping into a dark shadow near a large tree and waited to see him leave. It did not take long, he came out in a huff and quickly reached the end of the block and turned toward the rail line.

I set my portfolio behind the tree, walked back into the tavern and found the crumbled paper on the floor. No one paid any attention to me, not even the waitress. This time my foreign appearance was helpful. I retrieved my portfolio, hailed a carriage, and went to class.

Most of the same students were there again including department store clerk Frederique, but the female model was a large, heavy-set woman which was not as pleasant to look at, but much easier to draw in a fuller scale. The male model was shorter and scrawny looking, but even more impressive to the ladies especially when he took a classic foil fencing pose. They even insisted he hold it for at least 20 minutes. Both models were challenging to draw in my organic Expressionistic approach. I kept suggesting bits and pieces of clothing on them, but I do not know why. They both conveyed a feeling of being alienated individuals, sort of like they were psychological by-products of Berlin's urbanization – an emotional distancing from the greater community. I had seen the same look on the faces of women I assumed were derelicts or night women.

At the end of class, I joined everyone at the local tavern and was pleasantly surprised to see so many of the ladies also there. As I listened to their conversations I wondered where Choine was and if I was going to encounter 'Dünner Junge', ah slim-man again.

It was too cold to take an open carriage home so I hailed a taxi car and to my surprise several others asked if they could share it, which made it less expensive for each of us. They dropped me off at the corner of my block so it took only a minute or so to get to my door.

Before I could turn the key, I noticed a shadowed figure approaching. I dropped my drawing portfolio and inserted my door key. Choine was suddenly at my side. We embraced and kissed.

"Who are all those people you were with," she said.

"What are you doing here and why are you out so late alone? I asked harshly.

We stepped apart and took a moment to look at each other. Choine shivered. I put my overcoat around her shoulders.

"It's too cold to stand out here, let's go inside," I said.

I turned the key gently and gestured to her to be quiet. We entered and moved silently along the hall to my room. I unlocked the door and we looked at each other smiling before entering.

"Oh, it is so much warmer in here," she whispered softly even though no one was within hearing distance of us.

"The furnace for the entire house is on the other side of this wall," I replied.

She smiled at my bed and snuggled up against me "So, who were all of those people?"

"They are art students. It is not important. What are you doing out this late without an escort?"

She lowered her head and turned away from me. "I was out to dinner with one of my workmates from the antique warehouse."

"Who exactly are you referring to?"

She turned back toward me and looked up through the top of her eyes, "Herr Montu Sati."

I was not sure I recognized the name, but could tell Choine was concerned about how I was going to react. I decided she deserved the most understanding, good listener I could be.

"And what happened to make you come here? Did he insult you or hurt you in some manner?"

"No, no, it is just that I realized I should not be out alone with any single man. It makes them believe I am a night woman."

"Well yes it does, but he must have said or did something to make you come here."

"It was mostly his manner," she said looking ashamed. "He implied if I were to help him with certain business transactions at the warehouse, he would introduce me to wealthy men who would take care of me."

"Take care of you in what manner?"

Her tawny face was turning burnt sienna. "They will give me gifts like expensive dresses and take me to the best restaurants or even maybe to the World's Fair in Belgium," she said smiling cautiously like a young girl.

"It will be open through October, perhaps we can go together in the Fall." I could feel my own skin becoming fiery. "Have you allowed any man to do things like that for you?"

"No Asim and I will not. I know what most men presume and expect when they give a woman gifts," she blushed and looked at my bed again. "No, I just feel uncomfortable working around him every day and I am certain the business deals he is referring to are illegal or will cheat the owner of the business, Herr Har-shaf Uga. Have you taken women out in the evening?"

Before I could respond, we heard foot-steps in the hall. We stood motionless and silent until it was quiet again. "It's just the maintenance man tending to the furnace," I whispered while returning my arms around her and pulling her tight against me.

"Aren't there several women working there beside you?"

"Yes, but he believes because I worked for Herr Borchardt at the Amarna excavation, I understand about Egyptian artifacts."

I suddenly felt completely conflicted, holding her against me made my manhood stiffen while the continued sounds in the furnace room worried me and I desperately wanted to hear more about Herr Montu Sati's illegal import deals. I needed to get her out of the house and I needed to cool off before I made an advancement I would not want to retreat from.

"Come on, you must not be seen here, I will get you a taxi to take you home and we will talk more tomorrow evening," I said still feeling the need to keep my voice hushed. "Please invite Fräulein Romy to join us for dinner."

She smiled and we kissed again as my hands venture to the sides of her ample bosoms. She did not resist my attention. It took a while before we separated. As we stepped into the hall the maintenance man came around the corner. "Guten Abend Herr Lateef," he said as he nodded to us both and continued past us.

I did not speak until we were outside. "It'll be fine, he often brings the house maid to his room at night."

She crinkled her eye brows and said only "men."

CHAPTER 13

I unlocked the door to our new Darkroom and found several newly developed photographs hanging from the drying line. They were of a nude young woman. Her poses suggested a natural ease acquired from lots of experience in being photographed. She had darkish hair cut in the new short style with a clear forehead, intense eyes, high cheek bones and very desirable lips. I had no idea who she was and considering we were scheduled to photograph the Nefertiti bust this morning I was wondering where Anneliese had gotten to.

I left everything as I found it and locked the door. As I stepped back into the Studio the creaky sound of Herr Meierdiebrück's cart was approaching. I opened the door, but Anneliese walked in and gestured for me to hold it while she showed Meierdiebrück where to place the Nefertiti bust. Something about the entire action made me feel it had been choreographed or maybe it was the magic of seeing The Beautiful One again.

"Will your photographing take very long," asked Meierdiebrück. "It is not good for the sculpture to be so near the chemicals you use in your Darkroom."

"We keep the Darkroom closed and locked while we are photographing," I said.

He nodded and left wearing a sullen look.

Anneliese stood staring at the sculpture, her eyes filled with wonder to the point of looking hypnotized. A familiar feeling. I stepped back and let her indulge herself until I remembered the photos hanging in the Darkroom.

I gently nudged her arm. She turned and looked at me.

"We need more lights," she said.

"Not now, you need to clean up everything in the Darkroom first. That is our top priority."

It took a moment, but when it hit, she went into near panic. "Ach richtig, ah, yes, yes. I will take care of that right now."

She went into the darkroom instantly and it became my turn to admire The Beautiful One.

• • •

How much time had elapsed seemed meaningless when Anneliese emerged from the Darkroom carrying a large sealed envelope. "That job is completed, now what shall we do first?" she said as she put the envelope in her desk and locked it. "It's a shame they didn't find the rest of it."

"Are you referring to the eye and ear?"

"Yes and maybe the entire body."

"No, that is not correct. You will see. This sculpture was never intended to set on a body."

"What do you mean?"

"The longer you look at it, you will realize it was created as it is to bring you close to it. If it were on a body, you would always stand back from it."

She stood looking at it again and then walked around it several times. "I do believe you are correct. However, it should be at eye height and the lights need to be changed."

"These lights are too hard," I said interrupting her. "They make her look unfinished. Watch." I left on only one standing light and turned off the overhead ceiling lights. "Now look closer."

She walked up almost nose to nose with the sculpture. Tilted her head to the left, then right. Moved the standing light back further, aimed it off to the side and studied the effect.

"Wow, she is even more impressive, more regal, more mature, a real woman," she said glowing while quickly becoming pensive and thoughtful. "But is that what Herr Borchardt and the Director want? Are they and the world ready to see what a real Queen looks like?"

"Well we have enough time to shoot it with several different lighting arrangements. Let's do them all."

"I love the way the head extends forward, stretching the neck and causing the chin to raise energetically toward the front. It exudes an implied embrace of the person standing directly in front of it."

"Which is a tradition in ancient Egyptian sculpture, but in this instance, it is somehow more poetically graceful and feminine looking."

"Do you say these kinds of things to Chione?"

"I do not have the right to, yet."

There was a knock on the door, I opened it and the guard said "you have a visitor." I looked out and it was Hans. I stepped into the doorway, blocking the entrance. The guard stepped back so Hans and I were more-or-less eye to eye. "Herr Herbster, how may I help you?"

"I am here to remind you that at 4pm Herr Meierdiebrück is to return the Nefertiti bust to storage and you will need to inform him as to whether you will require him to bring it to you tomorrow." His quick shifting eyes surveyed everything.

Anneliese and I looked at each other and we both shrugged.

"We will not be able to determine whether an additional day of photographing will be necessary until we have developed and printed today's film."

"And perhaps Herr Director may wish to review the photographs as well before scheduling another shoot," said Anneliese.

"As you say," he said with a nod as he turned and walked away reluctantly.

After closing the door, I noticed Anneliese studying the sculpture again. "Turn all the ceiling lights off and let's take a few experimental shots quickly."

"Do we have enough film left?"

"Yes," she replied lost in studying how to stage the first shot.

. . .

Before we knew it, the sound of Meierdiebrück's squeaky cart ricocheted through the hall. "He is early, he must want something," I said. "Maybe Hans is waiting at the end of the hall."

Meierdiebrück arrived alone and quietly went about loading the sculpture, nodded to us both and left.

We told the guard we were going into the Darkroom and to not let anyone into the studio. He informed us he had instruction to only remain while the sculpture was in the Studio. He left.

I locked the Studio door and we went into the Darkroom and developed the film. I wanted to ask Anneliese about the earlier prints I had seen hanging on the drying line, but somehow it did not seem appropriate at the time. I thought perhaps she would bring the subject up herself. She did not.

As the hour grew late and we neared the end of developing the negatives I noticed her take out some additional film. "What is that for?" I asked.

"We are going to make a duplicate set of negatives," she said without stopping what she was doing. "We will also make duplicate prints including thumbnails."

"I see and they will be given to whom?"

"They are for the Photography Department's official achieves."

The look on my face must have said everything for 'us' was all she said. But, before I could ask for further explanation, a faint knock on the Studio door was just barely audible. We looked at each other. "I will go," I whispered, but I do not know why.

I unlocked the door, but opened it only slightly. To my surprise there stood Romy. I waved her in then closed and locked the door behind us.

"Anneliese is in the Darkroom. Is there something I can do for you?"

"Ah, no, ah she was to develop some prints for me," she said with a firm chin and smile as I watched the tops of her ears turn red. I knocked on the Darkroom door and said, "Anneliese, Romy is here."

Romy smiled as the blush spread from her ears to her cheeks. "Have you seen Chione?" she said with a rather demure grin.

The Darkroom door lock clicked and the door opened. Anneliese stepped out closing the door behind. "Hello, I thought we were going to meet later."

Romy appeared very self-conscious and tense as well as reluctant to speak.

"I was just on my way to the Library to check for the Holbein books," I said. "Ah, if you don't mind."

Anneliese's smile turned into a gentle laugh. "No Asim, let's all go for a drink."

"Why not come to my apartment," said Romy with a deep sigh of relief and a wink for Anneliese. "It's nearby and we won't need to worry about being seen or interrupted by anyone."

"So you're not modeling tonight?" asked Anneliese.

"No, I need a break from it for a while. You know it can get monotonous."

"Mmm, depends on your point of view," I replied smiling.

"Yes, I often think the entire process should be reversed. I should be dressed and the artist should be nude."

We all laughed. Anneliese and I made sure all the exposed film from the day's shoot was locked away and the Darkroom secured. Anneliese got the envelope from her desk and locked the Studio. We all headed for the side exit.

As we entered the last hallway, Hans came in the side entrance. "Good evening, ladies and Herr Lateef."

We all nodded to each other. "It's very unusual to see you using this exit Fräulein Stern," said Hans with a cocky smirk.

"We were hoping to avoid disturbing anyone."

"That is very thoughtful of you. I will be sure to mention your thoughtfulness to Herr Director."

"Yes, please do," replied Romy. "And be sure to explain how you just happened to be doing the same thing."

Spitefulness flooded his face and stiffened his entire body as he fast paced away, but I was more intrigued with how self-confident Romy was, especially since only minutes earlier she showed a complete lack of it. Obviously, the photos of the young woman had a much more personal significance to her than anything related to Hans.

"Why is he so unpleasant and malicious?" said Anneliese. "We have never been unkind to him. Have we Asim?"

"No, but it could be he somehow feels threatened by us."

"By two women and a…" Romy stopped in mid-sentence and stared at Anneliese and I.

"I was going to say and an Egyptian."

"Perhaps, what it really is, we are an up-pity woman, a Jew, and an Arab. Or a suffragist, a Jew and a Muslim. Whatever it is, he sees us as a threat to his world."

"Let's get out of here and get that drink."

We took a taxi car to Romy's apartment, which felt wrong to me, it was only 1 km from the Museum. She opened a bottle of white wine, which I had never drank before and set out a plate of cheese, bread, cut up bratwurst and pretzels. I was impressed and probably consumed more than a guest should.

Well, now we are all feeling more comfortable, how about giving me an update on how you both are settling in here in Berlin and at the Museum. You start Anneliese.

Anneliese finished her second glass of wine, took off her shoes and folded her legs up underneath herself to relax. "Keep in mind I have lived in Berlin on and off for several years. So, I have many friends and colleagues here. The biggest challenge I am dealing with now is adjusting to my position at the Museum, especially working with Herr Borchardt and you Asim."

"I am of no threat to you Anneliese. I want only to learn all I can while I am at the Museum. However, I think you have overlooked a concern we both share," I said. 'Dünner Junge', ah, slim-man and whatever Herr Meierdiebrück is involved with."

"What are you talking about?" said Romy.

We told Romy everything about what we believe Meierdiebrück and possibly Hans are up to as well as the stalking and attack by 'Dünner Junge'.

She blinked and finished her glass of wine in one huge swallow and said: "I think we need to open another bottle."

"If we just generalize for a moment it seems to me that Meierdiebrück and Hans are involved in making and probably selling copies of some of the Amarna artifacts, perhaps 'Dünner Junge' is controlled by the buyer? I mean you said Meierdiebrück talked about having to support his family. However, 'Dünner Junge' talked about threatening Chione if you did not stop going to the drawing class. I do not see a connection."

"Maybe it is time to tell Herr Borchardt about our suspicions," said Anneliese.

"I agree, but I am not sure the timing is good. It might be better to wait until after the Egyptian courtyard Amarna exhibit reception," replied Romy.

Anneliese and I looked at each other with an ambiguous gesture.

"Oh, I did not realize you are not aware of it yet. Herr Director and Ludwig are organizing an exhibition of the Amarna artifacts in the Egyptian wing courtyard for the Board of Directors and members of the German Oriental Society plus a short list of other important people and notables."

"Then we must tell him now," I said. "If he were to discover we were aware of something illegal happening before the exhibition and didn't tell him, he will fire us, maybe even have us arrested."

"Yes, I will tell him tomorrow," said Anneliese.

"Good. Now there is another potential surprise for you Asim," said Romy with no fun in her expression. "Herr Borchardt mentioned that Chione's uncle Youssef Sadek is now working in Berlin also for antique importer Har-Shaf Uga. Chione is having dinner with him tonight."

"Fräulein Stern you are surprising. How do you come into all this knowledge?"

"That is not important. What is important is for you to ask Chione if she knows why her uncle is here. I cannot explain myself, just trust that I am on your side… and let's drink to that and to tomorrow's rally," said Romy.

"Unfortunately, I will not be able to attend. Asim and I must complete making the photographic prints of the Amarna Collection and I must speak with Herr Borchardt. I would not be able to do either if I were in jail. My heart will be with you in spirit though."

"A rally? For what?" I asked feeling somewhat confused by everything she had said.

"The Social Democratic Women's Rally for our rights," said Romy as she stood and raised her glass. "Stand up Asim, you want Chione to marry the man of her choice, don't you?"

I nodded my head in agreement and stood even though I was not sure why.

Romy reached for one of the booklets on the table and handed it to me. "Read this," she said with a razor-sharp edge to her voice and smile.

The title read *Working Women in the Class Struggle* by Emma Ihrer.

"Who is this person?"

"One of the founders of the proletarian women's movement here in Deutschland."

"Human rights have no gender Asim," said Anneliese as she put her hand on my arm.

"But, haven't you heard about the British suffragette who was run over by the King's horse in London? She died," I remarked modestly.

They did not respond other than to stare at me. However, it was obvious my question frightened them. Their white faces remained composed, but their bodies stiffened.

"Let's have another drink," suggested Romy.

"I don't think I'll have another, thanks," I said as I reached for my coat.

"You're not leaving so early?"

"I am tired and have a lot on my mind. Good evening."

A faint laugh came strangely out of her unmoving face and Anneliese made a chuckling gasp noise in her throat.

By the time I arrived home I was exhausted and fell asleep instantly, but instead of sweet dreams of my Chione, marching women, Youssef and Uga filled my mind with puzzling, worrisome, thoughts and images. I was revved up and sweating profusely, endlessly tossing about. There were too many things to think about. Life seemed simpler somehow in Egypt; less pretentious and perhaps naiver. My night clothes were sodden when I awoke.

Evidence of the coming rally were everywhere as I walked to the Museum. Groups of yelling women carrying banners, placards and flags were at every intersection. I was even asked to sign petitions, which I politely declined stating I was not a citizen. I did not want to risk being deported. However, there was something refreshing about being mistaken for a local and for not having strangers shun or avoid me.

The overwhelming throng of women blocking the sidewalk and stairs in front of the Museum was astounding. As I pushed through them heading toward the side entry, I was shocked to see Romy standing arm-arm with Chione and both waving flags. I took the flag from Chione and threw it down the steps. "What are you doing here? You could be arrested!"

They both looked at me and said, "So what!" and continued yelling "Give women the vote!" Other women joined arms with them also bellowing.

I was pushed further to the side and stood amazed at the level of skreiching. Dozens of police arrived. I rushed to Chione and took hold of her arm. She pulled away from me and yelled "No!" I stepped back from her and moved away from the center of the mob. She and Romy were quickly seized by the Police who made a big show of their superiority by unnecessarily and excessively man-handling all the younger women while heaving them into a large iron cage-like carriage.

When the cage was full and started moving away, all the remaining women, mostly middle-aged, followed behind it and continued yelling and waving their placards and banners. I assumed they all would be incarcerated at the jail.

I felt angry and at a lost as to what I could possibly do to help Chione and Romy. As I went into the Museum and reached the Photography Studio, my mind recalled Marie Louise imploring me to notify her of anything Chione did that could cause embarrassment to Herr Borchardt or the Museum. But, how could I. She works at Herr Simon's office.

As I stood pondering, the door opened and Anneliese said, "Are you coming in?"

"Oh, you didn't get arrested."

"As I stated last night, that would put the Photography Department and our positions in jeopardy plus cause public embarrassment to Herr Borchardt and the Director. There is no upside to being on trial for a criminal offense. Especially since women's suffrage and our general class struggle does not have a chance in hell of succeeding yet. Maybe if a war does start, as everyone seems to believe it will, we might be able to show how valuable women can be. Maybe."

"I understand, however, remember I promised to inform Marie Louise of anything Chione did that could cause problems for her uncle and his family."

"Was she arrested?"

"Yes, with Romy."

Anneliese quickly took off her smock. "I will tell Herr Borchardt and he will telephone Herr Simon's office.

She rushed away.

I went into the Darkroom and discovered a dozen or more beautiful color prints of Nefertiti hanging on the drying line. Our experiments with the lighting had been the right approach to take. I especially liked the prints that showed the Queen as a mature woman. As I starred at them, the words 'class struggle' echoed in my mind. I pondered if Nefertiti felt she was in a class struggle or was only doing as Pharoah Akhenaten wanted.

Each image made me feel more and more as though I needed to be supportive of Chione's dream to be a modern woman in a modern world after all it is a new century. I wondered if the Museum's Library had a copy of Frauenwahlrecht und Klassenkampf by Rosa Luxemburg... one of the pamphlets I had seen on Romy's living room table. "Probably not," I mumbled. "It is not an art book."

As I studied the color negatives the Nefertiti prints were made from, I was reminded of an article I had read about French impressionist painter Claude Monet and how he approached depicting shadows. When he and Auguste Renoir left their light confining studios to go outside and paint in plein air ... which was a blatant rejection of the traditional protocols of painting under controlled lighting ... they were in the dappled sunshine of outdoors where their artistic eyes noticed the vast array of colors hiding in the shadows. In plain sight as it were.

They do not paint reality as a camera captures it, but as their eyes perceive it from one moment to the next including swift glimpses, blurriness, even fog and in that process, they try to duplicate the nuances of color within every shadow.

Looking at the color negatives it was easy to see what they witnessed and strive to accomplish in their paintings, especially in the shadows. They do not just wash or glaze black paint over say the folds in a piece of red fabric to make it appear shadowed, they put colors like blues and violets in the shadow area. I could also see how the type of light source used, be it candle, electric or sun had a very strong and individual effect on how shadows look.

The effect was so appealing to me I promised myself, someday, when I have my own photography studio, I will experiment with making impressionistic photographic prints. Maybe using nude poses of Romy. "Mmm, Azim you make Expressionistic drawings and Impressionistic photographs … what does that say about you and your future?" I murmured to myself again.

Somehow, as I stood there musing, I thought of my mother and father in Cairo surrounded by desert. The desert where my father taught me how to use it as a place to hide in plain sight. He said it was an old military battlefield tactic used to remain out of the line of view of your enemies. I wondered how one does that in Berlin; how can I stay out of the view of my enemies. Do I really have enemies here and why would anyone here consider me their enemy? Why would anyone be hostile toward me?

I have had moments of sublime bliss here, but not enough to dampen the constant pain of having left my homeland. It feels like a sort of liminal space between past and present.

"Ghorba," I uttered with a noticeable cry in my voice. I do not want my memories of watching the sun set over the Nile or the shadows of the pyramids stretching toward the east to fade. They have a magnitude that keeps pulling at my heart to return.

"There is no happiness without longing," I whispered.

• • •

When I came out of the Darkroom, I was surprised to find it was well past the lunch hour. I headed for a shady and intimate cellar space in the Ratskeller. Many on the Museum staff had told me it serves traditional German meals with contemporary twists to separate itself from other restaurants in the area. Its low-ceilings, with many archways and pillars throughout, encircled candle-lit tables and booths. I prefer the small tables at the back where you can see everyone who comes in.

As I locked the studio and headed toward the side exit of the Museum, Anneliese came around the corner. "Are you going for lunch?"

"No, I thought I'd see if the Library has any newspapers with articles about those who were arrested, but now that I think about it, it is too soon for them to be available."

"Don't worry, Herr Borchardt phoned Herr Simon and he sent his lawyers to the Police. They were able to get Chione and Romy released before they appeared before the Judge."

"They are waiting for us at Hollenbach Haus."

To say I was surprised would be a gross understatement.

"What is wrong with you? Come on let's go."

"You go, ah, I'm not hungry."

"Don't give me that. Chione is not angry with you. She insisted I bring you."

"She only wants to tell me to leave her alone."

"Don't you think you should talk to her about her uncle Youssef?"

"If he finds out she could have been arrested, he may send her back to Cairo."

I had not thought about that. "You are right. Let's go."

The taxi ride was quick and left only a blank in my mind. We arrived at the end of a line of cars in front of the Hollenbach. "Are you sure we will be able to get a table?"

Anneliese did not respond. She was obviously also surprised to see so many people waiting in line. "You wait here. I will go inside and see if Romy has secured a table for us."

I nodded and stood at the end of the line of people feeling radically out-of-place again among the upper echelon. My shoes had gotten scuffed badly by the rally crowd and my suit, though new, was decidedly un-impressive compared to all the men near me. I was feeling chilled even while standing in the sun. This was not a good example of hiding in plain sight.

"Herr Lateef?" asked a young man dressed like a waiter.

"Ja, das bin ich".

"Your table guests are waiting for you."

A sudden communal gasp erupted around me. One woman appeared shocked. "Why does he get to go before us?"

Walking proudly beside me, my escort took delight and amusement from the flare-up. I knew it was a moment I would always remember.

My three ladies were all smiling and looked gorgeous. "We ordered you a ginger beer and your favorite Sauerbraten." My day of living hell miraculously evolved into a glimpse of heaven. All praise is due to Allah, I thought to myself as the waiter seated me next to Chione.

She took my hand as our tear-filled eyes met. "Please forgive me," she whispered. I could see there was shame in her eyes, deeper than the knowledge of herself.

"No, I'm to blame" I said. While I was hesitant to speak further among newly acquired friends and the complete strangers surrounding us, my heart pined to express my apologies more fully to her.

"Our new home here is not like the land which yielded us and there is much that makes me sorry we ventured about before consummating our relationship. We absorbed fully those simpler times and must now address the many challenges and rewards of this place despite cause to feel sorrow or remorse for having forsook our youthful outlook. I apologize for imposing my concerns, my needs and myself on you without invitation."

She said nothing, smiled beautifully then ran her delicate fingers along my cheek and kissed me gently. Anneliese and Romy both applauded silently.

CHAPTER 14

Youssef sat in the far corner watching me approach and I fully anticipated his voice would be strident and words unforgiving for his eyes were piercingly angry like the stormy night sky outside with his mouth as sternly righteous as the cellar walls were hard. I walked toward him, but before I could sit, from the shadows, out stepped 'Dünner Junge'.

My first inclination was to look for a weapon, but the obscurity of the dusky warehouse revealed only shipping crates. I finally decided to do what Youssef kept indicating. I sat opposite him at a small table.

'Dünner Junge' sat in a third chair near a crate. He was self-assured and rough-hewn looking as if his face had been carelessly formed from a hard, bitter life which left him with a crude nose, thirsty mouth, and oddly shaped forehead. I found it troublesome to look at him, I turned away.

"I understand you have met my assistant Waaiz Zuberi," said Youssef. "He, tells me Europe does not suit him. Judging by your general appearance I'd say it suits you well."

His affability was new to me. At Amarna he normally exhibited a harsh surliness, but regardless of which was his true nature, I reminded myself, he is Chione's uncle and I would be wise to respect him.

"It can be perplexing and taxing at times, but there are many benefits too," I replied.

"Yes, Waaiz has told me of your many excursions. Which is fine for a young man, but not advisable for our Chione. Would you agree?" he said as a gray ash fell from his sloppy looking cigarette. His breathing was deep, racking and noisy. I wondered if his many years as an excavation digger had affected his lungs or perhaps it was the smoking.

"Chione's values are decent and honorable. You are to be praised for your principled up bringing of her. Any man would be honored to have her as his wife."

"You have an errand to complete," Youssef said to Waaiz through a cough.

Waaiz bowed and left via an unseen door somewhere in the obscurity behind me. I felt relieved at his parting and if I read Youssef's expression correctly, so was he.

"Does he work for you or for Herr Har-Shaf Uga?"

"He is a friend of a relative of Layla Uga."

That statement was surprising, but did not really answer my question. I decided to leave it for now.

"Is your work at the Museum for Herr Borchardt what you were expecting it to be?"

I wanted him to be impressed so I said: "Yes and more. I enjoy it very much. I am learning many new things. I believe I will be able to make a good living as a professional photographer."

His eyes looked up wearily, but he managed a believable smile. "Here or in Cairo?"

"That is yet to be determined. It could be in Istanbul."

He looked as though he was going to apologize about something, but instead he said. "You know me only as an overseeing of excavation workers."

"Yes and I'm surprised to find you here in Berlin working in the importing business?" I said interrupting him.

"Mmm, so am I and I could use your help."

"You need a photographer?"

He laughed with a low growling sound and leaned forward. "Ha, no I need someone on the inside of the Museum."

"For what?" I blurted without thinking.

"You and the lady photographer Fräulein Brantt are photographing all the artifacts from the Amarna dig. Yes?"

He had an ashy, pallid and slightly desperate look to his face.

"Yes, we are, but if you are suggesting I assist you in doing anything illegal, I will not."

"Good, I'm not asking that of you. I only want you to answer a few questions," he said with an awkward sideways leer as he exhaled smoke and searched for some clean air in the dankness surrounding us. "Have you found anything odd about any of the artifacts?"

The tone of his voice and his general demeanor had changed significantly. I quickly concluded I wanted to know more about what he was leading to. I replied: "Odd in what way?"

He squinted at me shrewdly. "I do not know. I have not seen them since they were crated for shipment."

"Uhm, you work for Herr Har-Shaf Uga, here at this warehouse? And he sells artifacts from Egypt, Iran, Iraq, and many other countries. What specifically do you do for him?"

"Inventory control. I communicate with all the supply chain managers to plan and maintain inventory and resolve any related issues and discrepancies. Plus, I supervise all our warehouse employees who are doing crating, shipping, and deliveries."

"That's very impressive, but doesn't explain why you are interested in the Museum's collection of Amarna artifacts."

"Asim, you and I have reached the point where we need to trust each other. Do you agree?"

"I have never had a reason not to trust you Youssef until now. I do not understand why you need to know anything about the Museum's Amarna artifacts."

He set his cigarette aside and took a moment to study my eyes. "I am not just an overseer of excavation diggers or a warehouse manager. If you love Chione and I believe you do, then you must promise me you will not reveal anything I am about to tell you. No matter what you decide to do. You must not tell anyone of this conversation. If you do, it could cost me my life."

I was speechless, but nodded my head in agreement.

"Good. I am an Egyptian secret police Captain assigned to find smugglers of our national heritage and I need your help."

The look on my face must have been priceless because his smile embraced his entire head. "I am so relieved you are not a smuggler," I whispered as if we were being overheard. "So this rough, uncouth manner you exhibit is not truly you? Is your name really Youssef? Is Chione actually your niece?"

"Yes, that is my name and Chione is my niece or at least we think she is."

I wanted to ask for clarification on that, but decided not to. "Does Herr Har-Shaf Uga know who you are?"

"It is because of his request, I am here. He wants to know if any of his employees are involved in the gang flooding Europe with original and fake artifacts."

This gave me pause and made me realize there was little reason to delay informing Youssef that Anneliese and I believe someone is making molds from the original Amarna artifacts in the Museum's collection. As I mulled how to address this idea Youssef said. "Oh, Waaiz does not know my real identity."

"Why not?"

"I don't trust him to keep a secret."

"Can you explain why he threatened me if I continued to meet with the art students or attend the drawing class?"

"He is a right-wing fanatic like Layla. They both hate Western culture."

"So did he follow me on his own accord or did someone tell him to?"

"It was probably Layla. She checks on every Egyptian and Turk who has any contact with her husband, especially the women. You need to concentrate on finding out who at the Museum is making the molds. Can you trust Anneliese?"

"Absolutely. She has told Herr Borchardt of what we discovered and he wants us to help him determine who else is involved, but he will not contact the police before the exhibit and reception in the Egyptian Courtyard for the VIP's is concluded."

"Is there anyone else you are leery of?"

"Hans Herbster. He knows Waaiz."

"What does Herbster do at the Museum?"

"He is one of the Director's assistants and does whatever is required of him."

"Besides knowing Waaiz, why do you mistrust him?"

"He acts duplicitous and shifty."

"That is not much, but I will try to investigate him. Tell me how you know he is acquainted with Waaiz."

I told Youssef about the two occasions I had seen Hans and Waaiz together.

"There must be something about Hans that Waaiz believes is immoral," said Youssef lighting another cigarette. "Would you like a ginger beer?"

I nodded and he led me into a small office. "This is where Chione works."

There were two other doors, one leading outside and the other to a back office. We went through to it. Both offices had a desk, two chairs and file cabinets. Chione's also had a small vase of flowers and a window, but it was too dark to see what was outside. I noticed a small note card laying near the flowers and glanced at it, but was not able to read the hand writing.

Youssef sat at his desk and took out a large bottle of ginger beer and two glasses from the bottom drawer of the filing cabinet. "Did you hear any of the conversation between Waaiz and Hans?" he asked.

"No, but Hans looked incensed both times."

"Have you met any of Hans other friends?"

I suddenly remembered Hans was aware of something I had said only to the tailor who assisted me in selecting a suit.

"That's it," I blurted out. "Waaiz knows that Hans prefers men."

Youssef looked mildly interested, snuffed out his cigarette and took a long swallow of beer then shrugged with a hoarse sound in his throat. "I knew you were smart enough to figure it out, but there must be more to it, that would not be enough for Waaiz to pressure Hans into helping him steal or make molds of artifacts. Besides, Hans is most likely a Christian which makes it doubtful Waaiz would care about his sexual proclivities."

"I will keep trying to find out more. It also could explain why he always seems annoyed by Anneliese and Romy."

"However, it doesn't explain why the Director hired him."

"As I said, I will find out more."

He stood up as did I and we embraced briefly. "May I meet Chione for lunch occasionally?"

"Certainly. Have you met Montu Sati?"

"No, but Chione has mentioned him. He is Herr Uga's assistant?" I was thinking he was probably the one who gave Chione the flowers on her desk.

"Yes and he is very close with Layla," he said with raised eyebrows. "Oh, if Hans or Meierdiebrück try to recruit you to help with whatever they are doing, you should agree. Otherwise, it may take too long for us to catch them. You would not want The Beautiful One stolen."

I unexpectedly felt anxiety, panic and dread all in one swift jolt.

He came toward me with his hand outstretched. I took it and he pulled me to him in a manly embrace and patted by back.

"By-the-way, did you know that 'The Beautiful One' is how Layla refers to herself?"

This implied Layla was conceited and probably arrogant. I wondered if she was Egyptian, how educated she was and what she did before marrying Uga. I recalled Romy saying Layla rarely appeared in public or at any of the many social events her husband attends and never wears western clothing on the rare occasion she does appear anywhere. All of which implies she is a stanch and devout Muslim. Committed to all its pious customs and traditions.

CHAPTER 15

All the elders in my family at the wadi where I grew up always proclaimed acknowledging fear was a good quality to have. It shows one knows what to do and self-doubt is a trustworthy ally. However, I was not confident Romy, Anneliese and I had any allies beyond my secret affiliation with Youssef. Nor was I convinced we understood what exactly we were looking for or perhaps hoping would occur.

These and many other trepidations caused me to carefully analysis how to approach Meierdiebrück. I concluded he would be more forthcoming at the Ratskeller than in the Museum.

My strategy was to linger near the side exit and pretend to be tying my shoe when he came out.

"What are you mumbling about?" asked Anneliese as we finished washing the last prints of The Beautiful One.

"Oh, I was just thinking since we have not heard anything from Herr Borchardt about our suspicions of mold making going on in the Museum, I will invite Meierdiebrück for a beer this evening. Maybe I can get him to relax and speak his mind a little more freely."

"Yes, this Warten, ah waiting is stressful especially as we get closer to the courtyard exhibit and reception. I will be meeting Romy this evening to see if any of her contacts have discovered anything. You go ahead. I will close-up here. You do not want to miss Meierdiebrück and remember to smile and be amicable."

"What does that mean?"

"Freundlich."

I nodded and left the Darkroom, took off my smock, put on my suit jacket and overcoat feeling a little more prepared for meeting mister grump. When I got to the side exit door, I untied my left shoe, walked out and almost bumped right into Meierdiebrück.

"Oh, excuse me, ah'm Verzeihung," I said as I bent down and re-tied my shoe. "I was just thinking about going to the Ratskeller. Join me for a beer."

A perplexed smile developed on his face and his head wobble as he said. "Danke schön."

· · ·

The Ratskeller was full of the usual crowd of men and the only women were the two waitresses. We each ordered a large beer. His flash of a thin smile had an icy tinge to it, but knowing I had to find a way to relax him I concluded I should speak first. I said: "When we were here last, you asked if I had noticed anything wrong with the artifacts."

He moved his head into the shadow near the wall as a pale quiver traversed his chin. "Perhaps I did."

"Well it is time to address that issue. I did notice something odd about several of the artifacts. How does it concern you?"

"I just want you to understand I did not do it."

"Alright, you didn't do what?"

He took a long swallow of beer and looked around the room to convince himself no one was paying attention to us. "I did not make the molds."

"Who did?"

Again his chin was quivering and beads of perspiration began to cross his forehead.

"All I did was let him in and made sure everything was right when he left."

He finished his beer and struggled to put forth a conciliatory smile, but ran his hand across it instead. I gestured to the waitress to bring two more beers. Her smile was wonderfully inviting and presented a disconcerting contrast to Meierdiebrück's state of mind. When the waitress set the beers before us, she deliberately leaned over and gave us a view of her full bosom. My mind flashed on the models in the drawing class, but Meierdiebrück's expression had all the crisscross makings of an internal collapse. The waitress winked at me and walked away.

"I have a wife and children, I must keep my position at the Museum," he uttered. I wondered if he assumed I had put the waitress up to her flaunting display.

"Your best chance of doing so is to tell me who you let into the Museum."

"No one must know," he said in a hushed tone. "Montu Sati. You know, Uga's assistant."

It was I who took a long gulp of beer this time. I could not conceive of how Sati could be making molds of artifacts without Uga knowing about it. "What does he do with the molds?"

He made a miserable sound like a child's sob and pressed his hands against his temples.

"I do not know and I do not want to know. It is getting late. I must go."

"Just a couple more questions. Do you know Uga's wife, Layla?"

I had hit a nerve for he began trembling all over. I found his eyes with mine, stared hard and said: "You are acting nervous. Tell me what happened between you two. Did she offer herself to you in exchange for letting Sati into the Museum?"

He started to lift his glass, but his shaking hand was out of control. Beer splashed everywhere.

"You are at the crossroads of your destiny Meierdiebrück and I believe you possess the spiritual power to save yourself from total ruin."

"It was only once, she gave me all her charms and we ..."

His head was on the table and his arms over it.

"I don't need to know all the details. Just tell me did you take her in the Museum or elsewhere and was Sati there when you did?"

"Yes, in the Museum and he watched," he said as his sobbing ceased and he lifted his head to look at my expression of disbelief.

I felt it was time we should move on. "Why isn't there a night guard at the side-entrance?"

He raised his head with a sigh of relief. "Each staff member has a key to their own office or work space. The only open place is the main entrance atrium." He stood up, still shaking and put forth his hand. "I'm depending on you to keep my name out of this entire business."

The corners of his mouth drew down and his face looked sulky. I shook his quivering hand. He left. I sat there staring at all the other men and wondered how many of them were discussing wrongdoings going on at their jobs.

The waitress came to my table. "May I join you," she said with a pleasant smile. "Your friend doesn't look well."

That was not what I was expecting her to say. "Oh, his wife does not like for him to be late for dinner. He probably should not have had the second beer."

"Do you need to be home for dinner with your wife too?"

Her smile was sweet and generous, not artificial like so many others I met in the weeks I had been in Berlin. "No, I do not have a wife. Did you grow up here in Berlin," I asked.

"No, I am from Bavaria. My aunt's family owns this tavern. Where are you from?" she asked quietly.

"Cairo Egypt."

"Do you dream of it often?"

"In a way, yes." I was thinking I dream mostly about one particular Egyptian, Chione.

"It doesn't get cold there in winter, does it?"

Several men came in and the waitress immediately put her hand on my arm and winked at me before she walked toward them. I took the opportunity to leave before I said something ribald to her.

I decided to walk home. I needed to mull over Meierdiebrück's revelation and how it may help Youssef.

First Montu Sati made molds from several Amarna artifacts; Sati works for Herr Har-Shaf Uga; Sati is probably Layla Uga's lover; Waaiz Zuberi is a right wing radical allied with Layla; Herr Uga requested Youssef's help to determine who is stealing and selling artifacts as well as molds; Youssef is an Egyptian secret police Captain assigned to find international smugglers; Hans most likely prefers men.

In all of that the only thing Herr Borchardt and the Director will care about is what Sati does with the molds from the Amarna artifacts in the Museum's collection and who allowed him to make the molds.

It seemed to me the only thing I could do was to inform Youssef about Sati, Layla and Meierdiebrück, but it would have to wait until after the courtyard exhibition and garden reception in two days.

The next morning Anneliese had left a note on my desk informing me she was meeting with Herr Borchardt and I was to complete development of the thumb-nail prints of the artifacts. As I hung the prints up to dry, I heard the Studio door unlatch and open. I stepped out and was surprised to see Anneliese holding a brand-new Makina compact bellows camera.

"This is our new camera," she said smiling broadly. "And you have the honor of using it on assignment first. It is a scissors-struts design made by a friend of Herr Borchardt."

"What am I to photograph?"

"Herr Borchardt feels it is appropriate for you to photograph the reception tomorrow in the Egyptian Courtyard since I, as a department head, will be required to converse with the guests.

"Do you mean I am to make candid photographs?"

"Yes, so you better start learning now how to load film and operate the camera. It is a completely collapsible and strong compact design with flexible bellows, flatbed track, interchangeable lenses and it can accept three different kinds of film. You are to use the roll film type. There are several rolls in your carry bag. Look how easy the optical viewfinder is to use," she said without stopping to catch her breath. "Oh, and it has a built-in a flash-synchronized internal iris lens shutter."

"I feel like I'm learning a new language."

"I suggest you familiarize yourself with how it works, go outside and shoot some test photos of people coming into the Museum then we'll develop them after lunch to see how well you did."

My mind instantly flashed back to the photographer who had accompanied the Prince and Princess of Saxony during the discovery of The Beautiful One. He used a similar camera and was very quick at taking candid photographs.

"I wonder if Chione will be in attendance tomorrow," I said out loud without thinking.

"Yes, she will be with Herr Uga. His wife does not enjoy formal gatherings," said Anneliese. "That's according to Romy."

"Good I want to talk to him," I whispered or so I thought.

"Him? I would have thought you would want to talk to Chione."

"What I want to say to her must be in private," I said as I finished loading the film into the new camera and headed out the door. I decided to exit via the side door so I would be less discernable to the general public. However, my mind was still reeling from thinking about Chione attending the reception on the arm of Herr Uga. I did not like it.

When I exited the Museum, to my surprise Hans and Waaiz were arguing almost right in front of me. I was already weary of these two as I walked right between them and turned to Waaiz, "Just let people live their own lives in peace. Your narrow-minded moralistic self-righteousness is not for everyone."

Both men appeared shocked and my first thought was to take a candid picture of their faces, but felt it would be a waste of good film. Waaiz's face was a red mask for an instant in stark contrast to his lifeless eyes as his whole demeanor suddenly turned tense and bitter with his hands forming fist and his back stiffening. He made an abrupt and sudden motion and reached into a pocket. I fully expected his hand to emerge holding a knife. As his hand rose the traffic noise from the boulevard became faint, but the roar in my head was deafening until Hans stepped between us and crabbed Waaiz's wrist.

"This is not the place or time. Leave now," said Hans as he pushed against Waaiz's chest.

Waaiz showed an empty hand and said: "You both will regret offending Allah."

We watched him walk away at a fast pace. Hans turned to me slowly, studied my eyes, then spoke while looking away from me. "I do not know about Allah, but I thank you for your concern on my behave Azim, you are an unexpected surprise. I am going to the spa tonight would you like to join me?"

In all this fracas, I took a moment to consider his invitation and concluded that since I had not had a steam bath since arriving in Berlin and would enjoy it, plus it would provide a more casual atmosphere in which to learn more about Hans, I said: "Yes, I would. Where shall we meet?"

In Berlin, I quickly discovered lodging rooms and most hotel rooms within my budget, do not include a bathtub so I was looking forward to going to the spa even though it meant being congenial to Hans. I was only hoping the spa, as he called it, meant a public bath house and not just a city swimming pool.

The taxi ride was not long so we only spoke about aspects of working at the Museum. When we arrived at our destination, I was pleasantly surprised the architecture was beautiful and enormous. "I had expected the building to be much smaller," I commented as we entered.

"Oh this place can accommodate thousands of daily visitors," he replied grinning.

I noticed both men and women coming out and going in causing me to raise my eyebrows. "Women have their own tubs, showers and pool," he said catching my expression. "You'll be with just men and this will be my treat."

He paid the entrance fee and a young man, who bearing a broad smile, escorted us to the changing room where we disrobed and placed our clothes in individual wardrobes. Hans appeared to be in very good physical condition and looked tanned all over as though he must sunbath often. I on the other hand was naturally tan.

"What do we do first?" I asked.

His grin was almost child-like. "Etiquette demands we rinse off in the cold shower before going into the sauna. If you do not, you'll get scolded by the Saunameister. Oh, and be sure to take two towels, one for sitting on and the other for drying afterwards."

"In other words, they do not want our sweat on anything other than the towels."

"And always speak very softly, talking loud or even normal is verboten. Do not worry, this time of evening it usually is not crowded so you will not be closely surrounded."

The interior was surprisingly warm even in the cold shower room.

"Come on, schnell, the Saunameister will be releasing the scented oils."

We scooped up our towels and hurried across the slippery wet floor to the large sauna room arriving just as the oil spray permeated the hot, wet air. I could not determine what the scent was, but I enjoyed it.

The crowd was not shoulder-to-shoulder but close to it and there were three levels of benches. It was several degrees hotter on the top bench. I moved down to the middle level. Every 15 minutes or so, one of the employees would fan the steam around by swinging a large towel through the air like a flag. Then around the end of the hour one of them gave out salt and honey to rub on your body. I was not sure for what purpose. When I looked around to ask Hans about it, I could not see him.

The sauna area was comprised of a couple of other smaller areas so I wondered over to them thinking he may be in one of them. He was, but not alone. There was man of similar size and age with him. As I turned around and walked back a young man came up beside me and was lavishly spreading honey all over himself. I was intrigued, but decided to get a cold shower and quickly realized getting honey off oneself is not easy to do alone. As I studied the young man again, I could see how a man washing himself would make for an engaging Expressionist drawing.

CHAPTER 16

The Egyptian Courtyard was overflowing with VIP's enthralled by the new Amarna Collection and all of them were so occupied with their group discussions few noticed me taking candid photographs. While I moved about making sure I captured each person in at least one photo, Chione was never out of my sight. In fact, I could often hear everything said to or by her.

This was the first time I had ever attended a social event for aristocrats and high society. As I moved through them, I felt almost invisible for few of them paid any attention to me. If they did, I simply turned so they could read the tag on my left shoulder listing my name and position title. Some of them, basically young men, were interested in my camera and asked a series of technical questions which I was happy I could answer.

The young women were also interested in the camera, but only in terms of facing it so I could capture the best view of them for they relished an opportunity to show off their haute couture, ah Hoch Modern.

One young lady, who I discovered was a reporter for Modes Magazine stuck to my side and provided me with a commentary about each woman and her ensemble. "Fashion has been moving away from a laced artificial figure toward a natural form supported by brassiere," she said softly. I was not certain what that meant, so I just smiled.

"The new style is called The Tango, which consists of adorned long, mermaid-esque dancing gowns with knee-high slashes on the sides. It has just emerged this spring as a result of the new music called the Argentinian tango," she said smiling brightly while doing a quick movement with her body and arms. It certainly looked like an unusual dance.

"The elevated waist and an asymmetrically formed skirt are typical of the tango style," she said smiling broadly. "Of course, pastel tones with a skirt converging conically downward and high waist with siren line are still very popular." I noted the women wearing that style of dress were considerably older than most of the others.

"Now, this is a tunic style." The name caught my attention.

"It consists of three lengths of fabric and a rose bouquet holds it. It was featured on the cover of the magazine in May," she said with a level of noticeable pride.

"It's a Boissy by Jeanne Paquin," said the woman wearing it. "It just arrived from Paris."

Most of the women had short hair, a bob I think it is called, and a broad-brimmed hat, softly-defined waist and curved-heel shoes with criss-cross straps at the ankles. I kept looking at Chione and if I did not know it was her, I would never have assumed she was Egyptian. She looked thoroughly European. Her corset was fitted to her small waist, while her buttocks, hips, shoulders and bosom were accented and looked possibly padded. I was not certain.

One thing was certain, she did not have the money to buy her stunning dress. I wondered if Herr Uga or Sati had paid for it or selected it for her. If so, I could see how she would want to have more contemporary dresses and attend lots of social events like this.

The magazine reporter drifted away from me when I started photographing some of the men. Perhaps because they all wore three-piece suits with a matching waistcoat. Their trousers were ankle length. They wore short gaiters or spats for shoes. Their formal shirts were pressed into wings at the collars and they wore ascot ties.

A few wore waistcoats or a sack coat fastened lower on the chest and almost all had a beard or moustache usually wide and curled.

As I stood starring at Choine I thought back to my first lady friend. When we first became lovers, I was fascinated to watch her take off layers of undergarments including pantaloons and a corset and in winter, she also wore gaiters over her shoes and lower pant leg, as protection from the cold desert air.

Herr Uga was expensively and conservatively dressed in a dark suit while his face wore an arrogant expression. His comments ranged from pompous to condescending and very disrespectful of many cultures. I was heated about Chione feeling obligated to stand at his side throughout the entire afternoon.

When I stepped away from the Courtyard to reload the camera Anneliese and Romy quietly walked over to me. "The exhibit looks far more impressive here than in our Studio," said Anneliese. "Let's take some photographs of it tomorrow morning."

"I'm somewhat surprised the labels do not indicate which artifacts will be returned to Egypt," said Romy.

"Yes, it is obviously still a very sensitive topic," I noted. "However, I find Herr Uga's comments aggravatingly stupid, senseless, and unwise. How can he possibly be considered an expert of ancient artifacts when he is so rash and reckless with his foolish comments."

"Asim, please lower your voice," said Herr Borchardt. "Return to the darkroom and develop your film."

As I looked about, everyone was gawking at me and Chione looked especially disgusted and repulsed. I nodded to Herr Borchardt and walked away feeling I had just ended my career.

• • •

Entering the Photography Studio, I went directly into the Darkroom. Having my eyes filled with darkness seem to calm the fury building within me and I needed to hide from everyone including myself.

"It's natural to feel angry sometimes," I said looking at my reflection in the dark liquid of the developer tray. "But losing your temper at work can have a negative effect on your career and work relationships dummy. Plus raising your voice was very stupid, stupid."

I heard the Studio door open and someone entered. It was most likely Herr Borchardt here to fire you, I thought to myself. You better go out and face up to your mistake like a man. I stepped out into the light and had to wait for my eyes to readjust before I recognized Anneliese.

"You know it can be the smallest things like somebody talking loudly on the train or tapping their shoe against a table. It just goes on and on and on while your nerves fray," she said softly.

"Yes and it rises within me when someone disrespects our own culture, but it was wrong for me to confront him in the middle of the reception. I only added to the impertinence. Should I resign in the morning?"

"Certainly not. You had expectations for the presentation of your ancient culture and one of your own belittled it. You have nothing to apologize for. If they fire you, I will quit. Beside several of the guests agreed with you."

That was amazing to hear. "Did they say so to Herr Borchardt?"

"Everyone heard them including Herr Uga himself."

"All of us boil over now and then, but we all return to normal after the rant dissipates. Just as you have now. It is healthier otherwise you will become depressed. You just do not want to allow your anger to become destructive or lead to violence, self-harm or addictions."

"Yeah, my father always says that leads to ending up in jail," I said.

By the time we finished developing all the exposed film it was well past 3pm. I sat at my desk reviewing how I would explain being discharged from the Museum to my father, but before I could resolve that dilemma, a hesitant knock sounded on the door. I opened it slowly and was astounded to come face to face with Herr Uga.

"May I come in?" he said while scrutinizing my face and glancing at Anneliese.

I did not reply, but gestured for him to enter. He was dark, florid, and stout with a slightly desperate look.

"We need to come to an understanding Herr Lateef," he said without any hint of emotion. "I have always favored the cultural value of antiquities and believe in preserving them for future generation to enjoy," he said as he looked at the candid photographs I had taken of visitors to the Museum. "I am adamant about sustaining that market within the legal confusion of international treaties, assorted trade entanglements and inconsistent regulations."

It did not feel appropriate to interrupt him so I simply nodded I understood.

"Aligning my business interest with those many shifting legal and cultural biases is demanding and exhausting. So, it is possible, occasionally despite every effort being made by myself and my employees, among thousands of ancient artifacts coming onto the market, a few enter illegally."

He paused again and again I felt uncomfortable agreeing or debating with him.

"I often use local consultants to verify provenances in source countries where I do not have employees. I have no way to determine if those documents are false and I am always willing to cooperate with police investigations."

While it was not exactly an apology about having slighted and degraded Egyptian history, he held out his right hand. I reciprocated and we shook hands. His hand was soft and chilly.

"I apologize for my thoughtlessness, Herr Uga and thank you for coming to talk to me."

I opened the door and he walked away without saying another word or looking back.

Anneliese and I stood looking at each other while shrugging our shoulders. We closed the Darkroom and Studio. I was still thinking it might be my last time.

The walk to my lodgings was one of the longest I had ever taken. I had even hoped Waaiz would appear somewhere out of the darkness and he would give me a reason to beat the hell out of him, he must have had something more important to do or was not interested in talking to me.

As the hour grew late, I circled back and stopped in the Ratskeller for a beer.

"Good evening, Herr Lateef. We will be closing shortly would you like a beer?" asked the waitress.

I nodded affirmatively and sat at the bar. There were no other customers and only one man cleaning up in the kitchen.

What is your name Fräulein?"

"Lena Marie," she replied as she placed a small glass of beer in front of me and smiled sweetly. "Have you had a difficult day?"

"No, not really. It was just my hartnäckig... uhmm, obstinate pride that made it trying."

"Was it for a good reason?"

That question caused me to reflect-back on what had made me angry. It really was not because Chione had to stand alongside Uga, it was because everything he said was derisive and ridiculing of Egyptian culture. Everyone there was admiring the wonderful display and enchanted by the history of a man and woman who tried to improve life and all he could think of was to laugh and deride. He is an Egyptian who detests his own heritage.

"Yes, it was. Had I not spoke, I would not be able to face myself ever again."

"Well then, I am sure others will come to realize you were correct. Relax and finish your beer." She said with a robust laugh.

It was easy for me to overlook her feigned toughness. She was a beautiful woman and her eyes told me she was interested in me. Her waist was slim, her bosom in full bloom and her hips, well they got my attention when her body shook with an ersatz chill.

"Maybe I had a wrong impression of you," I said as I noticed the man in the kitchen take off his apron and wave to her. "Is he leaving?"

"Yes," she said softly. "Why not move over to the corner booth. I will turn off the kitchen lights, lock the front door and be right there." I noticed she took off her apron as she headed toward the kitchen. I wondered how much more she would disrobe before getting back to me. I was looking forward to finding out.

When she returned, she had on less clothes and I certainly appreciated the change. "I hope you approve," she said in a lower, richer tone of feminine cajolery as she made a sexy curtsy and turned on her heel to walk directly to me. Her wide, dark eyes held all the life and energy of her face, but I stared at her red lips then dropped my eyes to her full bosom and taut waist.

"I'm interested in you in all sorts of ways," I replied.

"Where do you want me," she asked as she moved out of the light and into the shadowed corner of the booth. "You have a lot of energy in you Asim. Let's find a way to release it."

In the morning light, I felt prepared for whatever was to come. I walked to the Museum fully aware that I may be escorted out of the building. The air was clear, the sun warm and everyone I saw seemed normal. That is, until I entered the Studio. There was a uniformed policeman and a stern looking man with a heavy build, slick gray hair and thickened complexion.

"Herr Lateef, you are under arrest."

"On what charge?" asked Anneliese shaking.

"Murder. Turn around and put your hands together."

I did as I was told and the uniformed officer handcuffed me.

"I will inform Herr Borchardt," said Anneliese looking pale and shocked.

"Who did I murder," I asked the heavy man.

He scuffed and said: "One of your own kind. Herr Har-Shaf Uga."

"And how did I kill him?"

"You like to joke, don't you," he said with a sneer as he shoved me out of the studio. "You knifed him in the back."

Anneliese gasped with her hands at her mouth.

He was an oldish man with sad eyes and dissipated face that was beginning to go pouchy. He shook his gray head and straightened his hat as he paraded me through the front lobby of the Museum in front of staff and visitors, out the main entrance and down the steps to a waiting police car.

As we got into the car, I asked: "When?"

"When what?" said heavy man.

"When was he murdered?"

"Last night around 10pm. Where were you at that time?" he said through clinched teeth.

I did not reply. I had expected to be fired from the Museum, but not arrested. How will I ever be able to explain to Chione I was in a bar ah, ah talking to a young woman. It will break her heart.

. . .

The police headquarters was on Alexanderplatz. It was a large building filled with dark furniture and gray light. I was taken directly to a cell and told to sit. I felt restless and anxious like a caged animal. I began pacing around and wanted to escape myself, to get away from my thoughts and just sitting made time feel meaningless and my thoughts heavier than ever.

There were no windows I could see and the air stood still. I waited and waited and waited. A guard eventually came into the hall, looked at me, but said nothing and left.

Sometime later he returned with a key in his hand, unlocked the cell and told me to walk in front of him. We went through several halls and atrium spaces each got more and more filled with light and people.

We entered a private looking office outfitted with a row of empty chairs along one wall and a young Sargant seated at a desk opposite them, he told the guard to remove my handcuffs and suggested I straighten my suit and tie then gestured to me to sit in one of the empty chairs.

The lettering on a door at the far end of the room read *Director of Berlin Criminal Police.*

"Who will I be meeting," I asked the Sargant.

"Herr Ernst August Ferdinand Gennat," he responded sternly.

"Is he a policeman or a political appointee?"

The Sargant stopped what he was doing, looked at me with a stiff chin and said: "Herr Gennat was at the Frederick William University before he entered police service in 1904 and passed the examination to criminal police officer then started as detective assistant and was promoted to criminal detective very quickly. He initiated the creation of the on-call homicide service and it has had great success," he spoke with abundant pride.

"How many officers serve in the homicide division?"

"The department is organized as one standing team of detectives with two backup teams. The active team has one senior and one junior homicide detective plus between 4 and 10 criminal constables, a stenotypist and a dog handler. The backup teams have one senior and one junior homicide detective, teamed under what is known as the Mord-Ehe, ah marriage of murder plus 2 or 3 constables and a stenotypist. The make-up of the active team changes every four weeks to ensure each officer gains the proper work experience."

"Impressive. Very impressive," I said feeling exhausted from listening to him.

"Yes, so I recommend you set aside any thought you may have of escaping. Herr Gennat has reorganized much of the methodology by which our homicides are investigated. He follows the forensic science established by Herr Hans Gross, the first to recognize the importance of preserving all crime scene evidence," he said stopping to watch me catch my breath. "He has even written precise guidelines for crime scene procedures and established the inviolable principle forbidding anyone from touching or changing anything until the investigators have arrived."

In hopes of distracting him from his endless narrative, I picked-up an edition of the *Palästina* newspaper from the table and held it in front of my face while perusing the articles. On the second page was a description of Herr Gennat's custom built Daimler-Benz car. Aiming to facilitate thorough quick investigation work, he had it built as a standby homicide division car according to his own plans. He had the vehicle equipped with office and forensic technology and it was shown at the Police Exhibition where the public got a chance to visit the "murder car".

The murder car could be converted to a temporary office when necessary. A typewriter (complete with a steno-typist) was part of the inventory, as were collapsible chairs and a table for work in the open air alongside two retractable tables inside the car. For the immediate work at the crime scene there were materials for securing evidence and steel marking posts with sequential numbers; everything from searchlights to diamond cutters and axes.

There was even a seat especially designed for Gennat's great girth where he had a special brace included. Other-wise his weight would have disbalanced the car. The homicide division of the criminal investigation department in Munich has also been provided with a murder car and the corresponding equipment as well.

The article was informative, but my mind was preoccupied with my own problems, so I folded it and slid it into the side pocket of my suit coat to finish reading later.

"Please leave the newspaper here," snapped the young man. "The article about our murder car is to be placed in the central file."

"The what?" I asked.

"The death investigation card file. Detective Knauf would not like it if I told him a suspect had stolen the paper from his collection."

"My apologies," I said as I returned the newspaper to the table. "How is the file used?"

"Every violent death even outside of Berlin that is known to the police is systematically documented which allows for a quick reconstruction, in the shortest possible time, of any past case in order to identify potential links in the execution of the crimes. And it includes press reports and wanted posters besides original files for not just capital offences but also the indirect or cold murders like suicide following defamation or false accusations provoked by scammers, frauds, obscure fortune tellers or marriage impostors and blackmailers. Herr Gennat takes the view that driving a person to suicide is to be penalized as well. So, whatever you do when you go in, you better tell him the truth," he whispered as he nodded his head toward Gennat's office door.

"Beside the advances in organization and investigation techniques, is there anything about Herr Gennat's personality I should be aware of?" I asked in hushed tones.

"He is lauded in particular for his persistency and perseverance, his phenomenal memory, and the enormous psychological empathy for criminal profiling."

I wasn't certain what much of that meant so I said still speaking softly: "how about the use of forcible means of interrogation?"

"He is strictly against it and warns all his officers to not violate that code. His favorite saying is 'Our weapons are our brains and nerves'."

"He is surprisingly modern in many regards," I suggested.

"Yes, he stresses the importance of prevention as against the investigation of crimes. Being aware of the effect of capital offences on the public and of the opinion-forming role of the press, he strives to harness it for the purposes of impowering his investigative work.

Just do not be fooled by his striking corpulence he is actively involved with every case."

A buzzer sounded and he opened the inner door motioning for me to enter. I did.

To my great surprise and relief Fräulein Marie Luise Simon was seated in front of the Chief Inspectors desk facing him. She glanced over her shoulder at me briefly and said: did you murder Herr Uga?"

"No, I did not."

"Where were you at 10pm last evening?"

I hesitated, but concluded I must answer. "At the Ratskeller Inn, near the Museum."

"Why were you there?"

"For a beer and to think."

"Who saw you there?"

"The waitress and the kitchen aid."

"What time did you leave?"

"I'm not sure exactly, probably around 11:30pm."

"Where did you go next?"

"To my lodging room."

"What time did you arrive there?"

"Again, I am not certain, perhaps 11:45pm. The carriage driver may know."

"Did you go anywhere else last night?"

"No."

"We have enough. We will check with the witnesses to verify your answers. You may go now, but do not leave the city without informing my office," said Gennat. "Oh, do you have any idea who killed Uga, anyone who disliked him as much as you do?"

"No. Fräulein Simon, may I…"

She raised her hand and said: "We will speak another time. Good day, Herr Lateef."

I nodded, looked at the table set with 3 plates of gooseberry cake and left the office, but did not feel myself breathing until the guard escorted me out a side exit. I took a taxi to the Museum. I wanted everyone to see me as a free man. I walked through the front entrance directly to the Photography Studio.

Anneliese was standing at the display wall looking at the candid photographs I had shot of the reception. We embraced and she suggested we invite Romy and Chione to join us for dinner at Hollenbach Haus. I agreed. The telephone rang. Anneliese answered, listened, and handed the phone to me.

"This is Herr Leteef... Yes ... I will ..."

I hung up the phone. "We will have to have a short night. I must meet someone at 9pm," I said. "Please do not ask me to explain now and do not mention the meeting to anyone."

"Is everything in good order?" she said with a perplexed look.

"Yes, I believe it is, except I'm going to make a special effort to determine who murdered Herr Uga."

"So will I," she said still looking mystified by my behavior.

• • •

Anneliese and I closed the Studio and left the Museum at exactly 6pm. Within a couple of minutes, we flagged a taxi car and were on our way to dinner with Romy and Chione at the Hollenbach Haus, or so I thought. When we arrived at the restaurant it was an entirely different establishment. Apparently, I had been so preoccupied with everything from the past 24 hours I missed the name of where we were at.

We were immediately escorted to our table and found Chione and Romy seated there. Both of whom were overly friendly and joyously talking about everything from the wonderful weather to the new animals at the zoo; anything and everything except my encounter with Herr Uga or my day in jail. Each time a tried to explain myself, Chione expressed her belief that trouble is only compounded by talking about it. When I tried to question her about who she thought might have murdered Uga, she acted as though she did not understand what I was saying. Only when I inadvertently mentioned Fräulein Marie Luise Simon did both of them encourage me to speak further. However, by then it was 8:40pm and I had promised Youssef I would be at his office before 9pm.

"I apologize ladies, I promised I would assist the police with their investigation tonight. Please excuse me, I must leave now."

They appeared so surprised each was speechless, except Romy, she said: "Is this something you want to do or are you being forced to do it?"

"I want to help the Police in any way I can. Good evening."

It was 9pm precisely when I arrived at Youssef's dark office. As I neared the door, I thought perhaps I did not remember the appointed time correctly. The door was partially open. I pushed it further and stepped inside. "Youssef?"

"Close the door," he said as he turned on a small light. "Come here."

He was in the far corner behind several old, obsolete, large shipping crates. "Quick."

"Are you expecting someone?"

"Waaiz is meeting someone here at any minute. Stay hidden and do not make a sound, no matter what you hear or see."

As I squatted down and Youssef turned off the light. For a moment I felt like I was back in jail.

"Did you lock the door?"

"No, damn, I will get it," I said as I rushed back to the door.

"Hurry, I just saw a car light," whispered Youssef.

• • •

The warehouse was completely dark and we were well concealed as the lock clicked and the door opened. Two men entered, but they did not turn on the lights. One of the them carried a small portable dynamo shake flashlight and kept complaining it was not strong enough. They walked to the worktable area where several unfinished crates were scattered about. The man without a light struck a match and lit a small candle and placed it on the table.

It was Waaiz and Herr Uga's assistant Montu Sati. He was a big man who looked as though he had begun to lose his battle with age. His face made his graying hair seem premature. He held himself with dignity, but his jacket hung loose around the shoulders and his shirt collar was too large for his twilled neck. He obviously did not have the services of a good tailor.

"Did he have to die," said Sati. "You were told to just get him out of the way for a few days. There was no need to kill."

The candle light caused their shadow silhouettes to flicker and appear to dance about eerily. The effect quickly irritated me.

"He was disrespectful to everything we are trying to do. What difference does it make. Everyone is better off without him," said Waaiz in a huff. "You are much more self-sufficient and smooth-talking than he was. Besides there is now one less obstacle in our way."

"We have a treasure trove to plunder which has unleashed a rapacious frenzy of deep pocketed shareholders expecting to extract a fortune with every mold we sell them," replied Sati with the madness of extreme greed wavering in his dark candle lit eyes. "There is no need to get gluttonous or in a rush. Now, because of you, I will have to spend more time with Layla."

"They are perpetrating swindles by selling counterfeit artifacts," I whispered to Youssef. "The Museum is like a gold mine and they want to exploit its potential to the fullest."

"They cannot be dismissed as simple-minded crooks," he whispered back. "A man has been murdered and I'm not sure it was either of them despite what they say."

"I'm tired of seeing so many others get rich while we're plodding along and this could be our last big chance," said Waaiz. "Especially if there is going to be a war as you believe. During the confusion there will be many opportunities for slight-of-hand. We need to take advantage of every opportunity."

"Yes our odds are favorable and can be more lucrative now as opposed to waiting."

"I'll meet with him and give him a reason to get what we want," said Waaiz.

"No, another knifing will bring Gennat's homicide team and maybe even the international police down on us. Right now, they do not care because Uga was an Egyptian. I will talk to him," said Sati. "Is your alibi for last night set?"

"She will be ready for the Police if they ask any questions."

"Good. We better go and make sure the Amsterdam shipment left on time. Those dealers get skittish if we miss a deadline, they could cause trouble."

Waaiz blew out the candle, shook the flashlight again which came on as they walked to the door. "Old Uga was a fool all the way around." Both men laughed and locked the door behind them.

"What did that mean?" I asked Youssef.

"I think Layla has been having sex with Sati and maybe Waaiz too."

"No, I do not believe it. With Sati probably, but not with Waaiz, he is too conservative."

"More important right now, is we have no proof Waaiz killed Uga. If we went to Gennat, it would just be our word against Waaiz and whoever is his alibi.

"Let's try to follow them," I suggested. "Do you have a car?"

"Yes, come on. Who were they talking about? I did not hear either of them say a name."

"Neither did I, but at least we know it is a man."

. . .

Youssef managed to get within sighting distance from their truck as it wound through the warehouse district on the outskirts of Wedding, but when they stopped, we parked behind a wall and could barely distinguish them from several men loading a truck. One tall, lean fellow moved much like Hans, but we could not see him well enough to be certain.

"Let's go," said Youssef. "There isn't anything we can do here for now."

Though it was Sunday and the Museum was closed I had decided to use the new camera to shoot candid photographs in front of it. I was across the street when I noticed Hans holding a small package while waiting near the corner. Waaiz and another man approached him. Hans appeared better acquainted or friendlier with the unknown one than with Waaiz. The unknown one was tall, handsome and well-dressed though somewhat coy and cautious behaving. Hans was fidgety about the package, which by the body gestures of all of them intimated it held something of significant worth.

With feigned reluctance and a vague shrug of generosity, Hans handed the package over to the taciturn stranger. A taxi car arrived and they all entered it. I casually walked up behind it and was able to hear bits of their conversation between the intermittent traffic noise.

"You must complete the cast and return this to me by 5 am," said Hans.

"It's like reusing a Rembrandt engraving plate," said the stranger. "The flimflammers have suckered even the biggest collectors and notables, among them eminent business leaders, industrialists, and military commanders with their reprints from those plates. We can get a big slice of that kind of action too."

The taxi car started to move. Not wanting to risk being seen, I joined in with a group of people walking in the opposite direction. When we reached the corner Youssef appeared from somewhere. I was still not used to seeing him in a suit and tie.

"What are you doing here?" I asked.

"Following you, what else would I be doing?"

"Did you see Hans and Waaiz with that stranger?"

"Yes, what do think is in the package?"

"From the little bit of their conversation I overheard, it is an artifact from the Museum."

"I doubt it," said Youssef. "Hans is not stupid. He would not steal an artifact and hand it to someone on the street. Although, he would probably hand the guy a fake one."

"He told the guy he would have to return it by 5am tomorrow morning."

"Mmm, that is strange, but it does not proof it is an original artifact. It could easily be just another copy from a casting. Both Hans and Meierdiebrück enjoy reputations as conscientious, reliable men whose integrity has never been questioned. What could have possibly led them to try their hands at major crime and maybe murder?"

"The prospect of great wealth produces great wickedness, not just ostentatious mansions, dance-halls, gambling parlors, bawdy ribald houses, or opium dens," I said. "I wouldn't be surprised to find all the great cities of Europe filled with intrepid thieves, endless confidence men and pitiless killers like these."

"Yea, all of that can change even the best men," he declared to my surprise. "Tell me how you determined molds had been made of the artifacts."

"The discolored areas are not visible in my original photographs, plus they were damp feeling and smelled of fresh clay."

"Mmm, it's always the nuances that give the guilty away," he said.

"Let's walk over to Tiergarden Park and discuss where we are with all of this."

"Well first, we now know with Meierdiebrück's help Sati and Waaiz have made molds of some of the Amarna artifacts plus Hans appears to be helping sell some of them."

"And last night it looked as though they have sold either the molds or castings from them or both to a dealer or dealers in Amsterdam."

"While today we've discovered that Hans and Waaiz are involved with yet another man who they may have given a mold or fake artifact to."

"Or an original artifact," I said.

"Three suspects and one of them may be a killer," he said.

"To me, Waaiz still seems to be the most likely of them to commit murder."

"He is a right-wing fanatic, but he is not smart enough to make a decision of major consequences. Someone beyond Sati is determining the major objectives."

"This new guy was very well spoken. I am certain he is well educated," I said.

"He might be the brains behind all of this," replied Youssef. "To bad you didn't get a photograph of him."

"You know, I may have. I shot several random exposures of people in front of the Museum. He might be in one of them, I will develop the film tomorrow and check."

CHAPTER 17

Layla Snura Uga opened her mouth to tell me of her feelings, but something shifted rapidly and heavily on her mind closing off our casual discussion. "I'm afraid I don't recall," she said looking out the window with her black opaque eyes and a beautiful, but fallacious smile. "Why does it matter? He is dead now."

I was becoming interested in Layla. Something about her intensity bit into me while gazing into her classical Egyptian face. It crossed my mind why, Sati and Waaiz had probably succumbed to her as well as the University professor scribe and the unknown university educated receiver of the package from Hans. She had the kind of beauty that causes a man to want to explore her personal history.

"Waaiz tells me you have several lady friends here in Berlin. What could you possible need from me," she asked lowering her head and looking up though the top of her long dark eye lashes. "I must say, I was surprised Herr Gennat and his homicide team released you."

For a woman in her 40s, she certainly commanded the moment. "Ahm, well your evidence could be important to them."

"Evidence? Evidence of what? I have none." A kind of angry fear had gripped her face. "I have explained to him and you, Waaiz and I were here in my home when my husband was murdered. There is nothing else to clarify." She stepped a little closer to the window causing the olive drab imprints under her eyes to be noticeable. I wondered if perhaps she had been up all night. In any case she suddenly looked nearer to fifty. Her clear forehead had wrinkled, as if my question had taken her my surprise. I could practically see her resistance solidifying.

The phone rang causing her to walk across the room in a very feminine glide to answer it. "Not now... perhaps... no, do it as we discussed." She hung up and was showing signs of alarm. Her eyes and nostrils were dilated and her voice was unfriendly. "Now Asim, I have many business correspondences to complete. You are free to leave."

The ragged edge of her voice and use of my first name reignited my attention. "Yes, of course there must be much of your husband's affairs to address. Good day and thank you for your time," I said as I bowed and back stepped out of the room. She laughed a little and her eyes changed again as if something hard and scary had come to her mind. "Maybe I shouldn't have relied on your arrest so much, but I still cannot believe Gennat let you go."

It was unsettling to see her face change so rapidly and radically again. She looked at me pensively as if to make sure I was leaving. As I exited, I felt I had not learned anything of value except to confirm Youssef's suspicion that Layla was more involved than anyone knew or suspected. As I walked away, I could not visualize her and Waaiz or even Meierdiebrück's as sex partners, but I could see her with Sati and the man Hans handed the package to at the Museum. My mind was stitching pieces together striving to complete a comprehensive image of who did what to who before a momentous unimagined disaster came down on me like a giant whirling trap.

In the evening I met with Youssef at the Ratskeller to review our mutual findings and the candid photos I'd taken of people in front of the Museum. He looked at me stubbornly and his eyes were yellowish from some internal complaint or bad indigestion. I was not sure which.

"You must have noticed something illegal going on in the warehouse," I asked. "Do the items they put into those crates match the shipping invoices? Do the invoices match the antique shops sales receipts? Where do all the fake artifacts and duplicated molds go?"

He laughed and took a long swallow of beer. "Gennat believes the first thing to do is to arrest one of the men at the warehouse in Wedding."

"Why? What about Waaiz or Meierdiebrück? Why a man out in Wedding?"

"The men there get paid far less and have no direct contact with Sati or Waaiz and definitely not with Meierdiebrück or anyone at the Museum probably, except maybe Hans."

"So?"

"A Wedding man should be easier to persuade in helping us." Something deep in his mind looked out at me, gradually coming forth into the light.

"Do you mean to bribe?" I suggested.

"No, he means convince him he will be imprisoned if he doesn't provide usable information about how everything works there."

"Has he selected such a man?"

"He has an agent undercover there who thinks a guy named Mustafa will do as we ask?"

"When?" I asked getting excited about the potential action.

"Tomorrow night. Late around midnight. I will pick you up. Be sure to wear all black," he said with a grin full of yellow teeth. "Oh, better bring your own flashlight."

I took the envelop out of my coat pocket and slowly opened it while smiling at Lena Marie. "Here are the candid prints of the people I photographed walking passed the Museum. The tall man looks like the one Hans gave the package to."

Youssef studied each photo carefully almost as though he had never seen one before. "You took these, developed the film and made the prints all on your own?"

"Yes, you saw me take them."

"You have a skill you will be able to use to make a living with for your entire life."

"I hope so, but would it be most profitable here, in Istanbul or Cairo?"

"Your family and friends are in Cairo. Surely, you will be able to get more excavation commissions after you leave the Museum."

While I appreciated his opinion, I felt we should concentrate on finding who killed Uga so my name could be completely cleared. "How can we identify this man?"

"He appears to be wearing a very expensive suit, hat and shoes," he said looking at my suit. "Even more costly than yours."

"Hey, that is a good idea. I'll show this photo to the tailor."

"Be careful, didn't you tell me Hans and your tailor are friends?"

"Yes, I believe they are."

"Show it to Fräulein Stern first. She seems to know all the wealthy men in this city."

I nodded in agreement and put the photos back in my pocket just as Lena Marie returned to take our dinner order. When she took it toward the kitchen, Youssef said with a leer: "Pretty woman, do you know her well?"

His question caught me off guard. "Ah, no, only that she is Bavarian and her aunt's family owns the restaurant."

His eyes seemed puzzled as he spread his hands on the table and spoke in a cold voice. "Mmm, Gennat said she is your primary alibi for the time of Uga's murder."

I slowly finished my beer, straining to conceive a believable reason for having been in Lena's company so late at night.

"Do not concern yourself Asim. We are both men with a personal history. Just keep in mind, you have one more reason to find Uga's killer."

"We were talking about a book she gave me," I said calmly. "It's about walking around Berlin."

The look on Youssef's face was amazing, his mouth was agog and his eyes focused on the ceiling.

"It is entitled *Walks In Brandenburg* by Theodore Fontane. "She thinks reading it may help me improve my understanding of the German language and Berlin."

He took another moment before lowering his head and looking at me. "Is this what you told Gennat?"

"No, he didn't ask me why I was here only what times I arrived and left."

"He probably made the same assumption I did and having now met Lena I was certain I was correct. No one is going to believe you and her were discussing a book of that nature alone in the middle of the night. Is it really about walking around?"

"Yes, but it is also about being open to all impressions and experiences you encounter. It is not enough just to pass through a neighborhood. You must learn about its history and where its future may lead," I said as we watched Lena approach with our meals. "You have to risk strolling without a specific destination and open yourself up to unexpected adventures."

"Guten Appetit, ah enjoy your dinner," Lena said as she placed the dishes before us.

"I was just talking about the book you loaned me," I said smiling.

"Are you enjoying it, is it helping you?"

"Yes, although I haven't had much time lately to just saunter around.

She smiled at each of us and walked away. Youssef raised his beer stein and clinked it against mine then said: "Unexpected adventures. Yes, I believe that is true and I am sure it was. Just be careful. A mis-adventure could hit you with the kind of publicity you will never recover from."

I suddenly recalled, the young woman from the Egyptian Exhibition who writes about contemporary fashion for Modes Magazine. She may know who the man in the photograph taken in front of the Museum is.

Proving his stomach was churning, Youssef ate only apple cake and rice pudding, while I had a Jägerschnitzel with creamy mushroom sauce and fresh bread.

Mustafa was stingy with useful information, neither confirming nor denying the molds were made within the Museum. He hinted he may be disposed to entertain suggestions of selling a broken cast from one of the molds and he agreed to take us to where castings from some of the molds are made – but only if our eyes were covered in route. With the arrangement made, we boarded a carriage and headed toward the east side of the city. Our eyes were blindfolded as the horse drawn carriage crisscrossed back and forth for well over an hour. When we stopped, we were exhausted and confused while being pushed through a doorway and led down a musty hall, not unlike the one at the Museum or so I thought even though I could not see through the blindfold.

When our vision was restored, we looked upon several tables all filled with Egyptian sculptures, bas-relief fragments, amulets, amphoras and assorted shards of pottery. Some of which were conspicuous forgeries, while others appeared authentic despite the subterfuge.

I felt admiration for Mustafa's perspicacity and daring at having brought us here. Youssef appeared overly cautious, "Whoever is in charge is very sure of themselves. There are no guards," he said softly from the corner of his mouth as we happened upon a crate whose label indicated it was being shipped to Cairo.

Mustafa explained: "these cast will be buried at Tel El Amarna and re-discovered after the season ends. Obviously, to give them even more authenticity when they are smuggled to Paris or Rome and sold as originals."

A dumbfounded-ness could be read on Youssef's face. "This is audacious as hell. We must destroy all of it now," he garbled under his breath.

"Do you mean right now?"

"We can set this place on fire," he replied with a horrifying look taking hold of his face.

"How many swindlers are profiting from this elaborate subterfuge? What is the take from the fleecing? I asked our informer.

Mustafa shook his head. "You are not a policeman, are you?"

"No, I work for the Museum. Everyone there would be embarrassed by these revelations."

"At first, the plan was to simply steal the originals and replace them with fake copies. But Hans would not agree to it."

"Hans Herbster?"

His voice sank almost out of hearing as he twitched restlessly and said: "Yes. He makes sure all of the duplicates match with the originals."

To say I was surprised by that revelation would be a complete understatement for I was amazed and deeply saddened by it.

On the ride back to my lodgings Youssef was quiet, but I still had lots of questions.

"All of this is very good intel for Gennat's team, but doesn't help us find the killer."

"That's correct and it probably means he will not arrest anyone yet."

"Not even Hans," I asked.

"Especially not him. We need much more evidence. That is why I decided we would not burn the warehouse down. All evidence, no matter how small or inconsequential adds to the credibility of the case against the killers."

Being summoned to Herr Director's elegant office caused me some intestinal discomfort, but I had been expecting the order ever since my loss of temper at the reception. Upon entering I was prepared to be confronted by Hans, but he was not there. Instead, once again it was Fräulein Marie Luise Simon who received me in the outer office.

"Good morning Fräulein Simon. Please accept my sincere appreciation for your intervention on my behalf in maintaining a good relationship with the Herr Gennat."

"It is not necessary, I knew you could not possibly have been the killer," she said with a gentle smile and squinted eyes. "Now, I understand from Herr Director you have come upon some astonishing information concerning fake artifacts."

"Unfortunately, it is all too true."

Her face was half-shadowed by a shaft of sunlight coming through the window. "Herr Borchardt is certain all of the Amarna artifacts are genuine and you are just as certain some of them have been duplicated?"

"Yes, molds were made from the Museum originals. Then the molds were duplicated and distributed throughout Europe."

"Which artifacts are you referring to?"

"The amulets and bas-reliefs mostly."

"That is strange. I understood you discovered these duplicates are being smuggled in large shipping crates?"

"They are inside fake amphoras, mummified cats and old furniture."

She stiffened and her hand went up to her throat. "I see," she said, but sounded doubtful.

"All of this information is very unsafe to have Fräulein, please do not endanger yourself by sharing it with others."

"Your concern is noted Herr Lateef and appreciated. Good day."

Again her abruptness was unexpected, but somehow strangely appropriate.

"Should I wait for Herr Director?"

"It will not be necessary."

I returned to the Studio feeling unsure as to what I should be doing.

. . .

I took a taxi car to Chione's office planning for us to have lunch at the little café across from Tiergarten Park, but she insisted on walking through the park instead. We had much to talk about, but again she stated her dislike of discussing difficult subjects. I thought perhaps telling her about the walking book Lena had loaned to me would be a subject she would be interest in, but decided against saying anything related to Lena. We decided to walk toward the zoo.

"Do you know, visitors can either enter the zoo through the exotically designed Elephant Gate, the Lion Gate or the Egyptian style Straussenhaus?"

"No, I did not. Can we go to the Egyptian one?"

"Yes, certainly."

As we strolled, I asked her to tell me about her work and what she liked and did not like about it. She however, preferred talking about the social contacts she had made through volunteering as an interrupter.

When we approached the Straussenhaus, her entire face lite up with joy.

"This is wonderful and so unexpected," she said as we walked inside. "But it is not something the average Egyptian has ever seen. Are these paintings copied from a real Egyptian temple? I mean everything, the paintings, the sculptures, the architecture looks like it was inspired by ancient Egyptian art, but it does not look believable."

"Yes that is true, but isn't it encouraging to know others honor our history by being inspired by it on such a grand scale?"

She shrugged and smiled, but walked out of the building.

"Is this the oldest zoo in Europe?" she asked looking somewhat vacant.

"No, the oldest is the Tiergarten Schönbrunn in Vienna, Austria. As I recall, it opened over a 150 years ago."

"Why did the people here select the bear as their symbol for Berlin?" she asked in her sweet girlish way.

"I asked that same question at the Museum library and was told it is a pun on the city's name. 'Little bear' in German is Bärlein, which sounds like Berlin."

"What does pun mean?

"It's a Witz, ah, witticism or joke."

I had expected her to continue with this conversation, but she changed the topic again.

"Tell me about the amulets in the Museum's exhibit," she said with another of her sweet smiles and surprisingly seductive glint in her eyes.

"They are crafted out of gold and precious stones and served to protect the wearer or deceased."

"I like the winged scarab," she said as we approached a flower vendor.

"Please select what every you want," I said feeling good that I had more than enough money in my pocket. She selected a single red rose.

"Do you believe amulets have special powers?"

"They can, if you believe enough," I said as she held the rose up, for the scent to reach me. "That is definitely a regenerative aroma."

"You mean it gives rise to your ah, ah male energy?"

I could not resist. I took her into my arms and we kissed as if we were under the stars of Orion again.

"You know, the Roman natural history writer Pliny said amulets protect you from trouble," I said as I felt embarrassed pressing my manhood against her in such a public setting.

"Do you wear one?" she asked as she flung her hair back and pulled me to her lips again.

"I've noticed many people here wear a Saint Christopher pendant," I said trying to regain my composure. "In Egypt, an amulet's power is derived from a combination of its shape, decoration, inscription, color, material, and even words spoken over it. Plus, they are worn on selected parts of the body to transfer their powers directly to it."

"Yes, I've read they've been found on the tongue, eyes, heart and certain parts of male mummies." Her blush matched the rose. "This is for you, if you keep it near your heart, it will keep you in good health and fortune. I believe it is made of Egyptian faience."

It was a blue scarab beetle amulet, which traditionally represents the journey of the sun across the sky, a bringer of good luck. It looked and felt like an original ancient amulet. "How did you come by it?" I asked softly.

"It was my fathers and was given to me by my mother. I want you to have it."

"I will keep it near my heart," I said as I unbuttoned my shirt and slipped the delicate chain holding it over my head. Standing there watching her rebutton my shirt and adjust my tie was the most contented feeling I'd had in a long while.

We continued walking through the park along the Spree River and there were people everywhere. "This is a very popular area," I said. "Do you come here often with your friends?"

"It is always pleasant, but being here with you is the very best way to enjoy it," she said with a shy, sweet smile.

"Unfortunately, we must leave. Your uncle will be concerned about you and I should not give the Museum any further cause to discharge me."

"Have you heard of the bronze age hoard discovered in Eberswalde?" I said as we searched for a taxi car.

"No what is it?"

"It is the largest assembly of prehistoric gold objects every discovered in Germany. It was found less than 1 meter below the ground during excavations for a house near a factory.

"What kind of objects?" she asked looking enchanted.

"It was in a globular vessel with a lid and inside were eight gold bowls, which contained over seventy gold objects including necklaces and bracelets."

"That is strange, in Egypt such things are found only in tombs and sarcophagus while here they are just in a hole in the ground?"

We got into a taxi car to return to the Uga's office and storage warehouse. "Where else do you go with your friends?" I asked.

"Sometimes we go on the electric trams to take coffee in the Hotel Esplanade or the Hotel Excelsior," she replied thoughtfully. "Have you attended any of the gentlemen's evenings there?"

"No," I said. "That would be above my station and I'm not likely to be invited as a guest."

"Where do you go evenings and on Sunday?"

I was not going to mention the Ratskeller or the figure drawing classes so I just shrugged and smiled. I learned long ago that vagueness functions as a deliberate and effective strategy in many of life's unexpected interludes.

"Perhaps you would enjoy visiting the zoo on Sunday," I asked. "It is very large and has over 20,000 animals."

"Oh, yes, I have heard spring time is an interesting season to visit," she said with a surprising full smile.

The taxi car arrived at the Uga warehouse much quicker than I thought it would. Chione leaned to me, kissed my cheek, and quickly stepped out of the car. "Thank you for a wonderful day."

She looked back only briefly as she entered the building. I instructed the driver to take me to the Museum. Upon arriving I walked to the side entrance and was surprised to see a Guard. "Your staff identity card bitte," he said sternly.

I removed my card from a breast pocket and handed it to him. He had a small ledger book under his arm. He thumbed through a few pages, stopped, read a page, and said: "Herr Asim Khalifa Lateef, Photography Department."

I could see there was a photograph of me mounted on the page along with my name, position title and office location. The Guard then unlocked the door and held it open. I nodded, entered, and went directly to the Studio. The door was locked. I used my key and entered.

Anneliese was at her desk writing. "Did you have a pleasant lunch?"

"No. Chione insisted on going for a walk instead so my stomach is still growling, but my heart is content. What are you working on?"

"We are now to begin shooting color photographs of everything on display in the Museum. I am formulating a schedule and trying to determine where to start."

"It is good we will be able to move forward in a normal fashion."

"Well, almost. Did you come in the side entrance?"

"Yes, I did and I believe having a Guard there is appropriate."

"Mmm, he not only checks your identity card he also keeps a log of what date and time you enter or leave. How do you feel about those procedures?"

"I have nothing to hide, nor do you. Do you?"

"Ah, no, but it makes me feel as though I'm not being trusted."

"Perhaps he will only be there until the killer and the smugglers are captured."

She still appeared disappointed.

"There were always guards at Amarna."

"I haven't walked through the Museum yet, but I suspect there are other new guards stationed everywhere."

"Do you mean beyond the usual roaming ones?"

"Yes. Let's go see. If anyone questions what we are doing, tell them we are determining which art works we will photograph tomorrow."

We both put on our smocks and picked up are ledgers. We looked very official as we moved through each floor.

As we proceeded it appeared there were now three more guards, all stationed on the ground floor. One each at the side entrance, loading dock and in front of the Collections wing.

When we returned to the Photography Studio, Anneliese wanted to know what I knew about The Beautiful One.

"Of all the wonderful pieces in the Egyptian Collection, why are you interested in it?" I asked.

All the vagueness went out of her expression and she spoke between tight lips. "Several of the ladies in the proletarian women's movement here in Berlin were discussing asking Herr Borchardt to let them use one of our photographs of the Nefertiti sculpture for their campaign posters. What do you know about her?"

"What for example do they want to know?"

"Well the name Nefertiti, what does it mean?"

"It is written several ways depending on how it is being use, but it usually means The Beautiful One or The Beautiful One Has Come."

"And how is it you know this? I mean, I thought she was an unknown Queen."

"At Assiut, a small very old wadi near Amarna there is a local historian named Karim who has a vast knowledge of Nefertiti and Akhenaton. I spent an entire day with him asking, these same kind-of-questions."

"So this is oral history, not written?"

"It is both. Karim is the keeper of the regions oral history and he reads hieroglyphs, but you should not tell anyone. He would be arrested and maybe shot."

"For reading hieroglyphics?"

"Yes, it is against the law?"

"That seems odd, but go on."

"Nefertiti was the royal wife of Pharaoh Akhenaten. Some assume, she came to Egypt in her early adulthood, some that she belonged to Egypt's upper class. Either way, it is clear the couple had six daughters."

"Wow. It is remarkable she remained so beautiful."

"If you will recall, several artifacts discovered at Amarna show her and Akhenaten with their daughters. Which from what Herr Borchardt says, is unusual in ancient Egyptian art. Nefertiti is also shown supporting her husband by identifying herself with his cultural and religious reforms especially her support of the new Aten cult. When they moved into the new city of Amarna she became co-ruler of it with Akhenaten.

"So she played an important role in religious and political events which probably improved life for most women in Egypt."

"Yes, on several artifacts, she is illustrated in positions usually only a pharaoh is shown in, like in situations of combat or war. It is also assumed she was responsible for much of the government's administrative business plus her position was later listed as equivalent to Akhenaten with regard to overall authority and power."

"She sounds perfect, except I'm not sure the suffrage movement would want to be represented by a Royal Queen, but go on. What else is there?"

She was also known throughout Egypt for her beauty. She was said to be proud of her long, swan-like neck and invented her own makeup using the Galena plant. She also shares her name with a type of elongated gold bead, called nefer, that she was often portrayed as wearing. Some of the artifacts depict her and the king riding together in a chariot, kissing in public, and her sitting on his knee. There is even a hieroglyph of a love poem he wrote to her."

"Well this is certainly a great love story, but I still think it may not work as a symbol of political change."

"In the fourth year of Amenhotep IV's reign, he made the sun god Aten the dominant national god. The Pharoah led a religious revolution closing the older temples and promoting Aten's. Nefertiti played a prominent role in the new system. She worshiped alongside her husband and held the unusual kingly position of priest of Aten. In the new, virtually monotheistic religion, the king and queen were viewed as a primeval first pair, through whom Aten provided his blessings. They thus formed a royal triad or trinity with Aten, through which Aten's 'light' was dispensed to the entire population."

"So during Akhenaten's reign Nefertiti enjoyed unprecedented power, and she may have been elevated to the status of co-regent, equal in status to the pharaoh himself. Right?"

"Yes, she is even often depicted on temple walls the same size as him, signifying her importance. Perhaps most impressively, Nefertiti is shown on a relief from the Amarna temple smiting a foreign enemy with a mace before Aten. Such depictions had traditionally been reserved for the pharaoh alone and yet Nefertiti was depicted as such."

"That does sound revolutionary, but too royal for me," she said smiling.

"Akhenaten had the figure of Nefertiti carved onto the four corners of his granite sarcophagus, and it was she who is depicted as providing the protection to his mummy, a role traditionally played by the old traditional female deities Isis, Nephthys, Selket and Neith."

"How long were they in power?"

"It is unclear as to what happened after Akhenaten's death. Apparently, some archaeologists believe Nefertiti outlived her husband and ruled Egypt for a short period by herself under another name or her power may have ended early."

"Why?"

"In the regal year 12, Nefertiti's name ceases to be found. Some think she either died from a plague that swept through the area or fell out of favor. Shortly after her disappearance from the historical record, Akhenaten took on a co-regent with whom he shared the throne of Egypt. This has caused considerable speculation as to the identity of such a person. One theory is it was Nefertiti herself in a new guise as a female king, following the historical role of other women leaders such as Queen Hatshepsut. Another theory introduces the idea of there being two co-regents, a male son, and Nefertiti.

"How old was she when she married Akhenaten?"

"Probably 15."

"Hah, well we will not bring that up in the discussion. I mean we were thinking she would make a good icon for woman's rights, but 15 is too young for that. However, her poised face, objective in its beauty and allure could bridge the gap between antiquity and modernity."

"What about her racial identity?" I asked. "Will European women accept an African as their divine leader or even equal to them?"

"I don't know about her racial identity, but I do know several of Berlin's artists have begun making paintings and prints about her."

"Her cultural potency is enhanced by her mystique," I said wistfully.

"Are all Egyptian men as romantic as you Asim?"

I felt a wide smile spread from the center of my face to its outer edges. "In many ways, I believe all Egyptians share a responsibility to protect their shared past if only to hold on to some notion of our distinction, its specialness requires care and protection. At the same time, I question whether non-Egyptians can be trusted to understand and contribute to it. They may make Egypt appear inadequate and derisory?

However, I must admit, I had visited the ruins at Amarna twice before being hired to work there and never had I even given any thought so many wonderful artifacts could be laying there under only a few feet of sand.

In many ways I feel more Egyptian here in Europe than I did in Egypt and clearly, I am a foreigner here. I was born and educated in Egypt. I am an Egyptian citizen. I have family and friends in Egypt and know the country well. But, does my heritage mean I recognize the grandeur of Egypt more than others do? Does the Egyptian blood coursing through my veins reveal to me things non-Egyptians can never understand. To be accepted as a legitimate historian in Egypt, I would not have to prove my allegiance."

"So being identifiably Egyptian, whatever that means, increases the veracity of everything you say about Egypt?"

"I do not know. All I really know is when someone here flinches when meeting me I feel my Egyptian identity coming to the surface of my awareness."

"A kind of instinctive reaction?" she said.

I nodded, but did not respond.

"Well, let us leave that for now. I am going to the proletarian women's movement meeting tonight and they are depending on me to report on the Nefertiti question, so I have another favor to ask of you and if you do not want to do it, please say so," she said with a mixed look of apprehension and trepidation.

"I will not attend the meeting," I said firmly.

"Agh, oh, no, no it's not that," she said nervously. "I have another roll of private film that prints need to be made from."

"Prints of what?"

"Another artist's model," she said looking decidedly self-consciously embarrassed.

This felt like a turning point had been reached. If we got caught making these kinds of print's we would not only be fired we would be arrested and I would never get another museum position.

I stood staring at our enlarged photograph of The Beautiful One and thought about sculptor Thutmos working late in his studio while perhaps Nefertiti posed and guards stood outside the door. I wondered if he worried about what he was doing as an artist. Did he fear being arrested or persecuted? I concluded, at the very least, he had the courage to depict her as he saw her in the flesh and spiritually, but in the end, the evidence seemed to reveal he had to quickly abandon his work and flee.

"I can compensate you for your time, if that will help you to decide," said Anneliese breaking my train of thought.

"No, I do not want money, I will do it for you because we are friends and colleagues. But I do feel you need to get your own studio soon."

"I'm working on it and Romy is helping me to search for an appropriate space," she said with a determined look. "You are a treasure, Asim."

She quickly got her purse from her desk, removed the negatives, and handed them to me along with her desk key. "Put the prints into a sealed envelope and lock it in my desk."

I took the negatives and watched her leave and lock the door behind her.

I quickly went into the Darkroom and locked that door, took out the negatives, slipped one into the enlarger and focused it. It was of another nude women. I took out a piece of paper, exposed it and slipped the paper into the tray of developing fluid.

While the image was emerging, I looked at all the negatives. There were only six poses and even though they were reversed I could tell the poses were very provocative. I slipped the first print into the wash and then the fixative and stood staring at the image as it stabilized.

The woman was very attractive and seductive looking. I immediately thought the artist she had posed for was an extremely fortunate man and I felt privileged to be looking at her too. I hung the finished print on the drying line and proceeded to make the next one.

This photo shoot was different from the others Anneliese had shared with me. In the earlier ones the model was always isolated on the platform with a plain wall behind her. In this shoot, she was on a couch in the middle of the artist's studio and you could see his easel, congested work tables and paintings stacked everywhere. In fact, there was so much stuff it looked as though the place had not been organized or cleaned in years.

The prints were still damp and the hour was getting late, so I used my clean handkerchief to wipe the last of the water from them. There was something appealing, even captivating about using my hand to remove the wetness from the image of a nude woman. It was then I noticed lurking in the shadowed background of one of the poses an object out of place. An object that should not be there. It was so intriguing I decided to make an enlarged print of just that small section of the image. As I waited for it to emerge in the developer tray, I felt horrified when I could tell it was exactly what I assumed it to be.

It was an ancient Egyptian terracotta amphora the two-handled kind used as a storage jar for grain, olive oil or wine. It had the tapered bottom designed to lean it against a wall rather than stand upright. I immediately wondered if there were other artifacts in the background of any of the other photos from the six.

As the hour was getting even later, I was planning on studying each image in detail at home so I made another complete set of prints, put them into an envelope and tucked it under my belt beneath the back of my shirt.

I put Anneliese's sealed envelope into her desk and locked it.

It was 9:35pm. I locked the Studio and started for the side exit. I was worried about how to explain my late departure to the new guard. When I turned to enter the last hallway, I was struck on the side of the head with what felt like metal. I went down slowly and fell to my knees holding my head as a second blow hit the back of my neck and the hallway light went off or I blacked out, I was not sure which. I could feel somebody touching the pockets of my coat and warm blood running down the side of my cheek. I was flat on my back. I tried to get up, but could not tell which way that was.

Time seemed scrambled and I heard footsteps pass by me. I blacked out again. When I finally awoke there was dark gray light coming through a window somewhere. I got up onto one knee and braced myself against the wall with my left hand while touching the side of my face with the other. The blood was dry on both my face and back of my neck, but my head was pounding and turning it in any direction was extremely painful.

Hunched, I managed to stand and lean against the wall and walk carefully toward what I thought was the side exit door when I stumbled over something large. It was a body. On my knees in the dark there was just enough light to see it was the guard. I could hear him breathing, but my brain fog was not dissipating in fact it clouded over again. I sat back down and listened to his labored breath. When I got to my feet again, I managed to find the light switch and turn it on. The guard was lying on his face which was drained of color and his whole-body appeared flaccid with fatigue, he looked dismal. I rolled him over and shook him vigorously again and again until he came awake slowly as if he had been a long way from where we were. When he finally sat up against the wall he asked: "Is the door locked?"

I turned the knob and replied: "Yes. Let's move into the coffee room. Give me your arm."

He did not argue as we held each other up and walked through the hall. His body was couched some and his left arm dangled loosely at his side, but his eyes appeared clear. We went into the room and he went directly to the sink and splashed cold water on his face with his one good hand. "I will be fine, but my arm is broken. You phone the Police, but be careful who ever hit us may still be in the building. Maybe you should wash the blood from your face and neck."

He began to sway. "Sit down here, I will go to the phone in the Photography Studio," I said. As I walked briskly, I suddenly became aware of the envelope beneath my shirt. I could not allow myself to be searched by the police or anyone. When I entered the Studio, I went directly into the Darkroom, took out the envelope and placed it beneath the tray of developer fluid. I then went to my desk, took out my ledger and notes about the artifacts Anneliese and I had recently photographed placing all of them along with the thumb nail photo sheets in such manner as it would appear I had been working there.

The police informed me they would contact Herr Director, to make sure all the exits were locked, and to stay in the coffee room with the guard.

• • •

It was a long and wearisome morning. I felt exasperated I could not study the photographs I had hidden or even tell anyone about them, except Anneliese. We agreed we would leave both envelopes where they were.

As we stood staring at the photos on our display wall a knock on the door startled us both. Anneliese opened it.

"Herr Borchardt, welcome."

He walked in, took my right hand, and held it as he said: "Asim again you have been the right person at the right place and time. I am sure it is to you and of course our guard, nothing has been damaged or taken from the Museum."

"I'm sorry I didn't get a good look at him or get my hands on him."

"Why were you working so late into the evening," he asked.

"As you are aware, color photography is new to me. I often spend a little time after hours studying the photographs we have completed to see if there is anything I can do to improve my skills."

"Admirable. Well, Herr Director and I agree you are to go to the doctor to have your injuries treated and take the rest of the day off," he said smiling and handing me a note with the name and address of the doctor. "Have the bill sent to me."

"Most generous and thoughtful, thank you. I need only to speak with Fräulein Brantt for a moment."

"Certainly. Oh, and do not strain yourself, take a taxi car," he said. "I have one waiting for you in front of the Museum."

I nodded graciously and sat down at my desk as he left then whispered to Anneliese: "Lock the door."

She did so quickly and said: "What is it?"

I gestured for her to follow me into the Darkroom where I went to the Developer tray, lifted it, and pick up the envelope of photographs.

"I asked you to put those in my desk," she whispered harshly.

"These are the ones I made for me," I whispered in return.

"Right, copies for your personal use?" she said at full volume. "Asim I must say I am surprised at you. Let me guess you are going to use them to make figure drawings from."

"In many ways, it is unfortunate that is not the case. No this is much more serious."

"What is? This is just another model who wanted copies to show artists who may want to hire her."

"Which artist requested these?"

"Otto Dräger. Why is that important? Are they too provocative or something?"

"When you get them home, look closely at the background areas. But whatever you see do not mention it to anyone other than me. Doing so could endanger your life."

Anneliese appeared bewildered and lost in thought. I put the envelope inside my shirt and said: "We'll talk about it in the morning."

She nodded in agreement and I left.

I went straight to my lodging thinking I would go to the doctor in the morning. I made only one stop, at a small shop to purchase a magnifying glass. I wanted to get a good look at the photographs.

When I arrived home, I suddenly realized I was hungry. I had only half of a pretzel and a small bottle of ginger beer. As I ate, drank and studied each photograph I couldn't envision why this beautiful woman needed or wanted to pose nude for artists.

The amphora was visible in another of the photographs, but there didn't appeared to be any other artifacts. However, the photo where the model was leaning back on the couch with her right hand and foot up on its back and her left foot on the floor was not only sexually arousing it also showed a pistol on the small table behind the end of the couch next to what may be a self-portrait of Otto.

Now I had two mysteries. Why would an artist need an ancient Egyptian amphora and a pistol in his studio. I fell asleep with an incredible array of images flying around in my pounding brain including Chione, the nude model, Nefertiti, Lena the waitress and all the drawing models were mixed in with artifacts especially the blue scarab amulet, the broken amphora and a gun. When images of Fräulein Marie Luise Simon, Romy and Anneliese burst in on top of everything else in my visual cortex, I awoke in a frenzied sweat.

In the morning I went directly to the doctor. He put a bandage on the side of my cheek but not on the back of my head or neck and instructed me to go back to bed for at least 24 hours. Anneliese and I arrived at the Museum almost simultaneously. We were checked in by a new guard at the side entrance and walked quietly to the Studio.

"I did not expect to see you here today. Are you sure you are well enough to carry the camera and tri-pod around the exhibit halls? I mean we do not need any accidents occurring."

"If I am not, I will go home. Explain to me why you shot the photos of this model from so far back. All the other photos of models you have shot are close-ups with no background visible at all."

She appeared surprised by the question and shook her head. "She and the setting just looked more fine-arty than the others did. The contrast between the velveteen deep violet couch, the pinkish model and the disorganized gray-brown studio floor and walls captivated my instinctive need to be creative. Isn't that why you made those copies for yourself?"

"Yes, but you shot it in black and white."

"Oh, damn I gave you the wrong roll of film. I meant to give you the color roll."

"Just give her the black & white prints and tell her it will take longer to finish the color ones. Who is she?"

"Do you mean her name or what she does besides model?"

"Both."

"Why?"

"It will help me to think of her as a real person."

"I see. You are right, that is important."

"By-the-way, what did your women's group decide about the Nefertiti photograph and are those paintings near the gun self-portraits of Otto?"

"Yes, they are and the women's group are going to hire an illustrator rather than use any photographs."

"Are those portraits of Otto an accurate depiction of him?

"No, they present him as much younger than he is."

"Ugu, that is odd," I replied. "Well, since you have not, looked at the photos of whatever her name is, do you want to do so now before we get started in the Museum?"

"What am I to look for?"

"There is an Egyptian amphora on the floor and a pistol on the small table near the end of the couch. The amphora looks ancient and if it is, why would it be in Otto Dräger's studio along with a gun?"

She appeared to drift back to the night of the photo shoot and I hesitated to interfere, but we needed to get to work before someone comes looking for us. "Did you remember something?"

She wrinkled her nose and let out a little giggle. "Yes, when I finished the shoot, Otto picked up the gun and slipped it into his coat pocket trying to look nonchalant."

"What happened then?"

"Nothing he took us both to Club Cairo for drinks."

"Mmm, where is that and what is the models name?"

"The club is in Wedding and her name is Elsslin."

"What can you tell me about her?"

She looked at me pensively through her drowsy looking eyes. "Why, are you thinking of hiring her to pose for you?"

"Maybe, you never know. This city could probably use another photographer specializing in boudoir portraits," I said flippantly. "Besides her eyes are lively and alert."

She cocked her head on one side in an odd bird like movement. "Her eyes, ah, I am sure that is what got your attention. If you want to know anything further about Elsslin or Otto you need to talk with Romy," she said sharply.

"Would you consider these photographs Expressionistic?" I asked.

She smiled and looked pleased by the question. "To some extent, yes I do and I have to say I'm surprised by your interest in the movement."

"I have listened to several of the conversation's artists in the drawing class and at *Café Größenwahn* have when they talk about how the images are meant to convey a turgid emotional state reacting to modern psychological anxieties and alienation. This set of photographs seems to fit their description."

"You are right, they do and in the color versions there are plenty of bold vibrant tints and tones which is also an Expressionistic canon."

"Even the mess in Otto's studio could easily be interpreted as capitalism's role in the emotional distancing of individuals within cities."

"Wow, you've really been paying attention to everything going on around you."

"Yes, well, when somebody calls me a name, I listen," I said with probably too much force in my voice.

"Who called you that?"

"The drawing Kunstmeister referred to my attempts at rendering the nude figure as Expressionistic and now many of the other students do too."

"Oh, I see. Well, let's get to work, we can discuss this while we are setting up."

"The Expressionists talk about color as a form of salvation," I said as I loaded our portable lights onto the cart. "Is that something you responded to when you photographed Elsslin?"

"Absolutely," she said with a pleased smile.

"They also claim to not have a way for the viewer's eye to easily enter the setting like in a Cezanne landscape painting. I noticed you did the same with your compositions."

"Not exactly, the poses Elsslin selected lent themselves to capitalizing on that approach. Had she not chosen to pose as she did, I would not have been able to do so."

"Mmm, so she could be an artist as well as a model?"

"I doubt that, it is more likely she pays attention to what the artists talk about, as you do, and applies what she has learned to her posing."

Her conclusion or suggestion, that Elsslin and I think in similar ways struck an oddly agreeable, symphonic cord within me. "That's a very nice thing for you to say, did it come from your woman's intuition?"

"Now that you mention it, I believe it did. What else did you hear the artists say?"

"Oh, many of them come close to arguing when they discuss the fracturing of the picture plane. It seems to me, the only way you can achieve that effect in photography is to make double exposures or overlap negatives in the darkroom to make a print. What do you think?"

She stood staring at me, but did not answer.

CHAPTER 18

Club Cairo was at the end of a short street in the basement of a very old looking building. There were several men standing around the exterior smoking and talking. I walked down the outside steps to below street level and could see over the half-curtains into the large windows near the entrance. There appeared to be many men and women inside seated on wooden benches at long tables with an extensive bar stretched across one wall. I could hear music, but did not see the band or singer.

As I entered, the rush of warm air embracing me was inviting, but the heavy haze of cigarette smoke was overwhelming, caused me to cough and made the glow from the ceiling lamps appear murky green.

The fireplace flickered producing crowd silhouettes frolicking about on the walls. Based on their clothes plus the snatches of conversations I over-heard while passing tables, the patrons were mostly Egyptian and Turks, many of whom acknowledged me as I sauntered to the bar.

I found an empty stool and noted the dark wooden bar was worn and deeply scarred from centuries of use. I enjoyed reading the names and dates carved into it. The thought of the wood having been there for a very long time and having welcomed hundreds of men to congenially converse around it was heart-warming. This was how I often feel when inside the ancient temples of Luxor.

The barman approached and I ordered a beer. He set a generous full stein of Berliner Weisse in front of me and went back to talking with two women at the far end. Their contemporary attire told me they were not barmaids. I suspected the one roaming barmaid, who wore a dirndl, was not a real blonde. Lena Marie told me dirndl's were the traditional dress worn in southern Germany, Austria, Liechtenstein, Switzerland, and Alpine regions of Italy. I liked them, but this barmaids big sloppy red lips and heavily painted eyes were not appealing even though the dirndl was.

The band was an odd mixture of Egyptian and German musicians whose sound I found appealing. As I tapped my foot to the rhythm and swallowed another gulp of very enjoyable sour beer the young rosy-brunette woman at the bar left her friend and sat next to me. "Would you like to dance?" she said with a cautious smile.

"Ah, no, I would damage your beautiful shoes, I just enjoy listening to the music."

"Where are you from?" she asked as she swayed with the melody and played with a ringlet of her hair which under the light at my end of the bar looked red.

"Cairo. How about you, did you grow up here in Berlin?"

"Hamburg, the city of canals and the beautiful Elbe River," she laughed too loud and long. "I followed an artist here. What brings you to this metropolis?"

Oddly, the question made me feel uneasy so I finished my beer and said: "What artist, what is his name?"

"Do you want another beer," asked the Barman with a laid-back smile.

I nodded yes and he gestured to the rosy-brunette.

"What are you drinking?" I asked her.

"A Gin-Ricky with a little Turkish yogurt," she said with a sweet smile as she touched my forearm. I smiled in return and gestured my approval to the Barman.

"So you like artists," I said trying to appear casual. "Is the one you are friends with German or Egyptian?"

"That's a funny question, but as it happens, Otto's father was German and his mother Turkish."

I suddenly felt a hot rush. "Are you referring to Otto Dräger?"

"Say who are you?" she said with a suspicious glare. "Do you know Otto? Did he send you here to find me?"

"Asim Lateef and no, I have never met Herr Dräger, but we have a mutual friend."

"You mean a mutual girlfriend. Which one is it? Romy, Greta or that princess Elsslin?"

"Why would Otto want to find you?" I asked deftly. "Do you model for him?"

"What if I do. That does not mean I'm a slut," she said finishing her drink in one long swallow. "You men are all-alike. You expect every woman to share herself around."

Her voice was competing with the band and the Barman was getting annoyed. "You two take your conversation outside or move over to the corner table." He glared at her with an unpleasant sneer and coughed deeply.

"Would you like another drink?" I said softly as I took her arm and helped her off the stool.

"Oh, just one more," she replied as she allowed me to walk her to the table. It was then I realized several men were coughing in between drinking and talking. I suspected the flu or Tuberculosis was rampant in this section of town, then again perhaps it was just that the bar was full of Turkish tobacco smoke. I had recognized the aroma the moment I'd entered.

The Barman looked pleased by my order, prepared the drinks and followed us still coughing himself. I gave him some money at arms-length.

"So you know Romy. She is an interesting person," I said smiling. "She certainly knows a great many people."

"So what do you do?" she said regaining her composure and moving her eyelashes up and down to indicate recuperation, but there was still a smear of shame on her face.

"I'm assistant photographer at the Museum."

"Oh, I remember you now. You attend the drawing classes," she said as her facial expression morphed back to a pretense of happiness. "Will you be there tomorrow night?"

"Are you going to model?"

"Yes, it beats working here."

Her statement surprised me on several levels, especially since I did not realize she was working as we spoke. My mind was drifting and I found myself looking forward to seeing her nude again, even though I was not certain on which night she had modeled before until I studied her red eyebrows and recalled her red-haired pubis. "Ah, yes you are a natural red head," I said smiling, but thought I should change the subject. "So, tell me about Otto. Do you like his artwork?"

"His artwork. You must be jesting me," she replied looking puzzled. "He does those expressionistic figures. You cannot tell one model from any of the others in his work, they all look alike."

"Who buys his work. There are none of those kinds of paintings in the Museum?"

"I do not know, but he always has shipping crates in his studio. Sends his stuff to Paris and Amsterdam. Places like that."

It was not a time to interrupt her, I just smiled and shrugged.

"There's only one model he tries to draw realistically, that Elsslin bitch," she said with a sarcastic twitch. "She will never give him anything of herself. She thinks she is too valuable to be soiled by him. He even pays her twice as much as the rest of us and we all show him the same stuff."

"How do you know all this?"

"Because sometimes he has two of us model for him at the same time."

"So you've modeled with Elsslin?"

"Yes. He puts us together in very suggestive poses. He likes to look at us that way. I can tell. He is an artist, you know what I mean." The hurt in her eyes tried to erupt into anger, but did not quite succeed. She just wheezed a bit as though she has done so many times. "Lots of artists hire us to just hang around nude in their studios. They all are voyeurs who copy their leaders … you know Rodin, Cezanne, Matisse, Klimt … every one of them are notorious for having nude models laying about to watch them paint."

This was intriguing, but not going where I needed. "Mmm, paying for two models at the same time must cost him a lot of money. He must sell every painting and drawing he makes."

"Oh, he makes other stuff too."

"Like what?" I said quickly in hopes it would lead to some worthwhile information.

"Those weird looking vases and wall sculpture plaques like you have in your Museum."

"Are you referring to Egyptian amphoras and bas-reliefs?"

"Yea, I guess they are Egyptian. I do not know," she said finishing her second drink and watching two young German men enter and go to the bar. "It was nice talking with you Asim, perhaps I'll see you tomorrow night at the drawing class." She gripped my forearm, looked me in the eyes, smiled and sashayed away toward the young men. I suddenly realized I had forgotten to ask for her name, probably because she had a trait that bothered me, a certain doubt and dimness about her eyes, as if she had lost her sense of self a long time ago. I was convinced, she carried a deep sadness shrouding what remained of her delicate soul.

The Barman held up an empty beer glass as he looked at me. I shook my head negatively and walked out hoping I was not carrying any flu or anything worse. The stench of tobacco seemed to be following me as I moved into the night air. I was sure it was embedded in my coat.

It had been an informative and surprising evening in many ways, but I was tired. My head and neck were still aching causing me to fall asleep several times during the tram ride back to my lodging and the ringing in my ears only lessened when I plugged them with my fingers.

• • •

Thursday morning, I wanted to tell Youssef of everything I had learned about Otto, but I had to work at the Museum. When I arrived, Anneliese was ready for us to resume photographing the exhibitions on each floor. She told me reviewing the prints of Elsslin did not uncover anything unusual beyond the amphora and gun. When I asked her about seeing shipping crates in the studio, she replied it is not a secret Otto uses them for the cheap replica's he makes for decorator shops in Vienna, Paris, Amsterdam, London and Rome.

"Does he have a license to make copies and why does he need a gun?" I asked.

"Yes, he keeps it on the wall near his desk, but I've never bothered to see who signed it. Romy says he needs the gun because gets into fights when he is drunk and has been known to have affairs with prominent married women," she said. "However, I have to say, I'm surprised Elsslin seems interested in him beyond posing for him."

"What do you mean exactly?"

"She is articulate and talks as though she is well educated. She is not the kind of woman who you would think could be interested in his sort of man. He is coarse and behaves in a crude and rude manner. While she is refined almost lady-like."

"Opposites attract?" I said feeling I could learn to hate the guy without even having ever met him.

"That is what I saw when I photographed her. She looked out of place in his studio. The contrast between her physical beauty and Otto's scruffy, chaotic mess makes for a wonderful photograph. She almost looks like pure innocence in a war zone. Besides, posing is one of the most powerful tools available to photographers. Without the right pose, your whole image falls apart and Elsslin has an intuitive sense of how to strike an engaging pose. It is surprising she is not one of the new modern fashion models. I am certain she could earn more money if she were."

"Maybe she is an exhibitionist and enjoys having people look at her nude body. Where did she come from? Who is her family?"

"I was wondering the same thing. I asked Romy about her and she has not been able to find anyone who knows anything about Elsslin or so she claimed. She is a mystery. No one even knows her last name."

"Well, one thing I know for sure. Otto is a very lucky man. Hey, that raises another question. Does Elsslin pose for any other artists?"

"Who were you talking to about Otto?" she asked looking at me with puzzled eyes.

"I hate to admit I didn't ask her."

"You bought some woman drinks and talked to her for an hour, but never thought to ask for her name."

"I was tired and my head hurt as it still does, but I will see her tonight maybe."

"What? You have a date with her?"

"No, she is posing for the drawing class tonight; I think unless I didn't understand her correctly."

"Are you planning on taking her out for a drink after?"

"None of this seems to be helping to find who killed Herr Uga."

"That's true, but you are learning a great deal about the art community of Berlin and those are the people Herr Uga hung around with," she said averting her eyes.

"That's also true and this is exactly what Layla and Waaiz dislike about the antique business. According to them it attracts an undesirable element. People of low character and devious values."

"Look, it is obvious you are not feeling well and I've got a lot on my mind so let's just make four shots in the first room. After which we will go to lunch and spend the rest of the day developing whatever we have and call it a day," she said passing a hand over her eyes as if to clear everything else out of her mind.

When we completed the four shots and returned to the studio, I immediately phoned Youssef and arranged to meet him for lunch at the Ratskeller. Anneliese said she would be meeting Romy at Hollenbach Haus.

The four-color photographs we shot turned out better than we both anticipated. We concluded it was due to the early morning light coming through the windows, but I still had other things occupying my thoughts.

"Do you have any of the Elsslin negatives here?" I asked Anneliese as we finished drying the exhibit prints.

"Yes, what is it you want to do?"

"I would like to make a close up of her face for Youssef. He may have some contacts who know something about her."

"Right, well in that case, we should make several copies so he can spread them around," she said with a peculiar smile. "Are you sure you do not want to give him one of the full figure shots. You know to give him some incentive." Her giggle was almost childish.

The negatives she had with her were for color prints and we selected my favorite one because it was the only one in which Elsslin is looking directly at the camera.

"How big do you want to make it?" she asked still snickering.

"Wallet size should do. We can probably fit four on a single sheet of paper."

She looked at me curiously. "Correct me if I am mistaken, but in the past few months you have encountered three women who have really caught your attention. Chione, Nefertiti, and now Elsslin. Does that make you feel better about life or being a man?"

Her deep blue, meaningful eyes were focused on my face. I stood there trying to form a response, but thankfully the telephone rang before I manage to. She answered it.

"Hello ... yes, we will."

"Herr Borchardt wants to show us something in his office. Lock the portrait prints of Elsslin in your desk. I will put the negatives in my purse." We scurried about and were out the door within two minutes, locked the Studio and walked as quickly as we could to his office. The door was open and Herr Borchardt was at his desk studying something.

"Please come in, close the door and sit," he said solemnly. "Look at these."

He passed three black & white photos to us. We spread them out on his desk and looked at them. I said confidently: "This is one of the sunk relief carvings from Amarna."

"It does look like it, but it's a fake," Borchardt said. "It was confiscated by guards at an illegal dig there."

"Do you mean it was cast from a mold of the original that's here in the Museum?"

"That's correct and by having guards at the dig site take it away from the robbers gives the appearance of it being an original."

"How do you know it is fake?" asked Anneliese.

"The archaeologists at the site noticed several of the grooves are deeper than on the original and the blue pigment doesn't chemically match."

"Do you know if the casting was made in Egypt or here?" I said feeling deeply conflicted.

"I have given it a great deal of thought and concluded it was most likely made here in the Museum. There were always too many people around all the artifacts while in camp and in transit. Plus, had there been someone sneaking around, the guards would have shot them. But here, at night, there would be only two or three individuals at most and the thieves would be able to compare their copy directly with the original."

"They then ship the copies to Egypt and bury them. Why?" asked Anneliese.

"By having one or two men arrested at the site with an artifact in hand, the masterminds can then claim they still have lots of other originals the archaeologists didn't find."

"Plus it implies there are still many more undiscovered in the same site," I added. "So, what do we do now?"

"Bring all the prints, color plus black & white and all negatives to me now. We are going to lock them in our new safe."

"They are all together in our office filing cabinet. I will get them and bring them right to you," said Anneliese. "I would like to request Asim be allowed to leave early today. His head is still throbbing. He should get more rest." Her demeanor was calm, but her voice was edgy sounding.

"Oh Asim, by all means, go home now and take tomorrow off as well if you need to," said Borchardt. "Perhaps, you should accompany him Fräulein."

"No it is not necessary. I will be fine and will take a carriage home," I said as Borchardt looked anxious.

We excused ourselves and returned to the Studio feeling confused, saddened, and dismayed. It seemed this would be the appropriate time for Meierdiebrück to tell everyone of anything further he may know, but I left and took a carriage directly to my lodging.

When I arrived and stepped into the hall, I could see the door to my room was open. I approached it quietly and found a woman bending over my bed. The house maid was changing the bedding. She was a shy, timid brunette, very thin and taut with hungry dark eyes. Her straight long dress revealed only her slender knobby knees.

My whole body was feeling slack with exhaustion, I uttered softly "Guten Nachmittag Fräulein"

She blushed, kept her eyes down and quickly continued dressing the bed. I waited outside until she completed it and left. I was tired and irritable. When I reclined on the freshly made bed my mind was reeling with thoughts, but within minutes I fell into a sort of half-sleep where everything moved slow and was out of focus. It was only when I heard the maintenance man, I noticed how much time had elapsed.

I washed my face quickly, grabbed my drawing portfolio and rushed out to hail a carriage. Arriving at the classroom, my usual spot was still open so I wasted no time in setting up paper and charcoal sticks. The professor was talking about the tradition of elongating the legs in order to give the human figure a greater sense of grace. Something about making it 7 heads high, 3 above the waist and 4 below. I did not know what to make of that, but it did not matter for when the model walked out and disrobed, I was stunned. It was Elsslin.

The professor instructed her to walk around amongst the easels so we could all get a better understanding about how to use line to interpret movement. Again, I did not know what he was talking about, nor did I seem to care. I was focused on Elsslin.

"Good evening, Asim," Elsslin said to me. "Rosy sends you her regards and thanks you for the good time last evening."

I was sitting on a stool with my eyes at her breast level and felt stunned by her comment, but was unable to raise my head above the 4 heads high level and felt completely tongue-tied and famished for I had not stopped for lunch or dinner. My growling stomach was embarrassing, but Elsslin smiled sweetly, winked and said: "Rosy is feeling indisposed this evening. I hope you are not too disappointed."

All the students were astounded. As was I, plus felt I could not move, but did eventually manage to smile and nod.

The professor cleared his throat, Elsslin went up onto the model platform and took a pose facing right at me. My mind was in a trance and the entire room was filled with whispers. I was just hoping she would not say anything about the photographic prints I had made of her.

When I finally managed to clear my head and start drawing, I noticed the men trying to catch my eye to give me a tilt of their head and facial acknowledgment of having reached some sort of momentous achievement. I was going to need all their encouragement if I was ever to muster the courage needed to speak with her. Every pose she took was enthralling and thankfully left nothing to my imagination.

At break time, the professor handed Elsslin her robe and escorted her to his desk where they spoke quietly to each other. I gathered from his demeanor and hand gestures he was instructing her on some special poses he wanted her to do next.

"Will you be going for a drink after class?" asked Frederique. "You are welcome to join us."

"Thank you, I'm not certain what I will do," I said without taking my eyes off Elsslin. "I should go directly home. I was out late last night," I said without thinking. All the ladies near me giggled. I turned and looked at them, but before I could formulate how to respond they all became quiet and were looking behind me. I turned around and was face to face with Elsslin.

"May I speak with you for a moment Asim?" she said with a warm hushed breath and enticingly hesitant smile so gentle, so exquisitely pure I felt almost paralyzed by it.

"Yes, of course. Shall we walk to the back?" I said as I gestured toward a Bulletin Board on the far wall.

The moment we started moving, a tidal wave of whispering erupted throughout the room. The whole incident was unlike anything I had ever experienced. One I would probably relive over and over whenever I would feel the need to find meaning in my existence.

"We need to speak privately," she said as she stood in bare feet and looked up at me with her robe open just enough to fill my eyes with wonder. "Please join me at Romy's apartment after class," she said very softly and with her hand held loosely in front of her lips.

Her hands were lovely, like the rest of her. Even her beautifully shaped and polished nails seemed sexually rousing to me.

"Shall we take different carriages?" I asked while smiling back at the class.

"No, you find a taxi while I get dressed after the last pose."

My throbbing manhood wanted to make a risque suggestion it was not necessary for her to get dressed, but I thought better of it so I just nodded my agreement and walked her back to the platform. I wondered what her relationship to Romy was.

By the time the last pose was completed everyone seemed joyful. The professor even thanked Elsslin for her exceptional poses. I quickly packed my supplies into my portfolio and darted out to wave down a taxi. I was happy she did not want a carriage for it was too public. We needed privacy and besides it was cold. If ever there was a time to splurge, I felt this was it.

A taxi appeared seemingly from out of nowhere and stopped at the curb just as Elsslin appeared. Her long, heavy looking coat completely hid the robust, healthy, seductive body I had been captivated by for the past three hours.

The driver, a middle-age woman whose figure looked as though it had not recovered from child bearing, got out and came around the car to open the door for Elsslin who winked at her, stepped in, and slid across the seat to the far side. I got in and looked at the driver. She stared back, shook her head, and said: "I know the address."

She quickly started the car and looked into the rearview-mirror as she said to Elsslin: "Did everything go alright?"

"Yes, no difficulties."

That caught me by surprise. "Are you two acquainted?"

"We've worked together before and have known each other our entire lives," replied Elsslin. "This is my big sister Bertha."

"So this is why no one knows your last name or where you live. You two live together, right?"

"Yes, and I'm an undercover detective cadet assigned to Herr Gennat's homicide team." Her pride was palpable. My mind was instantly flooded with a cavalcade of nude images of her in the jail wearing only a policeman's hat while practicing her poses. "Does the professor know this?" I blurted.

"So far, nobody knows except Romy and you."

"Not even Youssef?"

"No."

"What about you?" I said to Bertha. "Are you a detective too?"

"No, just a Policewoman," she said with a wink that twisted her face.

A torrent of nude images was still running rampant in my mind as I turned and starred at Elsslin. "Ah, were you an artist model before becoming a detective?"

"No, I was a cadet at the police academy following in my big sister's footsteps."

"Why did you agree to do modeling? I mean surely there were other options."

"If I can help catch the killer, I will receive a good position in the Tiergarden District and I want to be the first woman detective permanently assigned to the homicide team."

I must have had a puzzled expression on my face for she said: "I was a student at the University, but both our parents caught the flu last year and died. There was no money to complete my education or for us to live separately. Plus, in the original plan, I was only going to model for Otto, no one else."

"What happened to cause the plan to change?"

"He told other artists and the professor about me, so Gennat was concerned it looked suspicious if I was only modeling for one artist."

"That is a reasonable assumption," I said looking into her eyes for some indication of her state of mind. "Have you found out anything useful from Otto?"

"I think so, but let's wait until we are at Romy's before discussing it."

"Why, is she an undercover detective too?"

Elsslin smiled, but did not answer. She starred out the window with somber eyes and a reticent mouth.

"Has Otto ever touched you?" I asked softly.

Again she did not answer, but a tear spilled down her cheek.

"I'm usually parked nearby in the taxi whenever she is posing for him," said Bertha. "And I have a gun. If he does anything improper I will shot him."

We rode in silence the rest of the way to Romy's apartment and when we arrived Bertha said she would remain in the car parked nearby and asked if I had a whistle. I did not.

Romy again had set out food and wine enough for four people, but Anneliese was not there. Elsslin had cleared her eyes and appeared confident again as she poured everyone wine.

"I've explained everything to Asim," she said to Romy. "Including about you and Bertha. I feel more comfortable having Asim know who and what I really am when surrounded by so many strangers," she said shyly.

We all nodded our heads in agreement and I put my arm around her shoulders for a quick embrace of affirmation. I did not want to let go, but I knew I had to.

"Well Asim, I hope you understand the gravity of having such knowledge. Please do not share it with anyone. Doing so could put us all in danger," said Romy.

"I understand, ah, almost, why hasn't Youssef been told?"

"I do not have the authority to do so. Only the Herr Gennat does. You will have to ask him."

"It just seems unfair somehow. Youssef would certainly like to know someone other than him is actively working to solve the murder of Herr Uga," I said. "Have any of you found any leads?"

"Yes, Elsslin found something which could determine who supplies the forged import and export documents for the trafficked artifacts."

"How did you?" I asked.

"By posing for Otto," she replied flinging her head back. "An old man I've seen before at the University came into Otto's studio panicked about some documents."

"Didn't he recognize you?"

"He was so embarrassed he only glanced at me for a quick moment, turned away and never looked at me again before leaving."

"What was he upset about?"

"Are you referring to my pose or the papers he was carrying?"

We all laughed and it was good to see Elsslin smiling again. "So, I assume Gennat has assigned a detective to investigate the man."

"We do not know," replied Romy. "Gennat does not share information with us unless there is a need for us to know about it. He believes if you do not know something there is less chance you will get caught making a mistake in front of the böse Jungs, ah, bad guys."

"I suppose there is some truth there, but it certainly makes it more difficult to know what to do next," I said feeling exasperated. "Tell, me about this old man. What kind of professor is he? What does it look like, maybe I have seen him before.

"He is a heavy man who swings his right leg stiffly from his hip and sort of rolls it as he walks. He is bald except for a little bit of hair above his ears and has ink stains on the fingertips of his right hand."

"Mmm, you are a detective and I have seen fingers like those before. All the scribes in Cairo have ink on their fingertips. He could be the forger of the shipping documents," I said as a recall spark struck my mind. "You know, I saw a couple scribes at Kafé Kairo last night who had them as well."

"You should visit the Café des Westens, on Kurfürstendamm most of the artists prefer it than Kafé Kairo. They call it *Café Größenwahn*," she said with a hearty laugh.

I think *Größenwahn* means "delusions of grandeur" or some such thing and it was not late so I decided I wanted to go there. "Perhaps I should go there now. We do not have anything important to discuss, do we?" I asked staring at Elsslin who starred back at me with a demure smile for a brief-moment.

"I need to make my weekly report, perhaps I can reach my contact officer tonight," said Elsslin as she stood and put her coat on. She looked disappointed I did not stop her but something deep inside my mind was telling me to go to *Größenwahn*.

When I got into a taxi and gave the driver the name, he nodded his head, drove away, and began mumbling. He seemed rather elderly to be a driver, but drove well. He was wearing an old crumpled hat with tuffs of gray hair sticking out in odd places. He slouched over the steering wheel and his blemished hands looked frail.

"*Größenwahn* opened about twenty years ago. It's in a lavish building in the Charlottenburg part of the Wilhelmine Ring. The fashionable 'New West' area next to the capital. It was originally named *Kleines Café* back then and was popular with the literary circle around Maximilian Bern," he said looking back and forth at me over his hunched shoulders.

He appeared to pause just to breath in and out slowly through his mouth. I recognized this exercise for the Doctor told me it helps boost the amount of oxygen in the blood, lowers blood pressure and heart rate, and reduces muscle tension. All of which would help my aching head. I wondered why this elderly man needed to do it, perhaps it is just because he is old.

"They keep enlarging it and changing the name," he said with a slight cough. "Only artists, writers and musician go there now. Are you one of them?"

"I am a photographer," I said as I realized I rarely refer to myself as such.

"You are viel zu jung. The Secession was an art movement established over 20 Jahre frürher during the Great International Art

Exhibition. When Edvard Munch's paintings were rejected. It was formed in reaction to the Association of Berlin Artists and the restrictions on contemporary art imposed by the Kaiser," he said sounding a little angry and pausing again to take another series of deep breaths.

"The new group is led by Max Liebermann and they even include women members. They had a big exhibition in 1908. Were you here then?"

"Unfortunately no. You must know many of the artists, you are very well informed about their history. Are you a historian?" I asked.

He gave out with a strange mixture of cough and laughter. "I was a member of the art academy, but nobody cares about my paintings anymore. The academy gave no support to the new organization. Now they give no support to anyone associated with the academy," he said through his yellow teeth. "Politik… there was much unrest in the conservative group towards the mixture of art in the annual salon. They believed immoral modernists art should not be mingled in the same gallery with traditional art and they do not like including foreign artists," he said shaking his head. "So now, I am taxi-driver and no longer care about what they think of my paintings."

I was not sure what his accent was and had not really paid attention to it until then. "But, all the artists, German and foreign come to *Café Größenwahn* now, correct?"

"Ja, ideas of nationalism and a political interest in art are more popular now. Everyone is interested in what it means to be German and what it means to have a cultural identity through artistic style."

"Does this mean people want Germany to have an individual artistic identity?"

"Yes, like Austria, France, Italy and England have their own," he said coughing again. "We are here. It is unfortunate you were not here during the 1910 Film Festival, a special showing took place of In Nacht und Eis. I've been told it is a masterpiece film about the Titanic sinking. Have you ever seen it?"

"No, I've only seen two movies," I replied while exiting the car.

"Try to see it as soon as you can," he said smiling. "It will help you."

That was an unexpected coincidence, for it was what I was told just before seeing my first movie, an adult film my uncle showed me and a few other teen-age boys from the wadi. It certainly helped us to understand a variety of things about life and relationships between men and women.

It felt late and I was tired, but the café was overflowing with a lively assortment of fascinating looking people. I thanked the driver for generously sharing his knowledge of local history and gave him a liberal tip. He said "Gern geschehen."

I walked through the crowd looking for the bar when a woman came to my side and wrapped her arm around mine. To my surprise, it was Anneliese.

"Hello Fräulein. You missed the party at Romy's."

"Did you ask the model her name?" she said smiling and looking up through the top of her eyes.

"No."

"Why not? Were you too embarrassed?"

"No. It was a different model. It was Elsslin."

Anneliese looked at me with a glow and her head tilted back as she said: "You must have enjoyed the evening." A smile moved imperceptibly from her eyes to her mouth, but did not stay long.

"Yes, I must admit, I did very much."

"More than looking at Chione?" Her taut voice deepened as her head tilted further up.

"I've never seen Chione in positions like those."

She raised her eyebrows, paused, and looked at me with a hard gaze for a still moment. "Well, let's have a drink to the day when you will."

She walked me toward a table where several men and women were sitting and drinking. "Welcome Asim, we ordered you a beer," said a high-shouldered and elegantly dressed young man who was handsome and seemed to know it. "Anneliese tells us you are an aspiring photographer and artist."

I nodded my head in a gesture of more-or-less and raised my glass of beer in salute. "Thank you one and all," I said with restrained enthusiasm before drinking at least a third of the glass and sitting down. "So, who among you is conservative, who is liberal?"

An angry flash pumped a blue streak across Anneliese's cheeks and she sneered at me with expressive nostrils. "Maybe you should rephrase your question, Asim."

I could not help myself, I looked from side to side for some polite way to leave, but it felt as though there was no escape open to me. As I stammered, someone else spoke.

"You tell us, Asim, are you a Naturalist or an Idealist?"

I was thankful for the question and extremely grateful for being able to recall everything the old taxi driver had told me.

"It depends on whether I'm making images for myself or for an employer," I replied looking as serious as I could. "The photographs I am employed to make have to be Naturalistic while the drawings I've made for myself have all been Idealistic or ah, should I call them Expressionistic?"

"Have you tried to reverse them?" asked a very young looking fellow earnestly.

"No, but I can see it would be relatively easy to make Expressionistic photographs and very difficult, if not impossible, for me personally to create naturalistic drawings."

"Which approach feels most natural for you?"

"Well I have a natural need to eat so I must be employed and I cannot imagine someone paying me to make drawings."

To my relief, everyone laughed including Anneliese.

"Not even if the Kaiser approved of them being included in the official exhibitions?"

That question caused me to pause and to remember something my father once said when someone asked him a very similar question. "Egypt does not have a Kaiser," I said as I raised my beer glass in a gesture of salute and sat down. I decided not to tell them Egypt had a Sultan.

Everyone raised their glass too. "Well said," a voice rang out from somewhere in the room. I felt as though we all were making a declaration of war on the classical ideal.

"Do you prefer drawing the figure clothed or nude?" asked a voluptuous young woman with raven hair.

"In subtle ways, a dress can serve to unveil a woman's individuality," I replied smiling. "It can tell, more about her persona than seeing her nude."

"So, you believe a dress is no less important than the nude model?" asked another woman and again I had to pause for my mind was reeling. Somehow, I felt every question was about Elsslin, not me.

"Have you seen Klimt's full figure portraits of women?" said someone in the group.

"No, but I would like to. The fashion writer for Modes Magazine here told me about them. She mentioned many artists in this new century have selected to react to and portray new discoveries and inventions, but visual expressions of how deeply the human soul and heart are affected by them are challenging to absorb and understand," I said gently. "To me, artists and fashion designers who portray and interpret such reactions in their art—have had the courage to give form to their imagination while employing full use of their poetic license—and are leading us all into a new world. I applaud them."

"Are you sure you are not talking about a taste for decadent aestheticism?" said a voice familiar to me, but I could not place why. Perhaps it was that of another undercover policeman.

Everyone seemed to finally relax and I suddenly recalled standing at the Developing Tray in the Darkroom watching color images of paintings of nudes on antique vases I had photographed slowing emerge from mysterious liquids; quickly followed by the artistic revolution ancient Egyptian artist Thutmose was involved in. I wondered if he had similar conversations with his fellow artists concerning his revolutionary ideas for the sculpture bust of The Beautiful One.

Before I could conclude my thought, a large middle-aged man who moved awkwardly, as if he was an intruder stepped out of the shadows and leaned over the table placing his blunt strong hands thick with hair on their backs, flat while surveying everyone until his sad eyes stopped at me and said in a rich baritone: "Do any of you know where I can purchase some falafel? I'd like a savory midnight snack."

He was as bald as boulder, heavy around the waist and hard-muscled with middle age. His eyes were fish gray and his nose was a burst of capillaries. No-one spoke-up, but everyone shook their head in the negative. I shrugged my shoulders at him. He frowned, his eyebrows drooped at the outer corners to match his mouth as he turned around and walked back into the shadows on the far side of the room.

"There is a sad man like that in every quiet bar in the world," said the oldest looking man at our table.

Again, every individual at the table focused their question tainted face back on me. "Why are you here?" said Anneliese as I too was striving to comprehend who or what falafel man was all about.

Her question surprised me, causing me to procrastinate, but I knew everyone expected me to answer. "I assume you mean here in Berlin, not just here at this café," I replied cautiously.

"Yes, why did you leave your homeland?" a voice close to my elbow said.

"In a way, I am following a dream. Although just now it feels more like an Alptraum, ah, nightmare."

"That I can understand. We are all doing that, but do you value where you are now?" said a plump fellow with bushy eyebrows and puffed cheeks.

The entire group became quiet and almost completely immobile. Their eyes were all on Anneliese and I. It felt as though it was a group effort, not a private conversation. I wondered if they have this kind of philosophical talk often or was it only because an alien was amongst them.

"I have progressed considerably since coming here and much of my improvement is due to our mutual friend Anneliese," I said smiling.

"Are you speaking about your skills as a photographer?"

"To some extent, but more about my outlook for the future," I said as I sensed a lessening of tension around the table finally. "Deliberate oppression and injustices often appear to be in the center of my life here, but so is a new kind of joy."

"Do you feel that is because of your education or cultural heritage?" said a man to my right with a dry, official voice and face to match.

I took a couple of swallows of beer as I perused all the other faces. "No, it is because of systems, ideologies and assumptions, both natural and artificial that embrace us all."

I felt it was time to go to my lodging and rest. I was tired and the discussion had drained what little energy I had remaining from the long day plus I was feeling disappointed at having not found anyone or thing related to who killed Herr Uga. I stood up intending to bid everyone a good evening just as a knife flew within a finger length of my shoulder and stabbed deeply into the wood post next to me.

Quivering loudly it spawned gasps and shrieks of fear from everyone at the table. Their high pitch intensified the throbbing in my head. The juddering knife, a flint Egyptian style dagger, put a spell on everyone as we all strained to look into the darkness from which it sprang, but no one was visible there.

Anneliese made a barely audible clucking noise with her tongue. It conveyed to us all the evening was over. I gave everyone a semi-apologetic nod, put my handkerchief over the knife and removed it from the post thinking Gennat may be able to lift fingerprints from it.

"Are you keeping it as a souvenir or for fingerprints?" asked one of the younger artists.

"The police may want to check it," I said then followed Anneliese to the exit door. It seemed odd none of the Café staff paid any attention to an attempted murder, nor did any of Anneliese's friends seem overly surprised. If this was a normal occurrence for them, I was not impressed.

The chilled night air felt invigorating and strangely reassuring life would go on with the morn, but Anneliese's whole demeanor radiated pending confrontation. "Whatever you've been doing is definitely stirring up hostility," she said between clinched teeth. "I can feel a strong devious will emanating from whom ever it is that wants you gone."

A quick forced cadence of fear had entered her voice as a taxi moved up alongside us. "My room is in the opposite direction, you take this," I said. "I'll wait for the next one. You know the knife could have been intended as a warning for your revolutionary friends."

"Are you certain? I mean that is an Egyptian knife in your pocket, right?" She stood up on the toes of her shoes, kissed me lightly on the cheek, entered the taxi and departed.

I felt rather vulnerable, standing out in the open so I moved closer to the café into the shadow of a large hedge.

I could feel the weight of the dagger pulling my coat down on one side. It seemed paradoxical to have had an Egyptian knife thrown at me while drinking beer in a German café, but it convinced me I was unnerving whom ever had killed Uga and was certainly mixing with the appropriate crowd. That thought made me revisit the entire incident with the large middle-aged man who moved awkwardly and spoke of falafel.

"What the hell was that about," I whispered to myself.

It did not feel like a threat or an invitation, but being the only one there who would know what he was referring to, meant the message was for me alone. The more I pondered it, the more I was convinced it was a deliberate attempt to appeal to my cultural heritage. To remind me from whence I came. In my mind, knife impresario Waaiz Zuberi, Youssef's aid and friend of Layla, emerged at the top of my short list of suspects. It also struck me, he had the stealthy-ness needed to throw a knife and disappear without a trace of having done so.

I wanted to examine the dagger to make sure it was genuine and not a tourist replica, but to do so risked smudging any fingerprints it may still hold. Why use an Egyptian dagger rather than a slim switchblade? Because the dagger speaks to culture as well as the finality of death.

I remembered my farther saying to me when I attempted to repair the broken chain on an old bicycle I had found. "When you are young, any problem is always much more complex than you allow yourself to believe."

But am I still too young, to unexperienced to fully comprehend what all of this is about? In my father's eyes, I always will be young. That thought shifted my mind to the cultural identifiable of the evening, falafel. A popular middle eastern meal comprised of chickpeas, herbs cumin and coriander mushed into patties, cooked then served with salad or fried eggplant. You can buy it from street vendors in almost every neighborhood in Cairo, but here in Berlin who knows where or if it can be found especially in the depths of midnight.

A dark man in his late 30s emerged from the side door of the *Café Größenwahn* and crossed the courtyard with military precision, as if each step he took, each movement of his arms were following orders. His bearing was making me nervous. His lean face featured a tired somber mood above a square-cut, clipped mustache. As he approached his gaze drifted past me as did his steps, stopping a meter or more beyond and facing toward the narrow end of the street. His clenched fists slowly relaxed as he said: "I do not know what is going on with you, but falafel can be had at the Kairo Kosh Café. It is open until 2am," he said in a broken monotonous cadence reminding me of several military officer friends of my father.

"I am going there now, you are welcome to follow."

Feeling I had said and done all the wrong things for the past 15 hours, I was dubious and slow to answer, but some invisible force was pushing me forward. I gestured to him I would accompany him.

The further we ventured from *Café Größenwahn,* the darker the streets became and my guide always managed to be several strides ahead of me and thus closer to it than to me.

"You are the Egyptian photographer at the Museum?" he mumbled under his breath.

"I am, who are you?"

"I was your waiter at *Café Größenwahn,*" he said with a tone of mingled anger and indulgence.

I felt embarrassed and disappointed in myself. I need to pay more attention to everyone around me, especially to those who specialize in being invisible.

"If you are seeking falafel, you must be feeling heimweh, ah, homesick. Do you know of Koshary? It is a dish that reflects Egypt's history of colonization, migration, and the miserable economic conditions of our life time."

I found his level of speech far more educated than the average waiter and was feeling suspicious. "Are you working undercover?"

He flashed a bleak look back at me which resisted further personal questions. We walked in silence until we were diagonally across the street from the Kairo Kosh Café.

"It is said when the British arrived in Egypt from India, they brought the earliest version of Koshary, an Indian rice and lentil dish, with them. The Ottoman influences added tomato sauce and Egypt's proximity to the Levant regions resulted in hummus beans being introduced to the dish. Finally, the crispy fried onions, hot sauce and garlic vinaigrette from Italy completed the dish. I hope you enjoy it," he said with a knowledgeable smile that appeared grippy and gave me a shivery apprehension.

"Of course I will, I've been eating it all my life, even if I didn't know the history of it," I replied striving to look into his eyes as he turned away from me. "Are you a historian or a chef?"

"Who and what I am is of no importance. You should follow every lead, no matter its dubious value," he said as he jumped into a passing carriage and vanished into the night shadows of the narrowing street beyond.

I stood starring at the Kairo Kosh Café. It looked much like a welcoming beacon in this city that does not sleep. I wondered if it too was filled with artists. I cautiously crossed the street thinking only the lonely would be out this late seeking falafel or Koshary and who would care what the difference may be?

. . .

Upon entering the café, a rotund man with a booming voice welcomed me. "Please to enter friend, there are many here from Cairo, Damascus, Beirut, Istanbul, Libya, Tunisia, and Iraq. We are the northern capital of Arab culture in Berlin," he said escorting me to a table filled with men who had a gleam of comradery in their eyes for the jovial proprietor. "These are artists, writers, musicians, actors, and filmmakers all of whom have descended on Berlin for the freedom to express themselves, without repercussions from a repressive government or conservative fanatics. Welcome."

I was beginning to wonder if the dagger incident was nothing more than a ploy to drive customers to this café.

"Did you know, it's thought falafel originated as Coptic Christians looked for a hearty replacement for meat during their seasons of fasting or lent?" I heard a man at the table eating a large plate full say between swallows.

"You should always avoid using canned chickpeas! Dried chickpeas that have been soaked in water for 24 hours are the important ingredient that gives falafel the right consistency and taste," said the man opposite me.

"Do you prefer patties or balls," asked a third man.

"It doesn't matter so long as they are fried in hot oil," replied the man at the end of the table. Everyone laughed.

"Do you have it for breakfast or dinner?" the man next to me asked as he looked at my suit and smiled.

"Well, considering its now 1:35am, I have to say both," I replied with a chuckle.

I was thinking about how often the duality of my life awakens fond memories of family gatherings at meal time. My mother washing grape leaves and molding rows of a mixture of seasoned beef and rice to fill them with. A cousin making sure the stems were all removed. An aunt spending hours, roiling a pot of broth with sumac and lemon. Everyone speaking Arabic because it was the mother tongue of all the gathered elders.

I remember thinking it was a way for them to reconnect with home and here I am in an entirely different habitat trying to find some way, some thing, some person to give me some pale reflection of that feeling, some deep insight of what it means to call Berlin home. However, I suspect a complete untethering from Egypt will never really happen for the reverberations of those long since gone days of my youth, will always be with me like the olfactory experience of my father's favorite breakfast simmering on the kitchen stove, or cool Nile waters passing over my bare feet, and scents of myrrh, cotton, and sandalwood filling the warm desert air, will always be within me.

The nearest I've come to feeling comfortable here is the commonplace smells of spring, such as flowering trees and vegetation. I find them heady, intense, and wonderful for they are almost non-existent in Egypt, but perhaps my most favorite of smells, are those of freshly baked breads no matter where I am.

CHAPTER 19

As I followed behind Chione and Anneliese through the flea market on Arkonaplatz I listened to their conversation about how popular it was and how one could 'find anything you wanted here including valuable antiques and paintings'. Even the artist Heinrich Zille, featured the hustle and bustle of the place in one of his recent paintings or so Anneliese said, but I was finding it odd the place was located so close to Berlin's city center. It was pleasantly shaded by numerous trees and surrounded by green spaces making it feel like an oasis away from the stress of the city. I would even call it comfortable and relaxed as we strolled in peace, stopping at various booths to browse calmly and talk with people who seem happy to meet and converse with us.

My ladies stopped at every clothing, jewelry, footwear, and accessories booth we encountered. There were even a few photography booths. At two of them you could have your portrait taken. I wondered what the rental fee was for a single booth space.

After two hours of strolling I suggested we stop at a bratwurst stand or visit one of the cafes around the outer edge of the square.

"Would you ever consider having a booth here?" I asked Anneliese.

"Maybe one to exhibit my fine art prints, but not one to take portraits. Dealing with the general public can be exhausting and then having to depend on them returning the following week to collect their print could be disastrous."

I turned to Chione and asked: "What were you talking to the antique jewelry dealers about?"

"I asked them about amulets," she replied.

"To buy or sell?"

"Both. I enjoy collecting them and I have several antiques ones," she said. "A couple of the dealers asked me to bring mine next weekend so they can appraise them for me."

"Are you going to?" asked Anneliese.

"No, I do not want to sell any of them now," she said looking immersed in thought. "I recognize some of these dealers. They come into Ugo's warehouse usually on Friday afternoon."

"That is intriguing, what do they buy from him, ah, from his business?"

"The shop staff keep a list of all items which have prompted little interest from potential buyers and they offer those to local small shop dealers, like the ones here today, at very low prices just to get the items out of the warehouse, but they still haggle over the prices. That was what Herr Ugo liked doing and he was good at it, his negotiating skills in several languages was an amazing thing to listen to," said Chione looking and sounding down hearted. "He would always say 'just be brave and tell them at least 20% more than they are offering'. He would even pretend to walk away if they did not accept his price. Then if they accepted it, he would offer them a special price for two or three other things they had shown an interest in."

"So they would have come in for maybe one or two objects and end up buying twice as many," said Anneliese. "Yes, and he would promise to have them delivered free to their shop before closing time."

"Did he issue certificates of authenticity or a provenance with each item?" I asked.

"Only if the buyer requested it. Which they rarely did," she said quietly.

"Have you ever seen any of the provenances? Do they arrive with the crates or separately?"

"They are always separate and arrive via Deutsche Post or the Professor."

I could not hold-back, I took Chione in my arms and kissed her deeply. She intensely returned my passion for a prolonged moment, but then pushed free of me. "Asim, what are doing? Stop. People are watching."

"Is he a short, bulky, older man?" I said.

"What? Oh, yes, he is and he always has dirty hands. You know like the scribes in Cairo."

I wanted to kiss her again, but I maintained a sense of decorum. "What kind of Professor is he?" asked Anneliese admonishing me with her eyes. "Do you know his name?"

Chione looked at us both with suspicion. "I don't recall his name, but I think he was a Professor of Literature."

"Was?"

Judging by the change in her eyes, she was trying out various answers mentally. "He does not teach any more, but is in charge of the old books in the University Library. At least that is what I think Herr Uga told me." Her smile was bright, but seemed anxious.

"That would be appropriate for an old retired professor," I said as I discretely allowed Anneliese to see me look at my watch. She made a sour face.

"It's getting late and I need to go home before meeting my friends tonight," said Anneliese. "Let's find a carriage."

"Yes, I should go home too," replied Chione.

"Do you have a date tonight too?" I asked harshly.

Chione looked guilty and bowed her head as she turned away from me. "It is a social obligation I must attend," she said sheepishly blushing and holding back tears.

"Right. I have one of those too," I said as I turned and walked away all ready regretting my foolish behavior.

"Asim, please wait..."

I did not look back, I wanted to get this information about the professor to Youssef and Romy, maybe even Gennat as soon as possible. I hopped into a carriage and as I considered what address to give the driver, I suddenly realized I had no way of contacting any of them except maybe Gennat. Youssef and Romy had telephones while I did not. I concluded someone at Police headquarters would be able to telephone Gennat.

As the carriage got closer to das Polizeipräsidium, I realized Gennat most likely already knew everything about the professor and I would look foolish rushing to his office late Sunday afternoon. I told the driver to take me to the Ratskeller instead.

When I entered the door the smell was foul with old cigarette smoke and rancid beer fumes, I took a deep breath of the early evening air before stepping inside. As far as I could tell in the dim light there were only a few men sitting at tables and no one at the bar. I sat at the bar and exchanged nods of recognition with the barman then ordered a beer.

Raising the glass to study its golden glow made me wonder what man Chione would be raising her glass with tonight.

"Ist da ein Problem," asked the barman.

"No problem, just thinking."

Barmaid Lena came up and leaned against me. "Good-evening Asim," she said through a pleasant smile. "Your friend was here earlier looking for you."

"Friend? Which one?"

"The older big Egyptian man," she said looking concerned about my apprehensive reaction. "He said he would be back later."

"When? What time?"

"Just later," she shrugged. "Why don't you have dinner and by then he'll probably arrive?"

I was feeling hungry. "Do you have any sauerbraten with Kartofel and Sauerkraut."

"Ja wirklich, Herr Asim," she said as she placed her hand on my lower back and snuggled her breast against my elbow. "We have some tasty desserts too," she said winking.

I wondered if her congenial friendliness was part of her job description. Though it did not matter, I was enjoying the pleasant attention. "Let's move to the table over there," she suggested. "You'll be able to see your friend the moment he comes in."

As I finished the wonderful meal, started on my second glass of beer and contemplated dessert the door opened as a man of about forty entered. He had fair thinning hair, bold eyes, and a wry mouth on a scarred face. His eyes searched mine. "You Youssef's friend?"

"I am."

"Kommst Du?" he grunted as he turned to leave.

I quickly placed money on the table for my meal and beers plus a little extra for Lena. Nodded to her and followed the man outside.

"Where are we going?" I asked as he lumbered toward a car and I could see his face closed-up had a blankness, almost stuporous expression although he did not smell of alcohol. I concluded he was striving to remember the place or how to tell me about it.

"Youssef." Was all he said.

He drove into an older section of the city I had not been to before. Most of the houses and commercial buildings were wooden framed with sagging roofs appearing untouched by human hands for decades. Grunt-man drove off the main road between two empty sheds and a tumble-down hutch next to a deserted-looking warehouse then stopped the car and turned off the engine near a large sliding, bolted, side door. When we stepped-out onto the gravel driveway I was surprised at the complete silence of the area. I was convinced we were no longer in Berlin.

Grunt-man walked under a large tree toward a thin shaft of light coming from a small house at the end of the gravel. I followed, wishing I had brought a gun, even though I did not own one. The light was slipping out a partially opened shuddered window near a very low door. He just barely fit through the door as he opened it without knocking.

When I got to the door frame I peered around the edge and was delighted to see Youssef sitting at an old wooden table with a bottle of beer in his hand. Unfortunately, he looked infuriated. I was hoping his anger was not going to be aimed at me.

"Ah, Asim, my boy praise to Allah you are safe," he said looking completely flushed.

"Why wouldn't I be?" I asked cautiously.

"Our beloved Chione has been taken," he said with a glare of hostility in his blood shot eyes. "We must get her back quickly before they …"

He did not finish his outburst. "Who are they? And why have they taken her?"

"They are smugglers and they will sell her as a sex slave if we do not provide them with what they want," he said throwing the beer bottle against the stone fireplace shattering it in all directions. "She is pure and has never been touched. It will drive her insane. You must give them what they want."

It was unsettling to see his face change so rapidly and radically.

"What do they want? Tell me!" I said as calmly as I could.

"They want the molds of all the amulets found at Amarna," he mumbled as he finally sat down fully red-faced.

Grunt-man appeared to be completely at a lost as to what to do. I told him to stand outside and guard the door.

I sat down in front of Youssef. "Do you know these kidnappers?"

"No and I do not understand why they associate Chione with me or the Amarna amulets. What makes them believe her or I have any access to them?" He shook his head like a child in a tantrum, whipping it rapidly from side to side until his hair stood straight out making his eyes bulge and appear fearfully puzzled.

Images of Chione showing me the amulet she wears and the one she gave me flashed in my mind. I told Youssef about them and that

Chione had told vendors at the flea market she had an entire collection. I showed him the one I was wearing, the one she gave me.

"Are all her amulets ancient like this one?" asked Youssef.

"Only Herr Borchardt would know for certain," I replied as I shook my head. "This does not make sense. The amulets are not the most valuable objects found at Amarna. Why would they want only molds of them and not the more valuable sculptures and wall reliefs?"

"They must believe in their ritual power," he said bowing his head. "People want to believe they can hold power in their hands. It helps them to endure their hardships and persevere or overpower their enemies."

"No, surely these people want to cast thousands of amulets from the molds and sell them for hard cold cash," I said. "We need to talk to Herr Borchardt first thing tomorrow morning."

"You think he will do it?"

"Maybe, especially if he believes we can catch these corrupted reprobates."

He got a little pale and tense, "I understand, but what about Gennat? If he gets involved it could endanger Chione even more."

"Yes, lets present the exchange idea to the fanatics. How are we to contact them?"

"We do not. We must wait until they contact us."

"Damn, I do not like that, but I guess that is to be expected."

Youssef got to his feet, his entire body making an angry gesture, "I do not like it at all either. He struck his thigh with his fist. "Let's contact Layla."

"Why her?"

"Despite what she says, I believe she and Montu are very involved with the smugglers as is artist Otto Dräger plus, Waaiz who even though he is a religious zealot works with them," Youssef was slurring his words with impatient directness.

"Kidnapping Chione seems very risky just to get a few molds. There must be something bigger going on," I suggested. "We need to talk with Romy, Anneliese, Elsslin and maybe Meierdiebrück before going to Herr Borchardt."

"Why do you always think these young women can be helpful?"

The emphasis he placed on their gender said much more than the question implied. He looked me up and down, the movements of his head as quick and instinctive as a loin revealing his brown teeth in an unnerving sneer of puzzlement.

I was uneasy feeling the full weight of my cold bones.

With enormous unwillingness, he rose and stepped in front of me putting his big hands, grained with dirt, on my shoulders and gripping them with his fingers closing like a metal vise. I knew at that moment, I was going to break the promise I had given.

"They are just like you, undercover police who work for Gennat."

His hands released me instantly and fell to his side.

"Romy and Elsslin are detectives?" He appeared stunned and sat back down. "This new century is making me feel tired."

I told him I would contact Romy in the morning to see if she has any contacts at the flea market. "Maybe I should resign my position at the Museum so I can help her and Gennat find who these crooks are."

"No, absolutely not, do not resign your position," he replied looking irate and livid again. "Don't you understand how important it is to our people to know an Egyptian works at the Museum? You must stay there."

CHAPTER 20

She was looking right at me, but could not see me. Her blue eyes were focused on something far away which gave her face an enchanted beauty, one I felt I should not disturb. I stood perfectly still holding my watch and observing it tick off each second of every minute until a knocking on the door caused me to speak. "I'll get it," I said jiggling my keys in front of Anneliese's face.

She shook her head and blinked several times while I opened the door.

"Good morning," said Romy as she stepped in quickly and closed the door. "Lock it, I don't want to talk to him."

"Who are you referring to," asked Anneliese still seemingly consumed by her own inner daze.

"Hans. His manipulative sweet talking makes me feel ill."

"What does he want?"

"Who knows, whatever it is, he isn't getting it from me."

We all stopped and listened to the approaching footsteps. They came to the door and halted followed by a moment of silence then retreated.

"I think he's gone," I whispered.

"Oh good," hushed Romy. "Now tell me what has happened to Chione."

Anneliese's eyes gradually became aware of what she had heard.

"What, something happened, what?"

I explained everything to them. Romy appeared irate, while Anneliese's eyes were tearing. "I knew I should not have left her there alone."

"Alone where," I asked.

"At the flea market. I had errands to do before my date and she wanted to talk to one of the vendors again so I left her. I am so sorry, I thought she would be safe in such a public place."

"Do you know the name of the vendor?"

"No, but it was in stall #3MADN."

"How did you remember that?" I asked feeling my mind rattled with frustration.

"Mensch Ärgern Dich Nicht', ah, hey, do not get angry," said Romy quickly. "Converting I.D.'s into words was part of my training as a police cadet. Were you ever a cadet," she asked Anneliese.

"Ah, no. I remember the stall sign because it reminded me of a game, I used play with der Opa, ah, my grandfather," replied Anneliese.

"Of course, that is why I was able to convert it so quickly. I'd forgotten about that game."

"Well Herr Gennat will be able to get the name of the vendor."

"Wait, if we bring him into this, it might cause the abductors to harm Chione or sell her out of the country," I said as I felt my panic level spike.

We stood starring at each other.

"I hate to remind you Asim, but if we don't start shooting photographs in the galleries, Herr Borchardt will be informed."

"Right, you two go to work. I will get Bertha to do some sleuthing and meet with Youssef. Bertha knows a lot of flea market vendors."

"Let's meet at the Ratskeller," suggested Romy.

"Ah, no, not there. Ah I am tired of that place," I said feeling awkward about Lena.

"How about *Café Größenwahn?*" said Romy.

"Too public. Hollenbach Haus would provide more privacy," I suggested.

"No, but it's not the right atmosphere for discussing how to get Chione back."

"Neither is the Ratskeller," I mumbled.

"Hollenbach it is then."

Romy gestured to me to open the door quietly, which I did and looked down the hall to make sure Hans was not lingering around.

"It's clear," I said.

Romy hugged Anneliese, touched my forearm and departed. I hugged Anneliese and said: "Which gallery are we shooting today?"

She smiled while wiping tears from her eyes. "I do not know. I am so worried about Chione. She is so innocent, so absolutely harmless," she said releasing a miserable sound like a strangled sob and pushing her hands against her temples. I started loading up our cart.

We worked throughout the day without stopping or even talking much, until we received a note informing us our lunch meeting was cancelled. In the late afternoon we ran out of film and returned to the Photography Studio completely exhausted and frustrated at having not received any updates from anyone.

Just as we finished unloading the lights and the camera from the cart, the phone rang. We looked at each other and Anneliese said: "You better answer it, if its bad news I'll die."

I picked up the receiver and a voice was talking rapidly… it was Romy telling me Bertha and Elsslin had determined where the kidnappers were holding Chione. My heart told me to rush to their aid as quickly as possible, but my mind said phone Youssef. I could not phone him at Uga's warehouse because that could inadvertently alert Sati and possibly Waaiz and they could be involved in the kidnapping. The best I could do was take a taxi car directly to Youssef's lodging house on the outskirts of the city in hopes he would arrive soon.

Anneliese insisted she was coming with me. Neither of us had a gun or weapon of any kind. I told Romy to bring Bertha and Elsslin with her so we all could devise a plan with Youssef.

It was completely dark by the time Romy, Bertha and Elsslin met with Anneliese and I at Youssef's, but it did not matter for he was not there. I suggested Bertha, who had a gun, and I go to the kidnapper's hideout to scope the place and make sure Chione had not been moved to a new location. Romy, Anneliese and Elsslin, who also had a gun, would wait for Youssef and then all of them would join us.

Bertha's knowledge of the city was remarkable, she knew exactly the most direct route to the warehouse where Chione was being held. When we finally managed to quietly open the back door and slip inside the interior of the long, narrow building was dim, grimy, and chilled. We could hear people talking at the opposite end so we moved between dozens of stacked wooden shipping crates, assorted wood planks and tools until we reached the outer margin of the shallow light shown from the nearest ceiling lamp. I could see through a small chink one man standing near a door on the far wall and Montu Sati seated in a rocking chair in front of a small fireplace's fading embers. Having not gotten a good look at him the night Youssef and I hid in Uga's warehouse, I was surprised to see he had deep-set eyes, surrounded by worn weathered skin with and an upper lip almost as long as his nose, that caved in when he spoke.

Looking from the opposite side of the shipping crate a saw Layla curled up on a couch with a shawl over her shoulders and her legs tucked under her, she said: "It's cold in here, if Waaiz does not return or phone soon, I'm leaving and you men can have the girl to do with as you wish."

Sati took the metal poker and shuffled vestiges of the small fire around causing sparks and ash to fly about. Layla huffed and sneered at him with a disappointed glare.

Chione was blindfolded and roped to a straight-back chair in the center of the gang. "I can think of a few things we will do with her before selling her to the east," said a bearded man standing over her.

I was experiencing a rush of fear, unlike any I had ever encountered before. Fear of the treacherous gang in front of me, fear of the life destructive terror they could bring down upon so many individuals I cared about, and fear of the unnerving panic I felt welling up inside me.

I heard a faint noise from behind us, held my breath, listened, and heard it again. Bertha, hunkered down behind the crate next to me, nodded and aimed her gun toward the shadowed area the noise came from. A delicate hand nudged out from the side of the nearest crate and waved. It was Romy scrunched down beside a pile of shipping blankets and packing materials.

"Damn Romy," I whispered as she crawled closer. "This is not a safe place for you to be especially unarmed."

"Elsslin and Anneliese are outside with Youssef, they have two guns and will charge in when you signal," she replied in barely audible tones.

A flabby, scratched-face man with a smudge of lipstick on his narrow chin and standing in an uncomfortable relation to the door, looked subdued as if there had been an argument he had lost. He took a handkerchief from his pocket and pressed it against the bleeding scratches on his throat. "Damn bitch, I get her first," he grumbled salivating with malice.

"Having been stupidly careless tying her up, you will be the last to poke her," scowled Sati stoking the cinders again and leering at Chione.

Scratched-man dropped the handkerchief and slowly moved his hand toward the knife sheathed to his belt. He opened his mouth wide as if he was going to scream at the top of his lungs causing the muscles along the line of his jaw to dimple, but no sound came out.

"You try to touch her and I'll use that thing to turn you into a eunuch," said Sati through clinched teeth. "Those bruise marks you made on her arms will cause us to lose money on this deal, idiot."

The two men turned to face one another. A sudden frantic pounding on the door caused everyone to tense up. Sati gestured to Layla.

Layla nervous, looked suspiciously toward the door and said cautiously: "Who is it?"

"Otto, let me in," he yelled battering the door.

Sati gestured to scratched-man who flipped the metal latch. The door flung open violently as Otto, hunched-over, staggered in smelling of whiskey with his shirt unbuttoned and sleeves rolled up. He struggled to level himself to his feet as he exhaled with a hoarse grunt.

"Where is she? Let me at her," he slurred through a swollen lower lip as a thin crisscross Mensur-like scar on his left cheek flared red. "I'm going to take her right now, right here on the floor and when I'm done with her, the rest of you cocks can fight over what's left."

Everyone looked at Chione including Otto and a sudden ferocious scowl twisted his face into dark knots. "Not her," he belched. "I want Elsslin. She owes me. Now where the hell is she?" His voice thick and heavy with liquor had a taut contemptuous snarl to it.

"What makes you think she is here?" asked Layla shuddering as she gestured to the other men to check outside. Scratched-man drew his gun and walked out cautiously followed by bearded-man who looked suspiciously toward Sati who pointed his gun toward the door.

Coughing Otto ripped off his shirt and pants to stand naked in front of the fireplace with his leather belt in his righthand while bellowing: "I'm going to teach her a lesson starting with a good old-fashioned whipping. Now where is she? I want her right here on her hands and knees." A glaze of dangerous confusion came over his eyes.

"Why do you think she is in here?" asked Layla again now standing with her hands on her hips. Her voice had lost its scornful stridency and had become tinny with fear. "You do not know what you are doing or saying. You are drunk. Sit down fool."

His lips drew back from his teeth and his voice rasped. "I followed her here. Right to this building!" His voice vibrated with an unnatural timbre as if he had reached the emotional level where murder could certainly be possible.

Everyone was motionless and silent. Elsslin, with a kind of shamed awe, aimed her gun at Otto.

"You do not want to do something you'll regret the rest of your life," I whispered. "Let's try to take him without gun fire if we can."

Elsslin shrugged, but did not lower her gun or take her eyes off Otto.

Otto looked at everyone with hostility and started swinging the buckled end of his belt toward Chione's head. "Bring her out or this-one gets scarred for life."

It was obvious, no one was going to get near him as he took a step closer to Chione.

A gun shot flashed from the darkness behind me. The bullet hit Otto in the chest and knocked him back against the fireplace mantle. He fell forward as two more rapid shots fired before his face hit the floor with a loud thud. Someone screamed punctuating the gun smoke saturated air.

Sati sprung from the rocking chair shooting wildly in all directions as he ran toward the door with a muddled look of fear streaking across his sallow face. A gun to my right fired one shot that struck him in the back. He slowed, his face became smokey, he turned with gun in hand and fell backwards shooting twice wildly again hitting a ceiling light. He reluctantly detached himself from the support of the wall, fell on his side curling up in pain and expired with a whimper. I felt a brutal pain and blood running down the calf of my right leg. I had been shot.

Bearded man, with a lean sour face and quick flashing eyes, rushed back in holding a blackjack in one hand and gun in his other. He appeared to be heading directly toward me wilding swinging the blackjack toward my head. I hit him with a left to the jaw, a right to the chin and a left to the solar plexus which bent him over. He lunged toward Chione in a sudden spurt of viciousness and fired one shot at Youssef hitting him in his left shoulder. Youssef shot back.

Severely hurt, bearded man slumped over Chione reaching down for the front of her dress. Shaking her head violently and screaming, her blindfold dropped off as my heart skipped a beat looking into her terrified eyes. I pulled her free from him dragging her still chair bound away from everyone's line of fire. "Don't shoot," he muttered in a voice as thin as death as his body crashed to the floor with a deep seeping exhale. I picked up his gun, it was empty.

More shots streaked back and forth across the dark space until Youssef yelled: "POLICE HALT."

In the fading glow from the fireplace, I saw Layla rise-up and run for the door. Bertha grabbed her by the hair, flung her hard against the wall and hand-cuffed her instantly. Her whole face twisted, trying to cover the nakedness of her emotions while her arms hung straight down by her sides with her hands together behind her, lending her an odd almost spell-binding air of stealthy dignity surrounded by blood splattered chaos.

Anneliese who had been standing completely immobile in the dark near the backdoor jerked about when she saw me looking at her. Everything she did seemed almost regretful, as if any action was a dangerous gamble she did not want to take. Stressed, she brought herself under control, brushed her blue-veined eyelids with the fingertips of one hand and turned-on a small light above the door, the only unbroken bulb left in the room. She now appeared petrified, possibly concentrating on what she might say and its implications.

It was obvious, her expression wore more grief than her mind was able to bear, but she had managed to keep our new camera in her hands. It almost seemed to steady her. As she raised it, I was sure, she was crying in tormented silent agony as she snapped a few quick photographs. The automatic flash of each shot startled us all and gave an eerie reality to everything.

I quickly freed Chione from the chair and caressed her. Romy lifted Otto's head onto her lap. Bright badges of blood made it obvious he had been shot three times in the chest and judging by the size of each wound it was by two separate guns. Blood was everywhere.

In the flickering fireplace light, I kneeled-down and said to him: "Who killed Uga?"

He was coughing up blood, but managed to slur out: "He was banging my girl."

"What girl?" I asked. My voice sounded strange; it had broken through into a tone new to me, deep as the sorrow I was feeling in my heart and the searing pain in my leg.

Otto did not answer, but looked around until he saw Elsslin. He strained to raise his arm and point to her, exhaled a deep death rattle, slumped to his side and died.

"Me," she shushed through clinched teeth. "I told him I could not have sex with him because I was Uga's girl."

"What? Was that true?" snapped Romy in an irritated huff.

"No, there was nothing between me and Uga, but it kept Otto from pestering me constantly. That is when he started banging you," she said pointing her gun at Layla.

"Mmm, well he was shot three times by two guns. Who among all of you shot him," I said to everyone as Chione kept me from falling over as I stood up.

"I shot him first, with just one bullet," said Elsslin, her expression alternating between being too personal and too official. I stepped forward and deftly took her gun from her.

"That would be the right shoulder bullet hole," said Bertha. The other two holes are in his heart and are from a smaller caliber gun."

"Let's see a show of guns," said Youssef pressing his shirt tail against his wounded shoulder.

Several hands raised, all with large caliber guns. I was surprised when I looked about to discover three of them were policemen. That explained why there had been so many gun shots fired. I assumed Anneliese had let them in the backdoor when the shooting started.

"Someone is holding out on us," Youssef said. "Wait, these wounds look as though they were shot from a low angle."

Bertha turned to Layla, searched her, and found a small hand gun tucked under her clothing.

"You were hiding behind the couch when the shooting started. You shot him," said Bertha. "Why?"

"I'd had enough of his cocky bragging about all the women he bangs." Looking murderous, cheaply elegant and epicene she made an abrupt angry motion and her eyes squinted with scorn as she spit on Otto's dead body.

A quick dragging noise sounded from along the outside wall and scratched-man rapidly stepped through the open door, he was wounded but still managed to hold his gun and aim it at Chione. I jumped in front of her. Youssef instantly fired two shots. One struck the man in his gun hand and other in the middle of his forehead. He fell over backwards dead.

"Make sure there are no more of them outside," said Youssef to the policemen.

Elsslin walked up to Layla and the two of them stood face to face. "You were sex partner to Sati, Otto and your husband, oh and Meierdiebrück. You had Otto kill your husband and you killed Sati."

Layla hissed in disdainful contempt and appeared to be teetering on the edge of hysteria.

. . .

After all the police questions were answered and the guilty taken into custody everyone agreed to meet at *Café Größenwahn*. We gathered around one table and ordered three pitchers of beer. Romy and Anneliese stood to give a toast. "Zu unserem Wohl," they yelled holding each other and swaying to the point of almost collapsing.

Everyone took a long guzzle and looked forlorn.

"I would like to speak," I said as I rose carefully holding on to my chair and waited for quiet. "I am grateful all of you are safe and none of us were arrested. However, I am not convinced all this happened because a few crooks wanted to make money from selling stolen molds of ancient Egyptian amulets and one sex crazed middle-aged artist wanted revenge for having been rejected by a young model. No something else is at the heart of this tragedy. None of it was an accident, there definitely was an unresolved prime objective to hurt or maline someone or some institution."

Everyone appeared thoroughly exhausted as they sat back and allowed me to ramble on.

"Otto and Waaiz killed Uga, Elsslin shot Otto, but Layla's shots killed him and she killed Sati. All of that seems understandable, but Layla had Chione kidnapped. Why? Certainly not just for some molds of ancient amulets and she obviously did not care about any money they could have collected should they have sold Chione."

"Because she believed Sati was having sex with Chione," said Bertha.

"Perhaps, but I believe she thought she would be able to convince everyone I was stealing from the Museum and Chione and I plus Youssef were in cahoots with an entirely different gang of smugglers. That would have damaged the Museum's reputation, Herr Borschart's and maybe even Herr Simon's as well. Further, to Layla, murder was just a small part of her wide-reaching cultural war against a modern Europe."

Chione sat forward her face warm and bright again, with the pride a woman takes in exerting peaceful self-confidence as she looked directly into Elsslin's eyes. "Layla wanted my ancient seal amulets, which she believes have the power to regenerate life, to make her young again; she wants all the men around her to desire her; she wants to look like you Elsslin; she wants to be as you are, the living beautiful one."

EPILOGUE

Har-Shaf Uga's import and antique business was dissolved and the Museum's curators checked its entire warehouse inventory for any original artifacts and destroyed all casting molds they found. Layla Snura Uga and Waaiz Zuberi were convicted of murder and kidnapping. Hans Herbster and Joseph Meierdiebrück were fired from the Museum. Youssef Sadek and his niece Chione Khnum-Rekhi returned to Cairo where he continued as a Police Captain and she married his lieutenant. Romy Stern resigned her position as an undercover detective and married a very successful Berlin businessman as did Fräulein Marie Luise Simon. Anneliese Brantt left the Museum and opened her own photography studio, in the Metta District, specializing in fine art nude figure studies and crime scene documentation photography. Store clerk Fredericka opened her own art supply store and art gallery featuring women artists. Bertha continued as an undercover Policewoman and her sister Elsslin married emerging Expressionist artist/photographer Asim Khalifa Lateef. Their home and his studio are in her birthplace, Aachen, where she opened a bakery specializing in Aachener Printen, a type of gingerbread and Asim's favorite hot cinnamon rolls.

AUTHOR'S NOTE

With so many major scientific, political, social, and cultural issues producing consequences world-wide in 1912/13 it is easy to question why the after-effects of the discovery of the Nefertiti bust continues to resonate with each new generation. This writer believes it is because artist Thutmose succeeded in his courageous goal of sculpting an individual who appears benevolent, kind and compassionate to all who look upon her. I honor him and his legacy as an artist.

ABOUT THE AUTHOR

U.S. National Endowment for the Arts Fellowship recipient M. Lee Musgrave has had his art exhibited in numerous solo and group exhibitions, was born in Australia and lived most of his life in Los Angeles. As a former professor of art and curator, he organized hundreds of exhibitions at museums and galleries involving artists, collectors, critics, gallerists and an array of related enthusiasts. His writings related to those exhibitions contributed to their success and to his ability to relate that community to others. Those many experiences and his ongoing art activities inform his creative writing about the exciting international art community. He is the author of novels *Brushed Off* and *Off Kilter* plus many short stories including *Quitessence*.

OTHER TITLES BY M. LEE MUSGRAVE

NOTE FROM M. LEE MUSGRAVE

Word-of-mouth is crucial for any author to succeed. If you enjoyed *The Beautiful One*, please leave a review online—anywhere you are able. Even if it's just a sentence or two. It would make all the difference and would be very much appreciated.

Thanks!
M. Lee Musgrave

We hope you enjoyed reading this title from:

BLACK ROSE writing™

www.blackrosewriting.com

Subscribe to our mailing list – *The Rosevine* – and receive **FREE** books, daily deals, and stay current with news about upcoming releases and our hottest authors.
Scan the QR code below to sign up.

Already a subscriber? Please accept a sincere thank you for being a fan of Black Rose Writing authors.

View other Black Rose Writing titles at www.blackrosewriting.com/books and use promo code **PRINT** to receive a **20% discount** when purchasing.